Also by
Paul Thaler

Fiction

Bronxland

Nonfiction

The Watchful Eye:
American Justice in the Age of the Television Trial

The Spectacle:
Media and the Making of the OJ Simpson Story

The Maddening

Paul Thaler

www.DarkInkBooks.com

www.AMInkPublishing.com

To Amy

For braving this story in the dark of night…
And for all of our life's stories we share in the light.

"Words have no power to impress the mind without the exquisite horror of their reality."

~ Edgar Allan Poe

OPENING

Poe hunched over a computer in the corner of his Harlem studio apartment, silently tapping at the keyboard. A pungent smell of rat poison mixing with the oppressive summer humidity hung over the room. Poe was oblivious to the stench and everything else about his surroundings. A blindfold covered his eyes as he faced the computer screen. He also wore earplugs and blue plastic gloves that stickily adhered to his hands. To stifle any possible light, blinds were drawn casting the bare room into pitch darkness. The only sign of light came from the screen illuminating his masked face that glowed like some ghostly image in the night.

Poe was frustrated and hesitated for the umpteenth time that evening, searching for the right words to finish his chapter. A writer in search of the truth, he bitterly told himself. Anne's story was coming too slowly. He needed resolution, but Anne was a stubborn one, refusing to die.

Poe had taken seriously an old *New York Times* profile. An up-and-coming writer recounted how he obliterated all sensory distractions to fully immerse himself into his story. And, so, Poe's own experiment. Not that it was doing him much good. A pile of crushed paper was proof of his deep writer's block, and he blindly slammed the computer in frustration almost knocking the machine to the floor.

It was just as well that he couldn't see the screen— whatever words already existed there were worthless. The earplugs and plastic gloves and blindfold had failed to do the trick. Just too many disturbances floating in his head. And then this incessant noise coming from inside a long, wooden box tucked in the corner of the room. Anne's banging and muted screams were getting on his nerves. He had grown used to her cries, but this was a bad time for such histrionics. The racket had even penetrated his earplugs. He was exasperated knowing that he had only himself to blame. No one else was responsible for the 30-year-old hysterical woman bound and stuffed inside the narrow sealed box for these past five days.

His plan had gone well, her kidnapping easy-peasy. She was some school teacher from Queens visiting the city when he came upon her that night leaving a comedy club on the Upper West Side. She seemed to have had a great time getting away from the baby and hubby for the weekend. The woman just wanted to break free. That's what Poe thought, anyway. Maybe with a little more attention and street savvy, she would have noticed the black Buick trailing her on her way to a friend's apartment where she'd been staying.

Poe hustled up to the building. The woman was there, waiting at the elevator. He offered a wide-toothed smile at the locked front glass door, rubbing his fingers together, signaling a problem—he had forgotten his keys, could she let him in? The woman wavered, cautiously smiling back, and then nodded, her natural trustworthiness and the man's apparent charm swaying her decision. But no sooner had she opened the door that she found herself dragged by her hair down to the grime-ridden floor. The chloroform did the rest.

The few passersby gave the drunk couple a wide berth as they staggered from the building into a parked Buick. Poe made his way to Amsterdam Avenue, stopping the car once to inject the woman starting to stir with a powerful dose of phenobarbital. Then the hassle back at his Harlem apartment, managing to half-carry her up the stairwell to his third-floor apartment.

Poe expected that Anne Sweeny would be dead by this time, clearly underestimating her resilience. The jumble of items in her pocketbook filled him in about her life. Pictures of Dylan, her husband; Amy, the adorable two-year-old; and a puppy, a Golden Retriever named Ennie. Just the cutest family, Poe thought. He had checked up on the woman the previous night after her screaming subsided. He opened the lid of the coffin-like box to find that she was still alive, her terrified eyes bulging from her head. Poe leaned over to brush away several large water bugs crawling on her neck and face that had made their way through the air holes. They reminded him of the 'death beetles' in one of Edgar's stories.

"A bit of company?" he said with a chuckle. Poe gazed at the woman tenderly, recalling that she'd looked much more youthful when he abducted her, but he supposed a price had to be paid for being entombed in the box.

"Please!" she rasped. Just a single word. Hoping he would understand—not that any word was about to set her free. Then she lurched, her head twisting violently as if she were trying to unknot it from the rest of her body. She reminded Poe of the young girl in *The Exorcist* thrashing about with the devil having his way, a scene that made him laugh at the time. He had to admit now seeing Anne's savage reaction, just how real a performance that had been.

Poe patted Anne's head, assuring her he had contacted her husband to let him know she was being cared for—though emphasizing there was no hanky-panky between them. Poe would never stoop so low to take advantage. He was not that type of man. Besides, other matters were on his mind. Poe was not altogether surprised that Anne didn't appreciate his thoughtfulness, bouncing madly against the narrow walls of the box.

Then she let out an excruciating scream.

Poe shook his head, finding her futility comical. "Now, now," he said. "This is not the time to make a scene."

Then he tacked the heavy wooden lid back onto the box, dampening her howling. Poe surmised that her death was coming along. Maybe another day or two. He struggled now with her story, but once she was dead he was sure to capture Anne's agony more vividly—the sheer terror, trapped inside these wooden walls, waiting to die in the darkness, the water bugs for company. Poe just needed an end to her. Then he would add her story to the others, in this, his masterwork.

He felt Edgar on his shoulder.

Poe was exhausted, bent over his computer, sensing it was closing in on midnight. It was then that Pluto jumped into his lap, clawing at him. He had brought home the stray, a wild black feline that he named after the main 'character' in Edgar's "The Black Cat." Pluto had the same vicious temperament as his namesake, but Poe was in no mood, swatting the cat away. The animal skulked over to the coffin, sniffing at the smell rising from the box, hissing and clawing into the wood. A sharp bang from inside the box sent him into a frenzy with his hair puffed, ears flattened, and fangs ready to strike—not that he had any way to reach the woman inside the box.

Edgar's stories had given Poe a mysterious word to ponder—'immurement'—meaning to be entombed alive inside a wall. It was a word that didn't exactly roll off his tongue, but stayed pictured in Poe's mind after reading "The Cask of Amontillado." What Edgar's Fortunato must have been thinking, finding himself shackled inside a narrow crypt wall where his friend Montresor had bricked him in, and where his bones would join the remains of others lying there.

Poe also needed to make his stories more vivid and real. The box he built from plywood and nails would be perfectly suitable. Then selecting the woman, the stalking, the drugging and kidnapping. More the immediate problem was Anne's desperate cries, pleading to be saved. The noise was enough to stir an elderly neighbor who came knocking on his door asking about the commotion. Poe conveyed to the old man—perhaps it was his black eyes—that he should avoid meddling in family matters.

It was Edgar who at last freed him from his current paralysis—this writer's block. His story would reveal itself soon. He needed patience with Anne.

It wasn't the first time his mentor had spoken to him.

"Your mind works differently," Edgar reminded him. "You live apart from the rest."

Poe understood. He lived in the dark, disregarded by those others who felt secure in their fantasies; that their lives made sense; their world was safe—that he, Poe, did not exist.

They would come to know him, though—their illusions gone—those who mocked him, called him a freak, as if he were something other than human.

Poe grinned, thinking of their lunacy.

It was well after midnight when Poe sensed the change in the room, the quietude. He tore away his blindfold and earplugs and ripped off his blue latex gloves, rolling them into a ball. Then he went over to the room's lone window and opened it, letting in the steamy street air. He threw the bundle out the window and into the black night, turning back into the room before the heap hit the sidewalk.

Poe breathed deeply. Relieved. Finally, he was ready to write their story. Anne's and his. He went over to the box and pried open the lid. Anne stared blankly up at him, wide-eyed and unseeing, a look of disbelief and terror. Her face, a contorted mask of death.

"Thank you," Poe said softly. "The fever called living is conquered at last."

Edgar's words stirred him once more.

He leaned over and kissed Anne on her lifeless lips.

Then he rushed back to his computer and began to write.

PART ONE

PART ONE

BONES

PJ Bones sighed, confronting the reality of his day, as he wound his way along the Upper West Side, moving past a flock of Sunday shoppers while sidestepping the sidewalk hawkers selling their stuff. His walk wasn't made any more pleasant at the sight of a beefy woman in spandex and a runner's bra scooping up some dog shit courtesy of her Shih Tzu, so appropriately named given the circumstances. It struck Bones that the dog and her owner bore a striking jittery resemblance and an intimacy shared in this public defecation.

Bones, in navigating the packed streets, grew only more irritated by the Bridge swarm ditching the weekend comforts of their ranches and colonials in Montclair or Teaneck, or wherever the New Jersey hell they resided, to make their way into "the city." Not likely the type to show up for his book signing taking place in a half-hour at the nearby Barnes & Noble. Most likely they were the Kindle crowd at best, believing that scrolling the almighty Amazon was a deep dive into the literary world.

So, PJ Bones was pissed, nagged by the street bustle, the empty faces, the shit—metaphorically and otherwise. He supposed he should be grateful. Not a single passerby recognized his presence by crawling up for his autograph or some god-be-damned selfie, those idiotic artifacts of celebrity. That celeb dance would likely come later at the B&N signing, the swap for the $28.98 paid for his latest and greatest. He abhorred the clamoring crowd, all too willing to stroke his ego. He was better off as another invisible New Yorker, but that wasn't likely with his fifteen best sellers, translated into some twenty-one languages. It was enough to make him rich and famous. Yet, always the critics. He did not write real books, only best sellers. Well, fuck the bastards!

Yes, Bones was not having a good day. And it was not about to get any better.

Bones pushed past the glass door into Barnes & Noble and paused to check out the recent popular titles stacked vertically at the front table. *Kiss and Kill* (a Sam Rock series) stood elevated atop the pyramid. Bones took a moment to glance at the cover with his name emblazoned in oversized 48-point Gill Sans Ultra Bold. His *nom de guerre* marked each one of his books. He'd let his readers ponder the identity of PJ Bones, though a quick search of Wikipedia showed that he was born Peter James to Liam and Margaret Bones, both from Staten Island and long deceased.

At this moment, however, he felt his blood rising, having noticed a thirty-percent markdown sticker plastered over the two initials of his name. It was one thing for the store to cut into his royalties, but burying part of his name under a damn discount sticker? A B&N sick joke.

Bones had mostly avoided the book-selling gallivanting around, leaving his publicity to some high-octane agency in Brooklyn. And then there were always the insidious tabloids that latched onto his renowned bad boy antics around town. His books spoke for themselves, he told himself, so he didn't need all the noise. Unfortunately, Bones' most recent hardcover, *Kiss and Kill*, did not speak loudly enough with its mediocre three-star reviews on Amazon. Even Bones' fervent loyalists had started to grow weary of Sam Rock, a hard-boiled private dick with a penchant to mete out his own tough justice. There were only so many bad guys to slap down hard and women to bed before finally getting to Part Three when Rock wins justice and saves the day.

Bones drifted back to his old days at the NYPD. He was more inclined then to use his wits than his gun, moving up the ladder quickly, making the detective rank in the elite Special Investigation Unit while still in his twenties. His rep took another leap when he brought down a Son-of-Sam-wannabe for a string of murders up in Washington Heights. The talk was of promotion when the internal scandal broke. Then came accusations of drug money and shakedowns that wiped him out of the department. He had nothing to do with those dirty cops but was swept out with the rest of them. So much for joining the force to "protect and serve" and "make the world right." He should have known better than to hold on to that bullshit—not that anyone was going to give a damn what he thought.

His one stroke of good fortune had come out of the blue. With nothing better to do now that he was out on the streets, he wrote his first crime-thriller—so Sam Rock was born, with his finely-tuned investigative sense and more than a bit of muscle. Reviews were good, not overwhelming, but still won him serious book sales. The second book was better, and by the third he was rolling. Bones had even found a way to kick the NYPD in the ass, depicting its fictional incompetence in cases only Sam Rock could solve.

At least, that was Bones' formula, and it worked well over the next dozen books that he churned out like clockwork. Funny how revenge bares its face. Still, Sam Rock was starting to show the strains of age, his boy scout idealism descending into middle-age cynicism. A Dorian Gray figure that did not escape Bones' attention each time he looked at himself in the mirror.

Bones snapped back from his thoughts, as a stubby, middle-aged man bounded up to him, grinning and waving his arms. Bones was in no mood for the bum rush.

"You like? See, we put your book on top of the stack!" the man said excitedly.

Bones warily eyed the stranger.

"I'm a big fan!" The pouched-belly store manager greeted his mega-star author with an outstretched hand. "Adolf, Adolf Himmelstein."

Bones reluctantly took the manager's hand, which was clammy and soft, like the rest of him. He then noticed a large Star of David around the man's neck.

"Adolf? What was your mother thinking with the name?" Bones said, pointing to the medallion.

Himmelstein blanched. "Well, uh…name's been in the family."

Bones shrugged. "Unfortunate."

Himmelstein winced, seeing his relationship with the famous author already trashed.

"If you don't mind," Bones said impatiently, "I've got a special bottle of Scotch at home that needs my attention. Can we get this afternoon going?"

"Yes, yes, of course," Himmelstein said unsteadily. "We should head upstairs to the event's area."

Bones took notice of the beleaguered store manager, for a second regretting taking out his bad day on this guy.

The two men walked by tables and racks piled with hardcovers, paperbacks, and store giveaways at three for ten dollars. Customers could take the B&N vibe home with coffee mugs plastered with Mark Twain's face or shopping bags with the store logo. The place was a sprawl, fashioning itself as a bohemian get-away for Upper West Siders that might find some nook and cranny with a book in hand before heading to the store's café to sip some joe.

Bones hurried past the pack of afternoon browsers trailed by Himmelstein and onto an escalator. As the belt inched toward the second floor, he found himself drawing closer to a young man waiting and wildly waving a book. Bones sighed for the second time that day, preparing for the assault about to come his way. Then he stepped off the escalator, coming face-to-face with the guy. Not a welcoming sight considering the acne plague that blighted his appearance.

Bones offered a cordial enough, "Hello, friend."

"I saw your picture in the store window!" the man exclaimed. "Real excited to see you in person. Read every one of your books!"

Bones, tilting his head in his bit of false modesty, replied. "Thank you. I appreciate readers like you."

Himmelstein happily chimed in. "I see you're joining us this afternoon for the reading."

"Wouldn't miss it," the guy said excitedly. "Jack Reacher just kicks ass. *Reacher's the bomb*, dude!"

Bones froze, shutting his eyes to blot out the cretin standing in front of him.

Himmelstein paled, anxiously reading the deadly silence radiating from Bones. "Oh, no, sir," he stammered. "Our window poster. That's Lee Childs. He'll be here Saturday. This happens to be PJ Bones. You know, the author of the 'Sam Rock' crime thrillers."

Himmelstein waved his copy of *Kiss and Kill*, needing to prove his point.

The man stared blankly at Bones, his eyes betraying his confusion. "You mean you didn't write this one—*Killing Floor*?" He absently held out his book as if he was expecting Bones to sign.

Bones smoldered, blood rising to his face. *Killing Floor!* He considered the poetic justice of killing the asshole on *this* floor where they stood.

Himmelstein tugged on Bones' arm. "Time to meet your readers, PJ," he said, aware of the quiver in his voice. "Mr. Bones, *please.*"

Bones glowered at the dimwit, shouldering past him. With Himmelstein's hand on his back, he found himself ushered into a backroom space where a hundred folding chairs had been set up. They were filled with store customers, most holding a copy of *Kiss and Kill.*

Himmelstein was momentarily relieved, eyeing Bones, still fuming.

"Great crowd!" he exclaimed, escorting his guest author to the front of the crowd. He crouched over to Bones, whispering in his ear. "Lots of books already sold."

Bones perused the audience, taking note of the misers who had yet to shell out cash for his book.

Himmelstein bounded over to a lectern that was set up for the reading. He surveyed the gathering before reaching over to a nearby table to align a stack of *Kiss and Kill* books— not that the books needed any such attention. He liked ramping up the crowd's anticipation for his grand event. At least Himmelstein thought it was a great idea. And then he took to the mic.

"Thank you all for being here," he chirped. "We have a *very* special guest today, the author of numerous, national *New York Times* best sellers. He will be reading from his latest novel, *Kiss and Kill.* Let us welcome PJ Bones."

To polite applause, Bones took over the lectern, nodding to the beaming store manager. "Thank you, Adolf...Mr. Himmelstein. By the way," he told the crowd, "my books aren't national best sellers," then turned to the store manager, "but international best sellers. Maybe I should get Sam Rock to take care of this guy for his disrespect. What do you think?"

Bones chuckled as if delivering a punchline rather than a menacing warning, giving his audience room for a small laugh. Himmelstein, his cheery façade quickly fading, faked a smile to convey he was in on the joke. It wasn't the first time that afternoon he felt unnerved by Bones.

"Well, good to see so many fans of our aforementioned hero, Sam Rock." Bones scoured the room, seeing heads nod their approval. "A private eye we all admire, yes? Willing to bring down those predators that lurk in the shadows set to cause harm. We need someone like that, don't we?" Bones could hear a murmur of approval from his audience.

"YEAH, SAM ROCK KICKS ASS!!"

Bones blinked, turning to the back row where a man was standing and raising a fist, exhorting the crowd on.

Zit-face.

Nervous laughter rippled through the room with the crowd unsure whether the pockmarked man making a scene was either a bit rambunctious or bat-shit crazy.

Bones seethed, glaring at the fool still on his feet and reveling in the attention.

Himmelstein considered whether Barnes & Noble was about to witness a homicide and anxiously grabbed the mic. "Please, *please!* We'll be taking your comments and questions later, but let's get back to our...*international* best-selling author."

Bones scowled, already worn out, just needing to get this fiasco over with and head home to let the Scotch drown out the misery of the day. He then reached over to a table to pick up a copy of his book—and stopped. A blood-red markdown sticker on the book's cover had obliterated his *entire* name. *Kiss and Kill by*...30% Off. He snapped around to Himmelstein, who flinched at the writer's sudden move.

"PJ...are you, are you...all right?" Himmelstein stammered, his forehead glistening with sweat.

Bones, fists clenched, had lost it. Enough shit for this afternoon; enough for his entire lifetime. His "fans" could take their marked-down books from some obliterated writer and go to hell!

Bones leaned back into the microphone, his anger bubbling over, and set to spit out his wrath.

"Mr. Bones?"

Someone had called out from the far end of the first row.

Bones growled at the interruption, pivoting sharply toward the voice, ready to confront this joker.

The sight of the young woman stopped him in his tracks.

"Mr. Bones, would you mind taking a question before your reading?"

Bones hadn't seen her before, but could not help from noticing her now. A cascade of dark auburn hair rippled down the woman's shoulders, framing her dimpled, heart-shaped face, but it was her translucent green eyes that mesmerized him. They zeroed in, and he could feel their impact piercing his body, at the same time silencing his rage. Suddenly, he was sapped of his pent-up fury.

Bones, bewildered, nodded to her to go on, strangely edgy to take her question.

"Mr. Bones," she began, her voice melodic with a trace of an Irish lilt. "You seem to have quite an imagination when it comes to choosing your killers. They seem quite vivid. Where do they come from?"

Bones drew in a deep breath, instantly beguiled by this young woman. He finally responded.

"Well, perhaps they are everywhere, even here in this room. How many of you have been swayed by the same passions, the same impulses that drive these killers? That given the circumstances, you might be capable of these very same acts of violence. We like to pretend to have a hard time explaining these people, that they are some aberrant beings, but maybe we aren't all that different—only that we refuse to believe it until that moment strikes us. That madness."

Bones paused, realizing he'd been rattling on. He glanced over to the young woman and shrugged, still feeling flustered.

"Are you suggesting then that *I* could kill someone, Mr. Bones?" she asked, smiling, the Irish in her voice more distinct.

"Actually, Miss..."

"Knox. Clara Knox, Mr. Bones."

Bones smiled back.

"Yes, Miss Knox, I think you have the real makings of a killer. I wouldn't want to get on the wrong side of you."

The crowd tittered at the intimate exchange between the author and the woman.

Himmelstein cleared his throat, snapping Bones back to his audience.

"Well, Miss Knox, since you asked." Bones graciously nodded. "Here's my latest psychopath," he said. "And our intrepid hero." Bones picked up a book from the pile stacked on the nearby table, turned to the opening page, and began to read.

"'Sam Rock first heard the crack of gunshots—boom, boom, boom—and then the swell of screams that rose in the air on the city streets. Twin noises of death and despair that echoed in the detective's mind long after fading into the night..."'"

BONES AND CLARA

Just a single, unsold book remained on top of the small table next to where PJ Bones was seated. He scanned the nearly empty room with just a few lingerers left, grateful that this "event" was over. His left hand was stiff after an hour anointing books with his signature.

Even Himmelstein was gone, likely crouched in a back room tallying the day's sales receipts—which, judging by Bones' cramped hand, must be sizable. Bones was certain though that he and Himmelstein were not about to celebrate, tossing back shots downtown at McSorley's. He caustically ranked this B&N experience just behind his two divorces and the death of his dog when he was eight.

He pushed back his chair and got set to leave.

"Could you write, 'To Clara, your devoted reader'?"

Bones, startled, turned and saw her standing there, awakened by the woman's perfumed scent.

Clara Knox eased closer to the table, a movement that set Bones back into his seat. She held Bones' book with both hands, then reached out to him, a gesture that unnerved him. This intimate sharing.

Bones fiddled with his Sharpie—Himmelstein's gift to him—silently eyeing the book. It struck him that Clara Knox might very well have leaped from these pages. This Irish lovely who had stolen Sam Rock's heart and soul, somehow materializing before him.

Bones felt her presence close to him, making him more uneasy.

He knew of writers losing it. Bones' favorite unhinged author was Hemingway, who wrote his own final chapter with a double-barreled 12-gauge shotgun to his head. It wasn't a death wish driving him at the moment, though he was seriously coming to grips with another confusing feeling taking hold.

Bones leaned into the book now resting on the table. He thought about an inscription, now desperate to find *something* to write to Clara Knox. Something more than just his cold signature. What was he thinking, anyway? Some endearment to his would-be lover?

Jesus. Had he lost his mind? He was way too old—approaching fifty—to have this bubbling up of adolescent angst. And she was way too young—he'd bet not even twenty-five. Pathetic. What was he? Some delusional reincarnation of Humbert Humbert? She his Lolita? How sick was that? She was just an autograph seeker, and here he was off the deep end. And sinking.

"May I have my book back?" Clara chuckled.

She bent over Bones, eyeing the title page. "You didn't sign," she said. Then she put her hand on his shoulder.

He flinched at her touch.

"I'm sorry," Bones stammered. "Just thinking of something else. Lost track."

"Yes, you look *very* serious," she said lightly.

Bones hesitated, thinking of what next to say. And then he said it. He couldn't have stopped himself even if he tried.

"Actually...I was thinking of you," he blurted out.

There. He had found the words.

They were the air. And no take-backs.

Clara Knox silently stood beside him, inscrutable. Bones cringed. Could there have been so humiliating a response? He was just another one of those assholes in her life hitting on her. Better if she had delivered a hard smack to his face. Better yet, a bullet to his head. Hemingway came back to his mind. Something, anything but this...silence.

"I'm very sorry," he said, licking his lips for his Scotch. He quickly scribbled his name on the title page. "Um, hope you enjoy Sam Rock." Then Bones forced a weak smile, a pitiful apology for his audacity.

Clara scrutinized Bones' barely legible signature, then came back to him, locking her eyes on his.

"I'd much rather enjoy you," she finally said.

Bones was dumbstruck, certain that he was the butt of her joke, but that wasn't the message this woman was sending. Clara Knox said she wanted him.

Impossible words.

Bones hesitated, not knowing what to say, but then stood up from his chair to face her. Clara's perfumed scent again enveloped him. He could see her more clearly now. She possessed a natural beauty. It was her iridescent green eyes that captivated him once more. Bones could hardly escape her gaze...then he did, his eyes drifting from the delicate contours of her face to the graceful curve of her long neck—only he suddenly gasped. Something was terribly out of place with this portrait.

An angry, jagged scar ran across Clara's neck from ear to ear.

Clara kept her eyes steady on Bones. The sensual atmosphere in the room had stilled.

"It's a long story," she said at last.

BONES AND CLARA

"I know a place," Clara said as they left the bookstore. Bones found himself unsteady as Clara looped her arm through his, drawing closer to him while they walked the short distance over to Amsterdam Avenue. The evening was growing more confounding. Clara then leaned her head against his shoulder as the cold night wind swept by tossing her hair and flushing her apple cheeks. Bones instinctively drew her closer.

Passersby might have mistaken them for lovers.

They settled into some earthy pub called The Dead Poet. The place was warm and dark with a burning fireplace that flickered about the worn wooden tables and chairs, with couples huddled closely together over drinks and hushed talk.

The getting-to-know-you conversation was worse than Bones had anticipated. Even before drinks arrived, he found out that Clara was all of twenty-three. I mean, what the hell was she doing here with him? What was *he* doing being here with *her*? Bones knew he had adoring fans pining for his attention, but this encounter was far more...dangerous. He couldn't put his finger on it. She wasn't some wide-eyed writer's groupie. Not at all. If anything, she seemed...in control.

Was she studying him?

Bones struggled, mystified by this Clara Knox. Was she just some virgin deciding "it was that time"? Maybe searching for her father's love? Even more questions spiraling through his brain, though Bones thought better than to ask them— lousy ice-breakers for certain. Besides, he wasn't sure he wanted to hear her answers. He wasn't sure of anything at the moment.

Bones badly needed a drink. He impatiently waited for the martinis, her choice, hoping to calm the shakes, a combination of being too dry and too anxious. By the fourth round, Bones had sufficiently liquored down his angst and half-drunkenly pronounced his personal theories to the ingénue sitting across from him. Clara didn't seem to mind. No, she wasn't a virgin—"There was this boy in college." As for Bones' dive into Freud, Clara bitterly laughed. There was nothing remotely alike between Bones and her father, except perhaps their mutual affection for Scotch whiskey. "Besides," she went on, "he's been out of the picture since I was a kid. Believe me, I have no wish to meet anyone that reminds me of good old Dad."

"Well, just sayin' that you'd better watch out for my type," Bones said, his buzz kicking in harder.

"And what type is that?" Clara replied brightly, also feeling the martinis hit home.

Bones pondered the question, shaking back his pending inebriation. "Twice divorced. A dropout at AA..." Then more softly. "And just way too old for you."

Clara grinned. "Not so fast. Remember that novelist, Andre Brink—what was he, 71 years old when he married this woman? What was her name? Oh, yes, Karina Szczurek. She was twenty-nine and beautiful and loved Andre. And they were happily married for ten years. So, screw Freud."

Bones shrugged. "Yeah, well, didn't he drop dead on a plane trip they were on? Poor guy was exhausted."

"So, that's it," Clara impishly smiled. "Afraid I'm too much for you."

They both cracked up, laughing loudly, liberated by drink and lustful talk. Bones could not bring to mind when he had ever felt this way. He surely desired this luminous woman, but there was something more. This is what it felt like being alive. That passion long missing from his life. Then why did he feel so helpless, unable to get past the verbal foreplay? Certainly, Sam Rock, his alter ego, would take the risk, the next step, he thought ruefully.

It was Clara who suddenly reached over to take Bones' hand. Strangely, her hand on his had the wondrous effect of quieting his nerves. Gone was the hellish day, his unrelenting anger ignited by the dog shitters, crazed fans, and the toadying Himmelsteins. Bones, defenseless, gazed at Clara, the heaviness of his old life slipping away. In its place, another feeling altogether.

He needed her.

"PJ...are you all right?" Clara said, her green eyes glimmering in the candle-lit room.

It was enough to bring him back from the jumble of emotions hitting him at once.

Bones tilted his head, contemplating this implausible turn in his life. "Not really." He sighed, shrugging his shoulders.

Clara softly laughed.

Bones watched the sound trickle up her throat, then shimmer on her face. Had he ever seen anyone as glowing?

If there was one hard fact that hit Bones squarely in the gut that night: he had fallen hard for Clara Knox. Too hard. He understood the absurdity, but there it was. Bones could not make sense of the feeling, so long gone in his life, and nor did he try.

BONES AND CLARA

Bones and Clara barely made their way into his West End Avenue apartment before tearing off their clothes and falling into each other's arms. Then, in a ragged dance, they staggered into the bedroom, toppling into a king-sized bed with all their pent-up sound and fury. Clara's orgasm shook the room with a crescendo of screams. She was insatiable, hardly giving Bones time for a breath, before bringing him into her a second time. Bones, overwhelmed, was thankful that his body parts were in working order, a serious concern considering his hard liquor diet all these years.

The musky air and stained, crumbled satin sheets gave evidence of their furious night. Bones considered how derivative the moment was—the older, angry author caught in the steamy throes of this much younger, mysterious woman. Had he ever dared to write such a scene in his book, *The New York Times* would have scalded him as a hack. (The paper was already leaning in that direction.) He chortled at the thought. Well, fuck the *Times*.

"What's so funny?" asked Clara, now puzzled.

"Just thinking."

"Not about another woman, I hope." Clara grinned, her body nuzzling against his.

"Well, yes, an old gray lady," he said, alluding to the newspaper's obscure nickname.

Clara playfully eyed Bones. "I guess I have some stiff competition for you."

Bones let loose a booming, joyful laugh. He willed himself not to bring such well-worn words to mind, but his semantic self-denial was an impossibility—could he possibly be in love with Clara Knox? This feeling was undeniable, one he hardly recognized. He recalled his first marriage years back to Suzy, a Vegas girl that knew a good time and no limits in bed. Bones found himself ensnared before coming to grips with her gold-digging and then the other men. Then there was Maura, their compatibility reflected in chain smokes and whiskey binges that quickly turned south with their ensuing all-out fights, sending curses flying and bottles shattering.

This, with Clara, was a world apart—intense, fiery, with their bodies yielding freely to each other.

They made love again, this time quieter, more loving than lustful. Afterward, Bones found Clara nestled in his arms, her leg snaking between his, her soft breath on his neck. He sensed every part of her, moving his hand gently along the curves of her body as if to reassure himself that she was real and there with him.

Bones felt so undeserving of this woman. He had been a bastard for as long as he could remember. The booze, the rage, the abuse he heaped upon friends, lovers, agents, publishers—most of whom had either given up on him or just stuck around for their next payday. Then he'd begin the cycle again, a temporary lull with new faces in his life, yet still the same bastard, only getting older, more embittered, with his better days spinning downward along with his book sales.

And now this woman, Clara Knox. Bones had no real idea who she was, but it was the not knowing that only fed his hunger for her.

Bones turned squarely to Clara, her face illuminated in the darkened room. He felt consumed by desire for this woman, a feeling he needed to confess—but Clara cut him short, placing a hand softly over his mouth, warding off any words that might complicate their intimacy. Bones eased back, vaguely disappointed.

Clara broke the silence, her eyes intently studying Bones. She needed to tell *him* something. About that day.

"It was two years ago at college," she began. "This man broke into my apartment, waiting. His arms, his entire body, covered with these hideous tattoos. He didn't say a word, just stood there, staring at me. Then he came over, took my hand. Told me I was beautiful. He held this large knife in front of my eyes. I couldn't move. I couldn't speak. Just terrified. He had this twisted grin, and said he *loved* me. Then he did...this..."

Clara traced the rope of scar that ran across her throat.

"He left me there to die in my own blood. My roommates came home early, thank god, called 911, and then the paramedics were all over me. Saved me. I should have died."

Bones listened silently, seriously.

"Did they ever catch the fucker?" he asked.

Clara frowned. "No, he's still out there," she said. "PJ, you write about these people. Why do they do such horrible things?"

Bones looked pensively at his young lover. He wasn't about to tell her that it was useless trying to find an answer that would make sense.

"I make up stories, Clara," he finally replied. "Psychopaths write their own."

BONES AND CLARA

They hardly left Bones' bed over the next five days except for runs to the bathroom and to the front door for the restaurant food deliveries. Bones had shut off his cell phone with its incessant beeps and messages and texts and all the crap that clogged his life. He had been amazed that Clara was in no rush to leave, settling in as if they were longtime lovers. By any stretch, a stunning turn for Bones. Clara Knox had not only stuck around but seemed like she just fit into his life. It was mystifying for sure, though Bones wasn't about to step into some deep mid-life analysis.

He knew plainly that he passionately loved this woman. Had he ever seen eyes as bright and penetrating or felt lips as soft? Had he ever met any woman that made him feel so...young?

Clara responded to his every touch, electric energy that sparked her cries of passion. Bones was bewitched, watching her stretch swanlike as she climaxed. He even went so far to imagine that Clara Knox might be falling for him as well! Should he even dare to consider that possibility?

Their pillow talk in-between their bouts of lovemaking was gentle and intimate. Clara seemed to be reading his mind.

"Do you think we are in love?" she said, cuddled under his arm.

Bones almost laughed at the off-handedness of her question but caught himself.

"I do love you, Clara," he said seriously. "But you already know that, don't you?"

"Yes, and PJ, I love you, too," she said.

Bones stared intently at his young lover nestled beside him, hardly able to grasp such words floating in the air. He was back to another lifetime when such feelings were bandied about in his youthful exuberance.

"PJ, can I ask you a question?" Clara asked softly.

"Of course, Clara. Yes. Tell me what you're thinking."

Bones never thought he'd be having *this* talk with any woman again—with *these* words that spoke of love. And, yet, Clara had miraculously appeared. It was all so perfect, he thought.

Clara squirmed higher to Bones' side, her face leaning next to his. Bones felt her warm body on his and gently squeezed her closer.

"How do they choose their victims?" Clara whispered into his ear.

Bones flinched, his peace of mind shaken.

"These psychopaths," Clara said.

Bones turned to her. A soft lamplight shadowed Clara's face as he reached out to touch her.

Clara backed away, lifting her head off his shoulder. She sat up in the bed, facing him.

"Why did he choose me?" she asked pointedly.

Bones was confused. How did this question find its way into their bed?

"This is important," Clara said, the lilt in her voice gone. "I can't figure it out."

"Clara, it's 3 a.m. Let's get some rest," Bones said lightly. "I need my strength to keep up with you." Then he tentatively smiled.

He felt Clara stiffen next to him.

"No joking, PJ. Why me?"

Bones was at once on guard, their lovers' murmuring gone. He turned to her, more perplexed. Clara, stone-faced and narrow-eyed, wanted nothing more to do with their intimate chit-chat. No longer was he her lover, but the cop he once was.

Bones grimaced, wishing *this* conversation away.

"Clara...these psychopaths search out people who are vulnerable, desirable."

"So that was me."

"Well, that's how your attacker sized you up."

"But why so vicious, so brutal?"

"They are sick, Clara," Bones said. "Living in a dark place they have created for themselves. Real life for them is humiliating. It is where they exist as outcasts, unwanted, unloved. They need to control, to dominate. Killing feeds the mania that runs in their bloodstream. That is their power."

"They are just monsters," Clara whispered more to herself.

"Well, that's the problem," Bones said. "They look and act like any one of us. They don't wear a tag identifying themselves as insane."

Bones felt himself sinking into his previous life as a young detective. He never did find a satisfying answer to explain these predators. No other creature on earth randomly kills their own. There was no Ted Bundy in the animal kingdom, a man who murdered and raped nearly forty women. Or John Wayne Gacy, another piece of work who played the clown at kids' parties, then went on to kill and mutilate some thirty teenage boys.

And too many others.

Bones shook his head, buried feelings of revulsion welling up from his days on the force. The disgust and outrage each time a dead body was pinned to his caseload. He'd been a good investigator and put away some very bad guys but other cases had run cold. Deadly mysteries that went unsolved. Anonymous psychos still out on the streets.

"Will you help me find this man?"

Another impossible question that startled Bones.

Where was this night going?

He desperately wanted Clara tucked back inside their cocoon before all this talk.

"Clara, I've been off the job for a long time," he said. "The police need to help you find this man."

"They have given up," she said sharply. "I'm not important anymore."

Bones knew she was right. Clara had survived, so that worked against her. It is the dead that get the most attention. She was just a buried case, forgotten in some detective's file.

"I can't let it go," she went on. "He still finds me in my dreams."

Bones had known too many survivors like Clara unable to break free from the demons that stalked their days and nights.

"It's best to move on," Bones replied quietly, hearing how trite he sounded.

Clara frowned, her eyes diverting to some distant thought. And then, inexplicably, she brightened, and was back to her radiant self.

"I suppose you're right," Clara said, smiling broadly. "I need to get on with my life. Correct, Detective Peter James Bones?"

Bones nodded, confused by Clara's sudden emotional turn.

"Yes, that's best," he said unsteadily. "And no thanks for giving me back my old job. My civilian life has been looking up of late."

Bones threw her a quizzical smile.

Clara grinned, oddly cheerful now, and gave Bones a long kiss before nestling up onto his chest, where she fell fast asleep.

BONES

Bones woke up the next morning to find Clara no longer curled up next to him—his last memory of her before falling into a restless sleep. A weird night for sure, but easing out of the bedroom he still felt a sweep of pleasure left from their lovemaking. He was happily looking forward to a leisurely post-coitus coffee chat with his newfound lover when he was struck by a darker feeling. Bones had not lost his intuitive sense that told him when something was wrong. And now that feeling hit him hard. The apartment was too quiet. Soundless.

The tranquility of the morning came crashing down, and Bones felt the rise of a stabbing headache. Not the kind that arrived after a bender, but one that spun wildly inside his blood before shooting into his waking consciousness. A premonition disguised as a headache. Like his bad old days on the force.

Bones thought to shout out Clara's name, but then instinctively held back. He did not need the silence to tell him. Clara was gone.

Bones turned back to his bedroom as if the empty space held an answer for him. Had he been some big-name author, just good enough for a fling with this astonishing woman? That couldn't be it. Not with the way Clara's body had meshed with his and the intimacies they shared over these days and nights. They were lovers, real together, of that he was certain. So, how could he explain why she was gone that morning?

He couldn't—only that he knew for sure Clara was not coming back.

Bones shuffled into the kitchen and stood there, leaning up against a counter, unable to rouse the energy to get his morning going. He felt sick, his head still pounding, accompanied by a crushing feeling that made him want to puke. And then he did, crunching over, the bile and booze from the previous night mixing and flooding the tiled floor.

Bones staggered into the bathroom and splashed some water on his face. Staring bleary-eyed into the mirror, he saw an old man's grizzled face that instantly reminded him of someone else: his father, another bastard. Milling in his brain something about apples not falling far from the tree. Had he dreamt up this Clara Knox? Was she some apparition that somehow flew into his subconscious to fill that vast, empty hole of his life?

Bones could not break away from his father glaring back at him in the mirror, angry at the world. Bones hadn't shed a single tear since he was nine when Liam Bones left him and his mother for "the other woman." Not that he would be missed. Certainly, not his alcoholic rage, his abuse, his viral unhappiness. It had been that other woman who much later informed him that his father had died. He'd been one of the jumpers from the South Tower that September morning. Maybe his dad's only moment in life when he felt totally free, a thought that haunted Bones.

Bones shook his head to free the memory, then headed to the kitchen for a coffee. There he saw the pink Post-it on the fridge door with Clara's scrawl.

"Thanks, PJ. It's been fun."

Clara signed off with a smiley-face emoji.

Bones read the note again, the pangs hitting him harder. Yeah, real fun. "You must be fucking kidding me!" he bitterly shouted out. Not exactly the shorthand love letter that spoke of Clara's undying devotion to him.

Bones crumbled the Post-it, pitching it across the kitchen.

He felt the old anger taking over.

"Are you some damn pubescent imbecile with a raging hard-on?" Bones scolded himself, but he could not sustain the emotion, already feeling drained.

Bones turned to open a cabinet, then pulled out a bottle, his whiskey. He drank straight from the bottle, readily letting the liquor overtake him. Suddenly, he was jarred from his stupor by a church-bell peal coming from his cell phone sitting on the kitchen table. He exhaled. Clara. He staggered over to the phone, tripping over himself, too late to pick up the call. A recording was left. Frantically, he swiped to hear the message. An anonymous caller babbling in Chinese. Maybe telling him to go fuck himself, Bones thought before heaving the phone at the kitchen window, shattering both.

He sat down at a table. He planned to make the whiskey his morning breakfast and huddled with the bottle over the next hour. His head reeling and his stomach in rebellion, Bones managed to make his way back to the bathroom. His father was gone from the mirror, and this time Bones saw his own blurry image staring back at him, the same angry bastard that deserved whatever damage came his way.

Bones barely made it back to his bedroom and collapsed onto the bed, smelling Clara before lapsing into the dark.

BONES AND MCBAIN

Bones was having a tough time with his forty-eight-hour hangover. The grand whopper, courtesy of his friend Johnnie Walker, had his different body parts crying out for mercy. A cold compress to his forehead seemed to have prevented his brain from exploding, but his bladder had a mind of its own. No sooner had he thought he had pissed the whiskey from his body, Bones was back to the toilet for another run. A stain lining the front of his sweatpants gave evidence to when he failed to make that rendezvous in time.

Bones hadn't slept but even the haze did little to blot out the memory. The damn Post-it note—with a smiley-face emoji!—had been the kicker, a punchline to his stupid adolescent fantasy, only he was nearing fifty, not fifteen, and what the hell was he thinking about with this Clara Knox?

Fuck, fuck, *fuck!*

He needed sleep badly, an impossibility. He had drifted on and off. The previous night brought his father back again, staggering home drunk, beaten and bloodied after a bar fight. Yeah, just a real nice visit to his subconscious. Both a waking and sleeping nightmare.

"Hey, Dad. Welcome to my world!" Bones called out to the empty apartment. At least no voices answered back, so he wasn't completely gone.

Bones swayed over to his cell phone. He vaguely remembered the phone buzzing during the past two days but had ignored picking up the calls. He knew for sure it wasn't Clara on the other side. Three messages flashed on his screen, all from the same number. Phil McBain, his partner from the old days, and the chief homicide detective at the 19th Precinct in Lower Manhattan. They were still tight from their early years as beat cops sharing a similar worldview. City streets were plagued by human garbage, and they were meant to clean it up. Not necessarily a sophisticated mindset, but it served them well in doing their jobs.

McBain's messages were short and not so sweet.

"Hey, dickhead, you might think about returning my calls."

Phil McBain wasn't the sentimental type.

Bones huffed out a deep breath, the day already growing heavier. He had few friends. In truth, McBain was it, the one guy he could confide in, not to mention set him straight in his fictional crime world. Bones had long been out of the loop regarding modern forensics and criminal investigation techniques, and McBain made sure his cops and perps and the rest of the inhabitants of Copland still walked the walk. More importantly, McBain was a trusted drinking buddy, the one guy who still put up with his bullshit.

It had mostly worked out for both men: Bones with his best sellers and McBain's steady rise in the city's detective ranks. McBain was now on the back end, getting set to cash out after his nearly twenty-five years on the job—awaiting him, a Mexican hideaway inhabited by expats that he'd been talking about. His career might have ended five years earlier—along with his life—after his squad stormed into a Chinatown drug den and the firing started. He survived, but two bullets were still lodged in his body from the shootout. The bad guy behind the door wasn't nearly as lucky, taking a full load from McBain's gun. Now the detective was almost done with that life with less than seven months left on the job. Then he'd pack his bags, brush up on his Spanish, and head south.

Bones knew they were both running on empty, a thought that did little to straighten his head at the moment.

He picked up his phone and punched in McBain's number. The detective answered the call just before it went to voicemail.

He greeted Bones accordingly. "What the fuck do you want?"

"Nice of you to call," Bones replied wryly.

"Yeah, three times," McBain said. "I guess you're alive. We should celebrate."

"To hell with you, too."

"Damn, PJ, why the isolation? They have monasteries in Tibet for that."

"Boring story," Bones said, already thinking the call was a bad idea.

"Okay, so a woman screwed you over. Not the first or the last."

Bones sighed. "Nice job, detective," he said. "Good to know you haven't lost your touch."

"Yeah, reading you is like a walk in the park," McBain said. "Actually, fortune cookies are tougher to understand."

Bones didn't have the energy to contend with his friend, the back and forth only compounding his headache.

"Hey, move your ass out of there," McBain said. "Beal Bocht at nine. No damn excuses."

Bones closed his eyes, shaking his head. Just the thought of the meet-up at the Bronx bar roiled his stomach, not that it needed much of a push.

Bones knew there was no use arguing with Phil McBain.

"Yeah, at nine," he grudgingly replied.

Then he hung up the phone, a stomach heave suddenly rising into his mouth. Bones gagged, but held back the acidy stuff, burning his throat. He stumbled back to his bed, silently praying for a few hours' sleep before meeting up with McBain.

BONES AND MCBAIN

Beal Bocht was a Bronx neighborhood drinking hole that attracted the locals and the kids from Manhattan College with its nightly music jams and craft beers. The two men lucked out finding a corner table away from the usual din that took over the small bar. The place brought Phil McBain back to his native Derry and he relaxed, easing back in his chair and taking in the ambiance. Bones faced him from across the small table, already on edge from a nearby electric guitar that pricked at his brain.

McBain's beer was one from the chalkboard. Bones hunched over his ginger ale, his punishment for his previous all-night bender. They sat silently, choosing to settle into the place. Then McBain got right to it.

"Hey, bud, you look like shit."

Bones smirked, not bothering to throw back the insult. The truth of it was, the years had not been kind to McBain either. He carried the wearisome look of someone that had seen too much ugliness on the streets. Bones still counted on him though, one of the very few reliables in his life.

"So, what gives?" McBain asked, cradling his beer.

Bones knew McBain was never one for small talk and saw no point holding back. Besides, the mess that was his mental state had only mushroomed since Clara left. He needed to talk.

"Eh, Mac, I can't explain it," he began. "This woman— young, gorgeous, smart, sexy, all that—but there's something else I can't put my finger on. Some mystery about her. I can't figure it out. I mean, it's stupid, yeah? Still, I can't shake her. How does this make sense?"

McBain sat quietly, listening. He had spent a career trying to figure people out. What made them tick. It never amounted to anything. Just a long line of thugs and victims over his twenty-plus years. He had decided to give up that waste of time. People were just too complicated, too capable of harm. They were never expected to make sense. It was a fact of police life that Bones should have known himself, and McBain felt sorry for his friend for believing otherwise.

Bones could not hold back, his story spilling out. The Barnes & Noble encounter. The drinks and flirty talk afterward. The rush to his place, and the next five nights and days, the frantic, frenzied sex. This enigmatic young woman declaring she loved him. Of all things, words that once were unimaginable. It did not make any sense—the emotional intensity of these days. Bones was certain of one thing—he had fallen too quick and too hard for her.

"Like some dimwitted schoolboy," he said scornfully.

"Given your track record...well, you know," McBain said.

"Yeah, but this was something else, Mac. This was...real."

"So, where's the problem?" McBain asked.

"That's it. I don't know. She left me a Post-it, telling me she had *fun*. She signed off with an emoji. Would you believe? A fucking, *smiley-face emoji*. For Christ sake! Last I heard from her."

McBain thought a moment. "Well, I could chase her down, if you want."

Bones snorted. "Nah, I'd probably graduate from lover to stalker, one of those real creepy, obsessive types. Then you'd have to step in with your gun."

They both laughed. It was enough to lighten the air for the moment.

"Damnit, Mac," Bones said. "Some asshole slashed her throat two years back. Messed her up royally. I'd love to get my hands on that guy."

McBain silently leaned back in his chair. His disposition had suddenly hardened as he lifted the pint to his lips.

Bones eyed his friend, mystified. McBain was seized by some distant thought. Bones recognized the look—the detective's brow creased in concentration, his manner on edge—that he used for his fictional Sam Rock as he confronted some unsettling news.

"What did you say her name was?" McBain finally asked.

Bones looked quizzically at his friend. "I didn't. Her name is Clara. Clara Knox… Why?"

McBain stared back then grimaced.

"Yeah, Clara Knox… She was one of mine."

"Just an ugly, violent attack about two years back," McBain said.

He had been the detective in charge of the Knox case, and his talk with Bones instantly revived old frustrations. He never caught the guy, nor did he ever make any sense of the incident. Clara seemed to be just another innocent victim who had the miserable luck to step into one of the city's shitholes.

"She was a real sweetheart," McBain said. "Then this bastard came along. Brutally cut her up."

Bones was stunned by the coincidence, but it made sense that his friend was the lead investigator in the case. The 19th Precinct was not far from Clara's old apartment in the Village.

"The case stuck in my head." McBain went on. "Just an innocent girl… She could just as well have been Becky." His thoughts drifted to his daughter, who had shunned him after Sarah died in the car accident. Her mother dead. Her father lost on the job. She was all of seventeen at the time.

"The case made a quick splash in the papers but then chalked it up as just another random attack," McBain said.

Bones wearily shook his head. "Clara told me some of the story. Really pissed that the guy was never found. Who could blame her?"

"Yeah, the case ran cold," McBain said glumly. "I made a point to keep tabs on her for a while. She had a tough recovery at the hospital. She was hurt so badly and wasn't right afterward. Just fenced into a dark place. Anyone could see that. Then her mother came and took her home to some small town in Kansas."

Bones thought back to his last night spent with Clara. McBain's account filled in missing pieces to her story, not that there was much more to tell. The deep scarring to Clara's body and mind were evident.

"Did you ever hear from her again?" he asked.

McBain hesitated, already regretting his response.

"Yeah, 'fraid so." McBain stared down at his drink. "She was arrested by one of our uniforms. About a year ago. She was around the Upper West Side, incoherent, out of control, dangerous, confronting people on the street with *a lead pipe*. She'd smashed up some cars, store windows. When I heard she was arrested at the scene and taken to Bellevue, I went over to the hospital."

"Jesus," Bones murmured.

McBain lifted his mug to take a swig. "I hardly recognized her, PJ," he said quietly. "She'd come back to the city. Still so young, but...hollowed out."

"And then what?"

McBain pushed his glass to the side, massaging the side of his head.

"She was in bad shape. In restraints at the hospital. We gave her a break after all she'd been through, but she wasn't well at all. The docs weren't keen on releasing her. They finally had no choice."

McBain paused, lost in the thought.

"That was the last I heard about her," he said at last.

"Until tonight," Bones said quietly.

"Yeah." McBain nodded. "Until tonight."

POE

Chapter 1
'Mary Jane'

"The death of a beautiful woman is, unquestionably, the most poetical topic in the world."
    Edgar inspires me.
    All stories have a beginning. How eager I am to start mine.

I admit to being a bit unsure, this being my first time out, but I knew she was the one from the start—nothing like those other spoiled college types. The ones with the incessant texting or those selfies or "Instas," or whatever crap they doled out on their phone. You know who they are—the whole "look at me" attitude, with their finger-swipes that beckon young men on their computers with the unspoken promise of getting laid. No, she seemed nice and cheery and also smart. I could tell that last bit since she'd carried a book about "existentialism" when I first met up with her at Washington Square Park. What a coincidence. I, too, had a deep view of our human existence. It was clear she was going to be very special to me.

"Mary Jane." I baptized her with a new name that was only ours to know.

Killing Mary Jane was never going to be easy, but the fact that she was dead now only went to show what can be accomplished when you put your mind to it. I may have implied that her death was random, like those military drones that wound up obliterating villagers minding their own business in some remote part of the world. That was just my natural modesty at work. No, Mary Jane wasn't the victim of some unexpected drone attack that blew her up…unless you were thinking metaphorically—that her killer was something like a walking time bomb set to explode when she came along. You would be right on that one. I do get that way. I mean, why fight your nature?

Don't assume, however, that I am just some fly-by-night killer. In fact, I find reprehensible those spur-of-the-moment killings, performed with such little thought and care. That sort of behavior only gives people like me a very bad name. 'Psycho,' for one, a slur that is piteously inadequate. I'm sure Mary Jane would have agreed with me given the attention I showed her.

Fate pointed me in her direction that afternoon at Washington Square Park. The neighborhood park was teeming with students and professors from New York University hustling past a large fountain, along with the usual deadbeats looking to score some shit to stuff up their noses. I felt in character in my tweedy jacket and tie and wig and mustache in place—I thought I bore a startling resemblance to Edgar. And there was Mary Jane standing underneath the park's marble arch next to a table with pictures of mutilated animals. She was chatting away with some animal rights' do-gooders spouting their political crap. She with her perfect teeth and perfect tits—not that I was being superficial.

Admittedly, I was uncertain—Mary Jane being my first, I needn't remind you—wanting to break away from the same old coed-killing storyline, the stuff of a thousand horrid horror movies. Nevertheless, I was convinced that she had called out to me. So, I ambled over and casually struck up a conversation, just like that. I admit to being taken in by her from the start. She was nothing at all like the girls I had known at the home long ago with their spiteful jokes and squinty eyes that told me I was a walking contagion to stay away from.

And me the sensitive type.

But that was then.

Mary Jane had this pleasant manner and respectful tone once I introduced myself as this bullshit professor. She told me her name. Clara Knox. Her eyes glowed happily. I took this as a sign of her feelings for me. She chatted on, telling me she was an acting major but still intended to save the children of Namibia or Haiti, or wherever. More crap like that. Then her lips pursed, and told me in a hushed voice—I suppose this was our secret—that she was thinking of changing her major to English Lit. Not practical but she just loved to read and live inside a writer's imagination. So, we had that in common, though Clara did not strike me as a fan of Edgar's. I wasn't about to hold that against her. Instead, I told her how impressed I was, that her future was as clear as day—I mean, was I lying? And she happily smiled back at me with those perfect teeth.

I then noticed a necklace around her neck and leaned forward to take a closer look. A small charm—a golden bird in flight—dotted at the center with a tiny turquoise stone, hung on a thin chain around her lovely neck. I was tempted to reach out to touch the bejeweled bird, but there would be time for that later. Instead, I asked her what it meant to her. Young girls love such nonsense.

"Oh, it was from a boy back home in Kansas," she said with a giggle. "He told me he thought I just needed to fly free of Willow Brook—that was the town in Kansas where we both grew up."

She thought a second, and nodded. "He was right. Here I am in New York City. And free!"

I nodded back, though I would not be surprised if she had been a bitch with this guy, letting him hang around with his hard-on. She knew her power. I could tell.

"Yes, I can see that you are very much a free and extraordinarily beautiful young woman," I told her, gazing at the delicate curvature of her face that ran from her high cheekbones to her soft, dimpled chin—such perfect symmetry that marked her beauty. It was all I could do to stop myself from fingering her moist, ruby-red lips. Of course, that might have been considered a hasty move, this being our first getting-to-know-you encounter.

Clara's smile instantly faded. Maybe it was the way I kept staring at her.

I could see her forehead crinkle, her manner suddenly confused. Was this guy—this "professor"—hitting on her?

"Well, thanks, I guess," she said shakily, narrowly eyeing me. "Gotta run to class now. Nice meeting you."

I couldn't miss the quake in her voice. Not quite as cheery as a few moments before. She quickly hustled off. At least I had broken the ice with her—and then, of course, there was no turning back.

Naturally, I needed to know her more intimately and saw right off that she wasn't one of the shy ones. The Instagram pictures at parties, the drinks raised to the camera saluting her inebriation, and always the boys flocking around her. Bees to the honey. I saw in their eyes their desperation, wanting her for themselves, not that they would stand a chance.

I scrolled through her zillion "friends" and "likes." I even posted an anonymous message to her page, telling her how beautiful she looked in her pictures. And she got back, with a question: "Who r u?" And then a smiley face. I could tell that things were going so well between us.

Hunting her wasn't difficult at all. I enjoyed the fun-loving photos of her posing with girlfriends outside her apartment building off Cornelia Street. I admit, my obsession was growing, stalking her around the neighborhood. I had to be careful though. One night while walking back home, she abruptly stopped and turned, sensing my presence in the shadows. I could see a flash of worry on her face as she nervously scanned the empty street.

It was time to take the next step in our relationship. So, I broke into her ground-floor apartment, a small, three-bedroom job that she shared with two roommates, and patiently waited. I had to give her credit—the place was spotless, with beds made and dishes stored away. Hardly what you'd expect from some college kids. The roommates, as I had expected having surveilled the place, were gone—and just as well, since I didn't want to complicate the afternoon with more commotion. I just needed some quiet time with Mary Jane.

I settled into her bedroom, tossing aside a stuffed panda lying on her pillow. The room was decorated with a few posters of long-haired, emaciated, pockmarked rockers from some previous generation. I remembered hating these fuck-offs back then, pretending the shit coming from their guitars was something we needed to hear.

I had previously shed my wig and mustache and oiled my body and shaved head. I felt like my old self, checking out my appearance in a large mirror that hung over a dresser. My body was a glorious covering of tattoos imprinted on my chest, back and arms. Edgar was with me, his images and words. I was particularly proud of the black raven that draped my left shoulder and upper arm. I had already planned to ink Mary Jane above my heart. She was deserving.

But Mary Jane was running late. I glanced at my watch—she was usually back after her afternoon class. I was concerned until I saw her through the window striding down the street. Kind of a skip to her walk; not a care in the world. Seconds later, I heard a key in the front door, and she bounded through and into the living room. It filled my heart to have her here with me. She was so young and shining and full of life.

Of course, Mary Jane froze when she saw me standing there. A pillar of stillness. She didn't, or couldn't, utter a sound. Her darting eyes revealed her deepest fear. I could see her thinking. This stranger, here in her house, his bare body shining and painted with tattoos. And he was coming toward her with a large knife in his hand...

I was quickly by her side and could see she was already riveted by my black eyes. Her pale face accentuated her ethereal beauty. She was shaking uncontrollably and gathering the strength to let loose a scream. I put a finger up to her red lips to make sure she understood our relationship.

It struck me what it was about Mary Jane that so powerfully stirred my obsession. She was my "Ligeia" that Edgar described in his story as his "spirit-lifted vision." She also dies young, tragically, though her spirit does return to life. So, maybe Mary Jane will find some comfort there.

I saw Mary Jane more clearly now as she trembled in front of me. This was different from that day in Washington Square Park. She was so childlike, budding into a rapturously alluring woman—and I was meant to kill her.

Mary Jane had yet to utter a single word, but finally asked me what I wanted. I appreciated that she had mustered up the courage. Her question, of course, was predictable. I imagined each and every Mary Jane asking the very same question, though I didn't see the point. It was clear what I had in mind with the knife in my hand. Still, I fervidly loved Mary Jane then and felt her quivering vulnerability.

I will respect her privacy in this journal given our subsequent intimacies—only to say I felt quite relieved when it was over. She was my first, and it hadn't been easy bottling my emotions for all this time, but then the release, the pure ecstasy. She had been exquisite.

Perhaps, though, I should not have been surprised just how quickly those feelings take hold again. After all, I am only human. The first only made me want to feel the exhilaration again. The addiction settling into my blood.

Edgar would surely understand this passionate craving—to still the beating heart of those others to come.

POE

Chapter 2
'Edgar'

I had been a kid when Edgar came into my life. He just seemed to appear in the dark of night as I huddled under my bedcovers at the children's home. By flashlight, I read his stories well into the morning hours. How do you find sleep as a child after picturing a killer that dismembers an elderly man, then buries the corpse under the floor planks of his room? I imagined Edgar's words, closing my eyes in that dark space, seeing the killer's story come alive.

> I think it was his eye! yes, it was this! He had the eye of a vulture—a pale blue eye, with a film over it. Whenever it fell upon me, my blood ran cold; and so by degrees—very gradually—I made up my mind to take the life of the old man, and thus rid myself of the eye forever.

And then the killer, so assured of his perfect murder as police arrive to investigate. That is, until the sound of the old man's heart beating from beneath the floorboards echoes in his ears.

> Oh, God! what could I do? I foamed—I raved—I swore! I swung the chair upon which I had been sitting, and grated it upon the boards, but the noise arose over all and continually increased. It

grew louder—louder—louder! And still the men chatted pleasantly, and smiled. Was it possible they heard not? Almighty God!—no, no! They heard!—they suspected!—they *knew!*—they were making a mockery of my horror!—this I thought, and this I think. But anything was better than this agony! Anything was more tolerable than this derision! I could bear those hypocritical smiles no longer! I felt that I must scream or die!—and now—again—hark! louder! louder! louder! *louder!* "Villains!" I shrieked, "dissemble no more! I admit the deed!—tear up the planks!—here, here!—it is the beating of his hideous heart!"

Not exactly the bedtime story that mother read to me when I was an infant. A time when she might have loved me.

I took out a pad and pencil and under the beam of my flashlight drew sketches of Edgar's tales. Soon I was using my body as a canvas. Childish ink drawings ran up and down my arms. Later, I would properly puncture these images into my skin.

Edgar made me think about the thin line between life and death. And, so, I began to write, stealing an empty notebook from some kid's desk, and dreamt of my own stories. I started with Edgar's words.

"The boundaries which divide Life from Death are at best shadowy and vague. Who shall say where the one ends, and where the other begins?"

Edgar understood with such clarity that each of us exists in the shadow, hovering between the tugs and pulls of life and death. The chaos that lies between the light and dark. The hope we cling to on one side and the terror that beckons us on the other. We live and suffer here, helpless against the buffeting winds of our existence that sweep us back and forth.

I gave this place a name. The Maddening.

It was then, as that boy, I decided to *become* Poe, a fateful decision—not that I had a real choice. I was barely visible at the children's home, a "freak" that other kids spitefully called me. They would never understand me, or care to. Neither would my counselors or anyone else. Only my parents tolerated me, but that was earlier on. I guessed they felt obliged, though I saw the confusion in their squinting eyes—how they could have possibly brought this person into the world. It didn't matter anyway since they were dead after the accident. Then I was taken away to live with these other kids with their own dead parents.

It was here at this "home" where Edgar and I bonded, having even more in common than I thought at first. Edgar's father had abandoned him when he was nine years old. Then his mother died a year later. Both of us were orphans of the world, and he understood me as he saw himself. There, in his poetry, he spoke to me.

> From childhood's hour I have not been
> As others were – I have not seen
> As others saw – I could not bring
> My passions from a common spring.

Edgar. I saw your life's suffering in the photographs. Your eyes diverted from the camera lens as if something else was preying on your mind. The dark circles that sagged onto your sunken cheeks, signifying your inner despair. There is only unhappiness in the thin, crooked shape of your mouth. I know all about you. Your drunken binges and failed suicide attempts. Your anguish built on the fear that you are alone in the world, as you were as a child, not even three years of age, when your beautiful mother, Eliza, a star of the stage, dies at twenty-four from consumption. The dreaded tuberculosis that attacked her lungs. So cruel, the coincidence, when the disease takes your beloved wife, Virginia, also at twenty-four.

Then the other women, but you were rejected or bereaved by them all. So, they are disguised in your stories and poetry—Annabel Lee, Berenice, Madeline Usher, Rowena, Lenore, Ligeia. Yes, they all die on your pages and in your life, so lost are you in the "death of a beautiful woman."

To live in such darkness. They found you delirious, shabbily dressed, penniless, and lying in a gutter after a bender at the Gunner's Hall tavern in Baltimore. You spent the next four days in a state of frightening hallucinations and incoherence. So ignominious. Your official death at the hospital: brain congestion. A stupid euphemism for drowning yourself in alcohol. At forty years of age.

How you must have anticipated and feared those last tormented moments of your life, crying out your last mortal words. "Lord, help my poor soul!"

Take solace, Edgar. You live in me.

I am amazed at how much I have transformed into you in my black wig and mustache, but I will never be able to inhabit your fictional world. That is where you are safely guarded, deeply ensconced inside your stories, hiding behind your *dramatis personae* from those malignant spirits. I don't begrudge you, yet I can't be satisfied just imagining your world. I need to feel more, to live inside of it—to be among people as an all-powerful manifestation of your subconscious.

So, I will write *my* stories. The world needs to know me for who I am. My purpose. My passion. My power. Someone whose mind works differently. Like yours. We are the same. You. Edgar. And me. Poe. We both exist in the darkness.

POE

Chapter 3
'You Mock Me'

Mary Jane still lives in the world.

How am I supposed to be okay with that?

You are alive! To deny me my "first"!

Cunt!

You are called Clara Knox. To me, you are only deserving of the name I gave you—Mary Jane. It was meant to be your dead name.

I take your current state personally. Lying there in a pool of blood, pretending to die. I hate such teases. You are one of those, aren't you?

I admit that I hadn't been entirely honest with you in the professor's guise and all, but fate brought us together that afternoon at Washington Square Park, and you chatted on about saving the world, and that you loved writers, and everything else. Just trying to impress me. I remember your eyes, magnificent. They glowed—like emeralds. I'm sure you must have heard that line a hundred times before, maybe on your slutty sleepovers at NYU. And yet, I listened to your bullshit, and didn't I even tell you how special you were?

And then later, at your apartment. There you were—you could barely breathe when you came through the door and saw me. I hid none of me from you. You were a picture of loveliness—the most beautiful woman I'd ever gazed upon. I opened my heart and loved you. And you loved me, too—didn't you?—so shy, you just didn't want to show it, though I could tell you weren't entirely comfortable. That must have been the knife.

Then the deed was done quickly. I bet you hardly felt a thing. I assumed our relationship was a thing of the past—these things happen—but then you survived.

It wasn't all your fault that you lived, I suppose. Just bad timing with your roommates showing up and then the whole emergency save-your-life thing. Regrettable. You've become a big splash in the news I see now—front page, your picture, and headline, "College Student Survives Slasher." Makes you a big deal celebrity, right? The article says you nearly bled out, but paramedics saved you. A lesson learned on my part. My new rule number one—never take for granted that a relationship is over until the very last drop of blood is spilled. Sounds dramatic, I know. But a rule to live and die by.

I'm off topic. It's the exasperation that's talking. I must see you again. We are fated. You must know that deep in your heart. I suspect, however, you might be left with the wrong impression of me. That I am a failure. That I am not enough of a man to get the job done. Impotent.

How you must mock me.

Like others I had known who tried to humiliate me.

You are out there, somewhere, Mary Jane. And I will find you. We will settle our differences. Your need to live. My need to see you dead. To have you one last time.

I must finish our story.

CLARA

New York was meant to be Clara's dream destination, the break from Willow Brook, population 8,053, where she was born and lived her entire twenty-one years before coming to the city. But then the monster came, cutting her body, taking her mind. The knife-rape that penetrated deeply.

At the hospital, she heard the same patronizing words from the doctors, nurses, her mother, Rose. "You are lucky to be alive." Clara wanted to respond. "Why?" Wouldn't she have been better off dead?

Rose was in New York to take her daughter home after three weeks in the hospital. The horrific wound around Clara's neck had healed as best it could, the doctors told her, though she'd always wear the thick, jagged scar across her neck. This macabre necklace. The blade had ended at the edge of her jugular. Just another inch. So, she was lucky to be alive.

Nothing about this was fair.

Clara had played by all the rules. A good girl from a broken home. And now she was being taken from the hospital back to Willow Brook, broken herself. Rose pushed her wheelchair through the corridor, out an exit door, and onto the city streets. Clara had insisted on walking, but there were the hospital rules. Gusts of cold air hit them as they left the building, sweeping Clara forward as she lifted herself from the chair. Rose caught her before she fell to the sidewalk.

"Everything is going to be all right," Rose said, hugging her daughter.

Clara clasped onto Rose, whispering in her ear, "Nothing will ever be right again."

She sensed that her mother knew that already.

Home was a 1,400-mile journey from New York, but Willow Brook existed in some time warp where families kept their doors unlocked and everyone knew everyone else's business. There were "the problems" that were ignored until there was no other choice. The crystal meth did a good job stoning the kids at Willow Brook High, and then something far worse when Joe and Molly went too far in their senior year. The drugs came pouring in, with crystal meth replaced by fentanyl meant to fix the kids' boredom in between the video games and the life-sucking hole of social media.

The small-town veneer was pleasant enough to hide the truth of the place. Clara's father, Wendell Knox, had played a leading role in the fiction as the upstanding president of the town council before word got out that he was screwing a high school intern in his office.

He hightailed it out of Willow Brook after the seventeen-year-old told him she was pregnant and the local papers got wind. Rose was sympathetic toward the girl, but she kept a shotgun loaded should her husband dare show his face at home. Clara got to see the baby girl, her half-sister named Leah Beth, after the former intern visited one afternoon. Clara was startled to see that the kid had her dad's bright sea-green eyes that she, too, had inherited.

Clara easily played her part growing up in town. She was *the* popular girl of Willow Brook High, at the center of her school's chatty, flirty crowd. The only time she'd pushed the line was letting Billy Bruster feel her breasts at the local drive-in before making the move to shove his hand down her panties. She'd slapped his hand away, and Billy pouted, but she would have none of that until they were "official," though she wasn't even sure that Billy was the one. In fact, she was sure he wasn't, but liked the idea he quarterbacked the Trojans and was the "big man on campus." The team name even sounded dirty and made her giggle. Clara enjoyed bringing up the "Trojans," giving Billy her wide-eyed wonder look. Billy wasn't all too happy seeing his team disrespected, much less Clara's cock teasing, but Clara was the most beautiful girl at the school, so he'd put up with it.

Not that he had a choice.

Clara understood her power, catching the incessant gawks from the senior boys with one thing on their minds. Boys were so predictable, she scoffed, smiling to herself. In any case, she planned to hold onto her virginity until the "right one" came along, and that wasn't about to be Billy Bruster or any of those hicks.

Her high school graduation marked Clara's intended flight from Willow Brook, but that meant having money, so she stuck around. She first took care of business, letting go of Billy and the rest of the crowd. Then she helped Rose run her flower shop in town. Her nights were devoted to community theater, and audiences agreed she was "a star," a point raised in the *Willow Brook Gazette* heralding her as the next Vivian Leigh, should a remake of *Gone with the Wind* be in the offing.

It took two more years, but with enough savings Clara was determined to go west to Los Angeles. No doubt, she was destined to be "discovered," as her incandescent beauty was made for the Hollywood screen. That all changed the day a mail delivery came with an unexpected scholarship to New York University. She had applied on a whim. A great acting school there. This good fortune was meant to come her way— and it was New York City!—and no doubt she would make her mark there. She was convinced.

At the start, "the city" was overwhelming with more people living in four-square blocks than in her entire town! University life shook her Midwest provincialism. Clara embraced a new circle of friends that spoke languages and had skin colors other than her own. She had found a second life brimming with possibilities.

Her first decision was to shun the dorms in favor of an apartment on Cornelia Street with two other girls, and a stone's throw from Washington Square Park. She loved the laid-back ambiance of Washington Square, hanging out with hippies strumming guitars around the big fountain amid the familiar sweet smell of marijuana wafting through the park.

Soon she was taking center stage at the university theater, and finally giving up her virginity to her opposite lead after the high of playing Lady Macbeth. Clara was also finding more to her new self, joining protests against climate change, racial injustice, and political corruption—a far cry from Willow Brook where politics was as welcome as a bad virus. With fifteen other seminar students, she sat around a long table to talk about great books that opened her mind and imagination. Words that inspired her.

It was all going so well. Her life was impossibly right.

Of course, that was before her life was obliterated by the knife, a never-ending spool of traumatic memory, always ending with her dying, choking on her own blood. He had been waiting for her in the shadow of the apartment. She'd sensed something wrong before seeing him. And then she did. He was statue-like and smiling as if he was greeting some long-lost friend. She saw him in parts. His glistening head. His muscular bare torso. Tattoos running across his chest and down each arm, a phantasmagoria of horror. She stared at his outstretched hands, beckoning her. In one hand, he held a long knife that shimmered across the room.

And then he came over whispering how beautiful she was, as he gently pulled her down to the floor. She couldn't resist, just powerless, her eyes transfixed on the knife he held up before her eyes. He reached over to touch the charm that hung on a chain around her neck—a golden bird in flight. Then he ripped away the jewelry, laying bare her throat. She looked into his black marble eyes. Soulless. And waited to die.

Clara could still feel the sensation of the cutting as the cold blade entered her neck. He started below the ear on her right side, deliberately taking the knife across her throat to her left ear. She felt she had been decapitated with blood spurting from her neck, a torrent of blood that wouldn't stop.

But, somehow, she was still alive, holding on, the killer caressing her, as she choked and convulsed. And then it went black, until the hospital, where she awoke in a frenzy, screaming. She remembered them strapping her down before the drugs took over.

And when she finally calmed down, she was certain that Clara Knox—the young woman she'd once been—was dead and gone.

CLARA

"Do you want to talk about what is going on?"

Clara despised the shrink with his imbecilic probing. What was this, her tenth or hundredth session over the past year? This same asshole. She had grown tired of playing with him.

"Your mother told me about the other day," he said. "You wrecked the house pretty good."

"Yeah, I was pissed off. You see, there was a call from this shrink. He was going on, asking me whether I was still on the meds that he'd prescribed. I told him to fuck off. Wasn't that you?"

Clara chortled at the sight of Doctor Glotzer sitting across from her in his office. She disdained his fake, feel-sorry facade, no doubt looking to impress her, spouting his psychological mumbo jumbo, pretending he understood her rage, but the bastard was interested in more than her brain. Him with his ogling eyes. Another Billy Bruster who wanted to stick his dick in her. She was sure that was it.

"Since you've been home—it's been a year now, right?—you've isolated yourself from your friends and everyone else," Glotzer said. "And you're very angry. This can't be good for you."

Clara smirked. What could this man possibly know? She only had enemies around her. Her old girlfriends, with their phony sympathies, looking at her as if she were damaged goods. Feeling she deserved what she got, leaving Willow Brook for New York City, thinking she was better than the rest of them. But she wasn't around for their amusement and let them know it. Yeah, they were shocked when she told them to go fuck themselves and get the hell out of her house.

"You are lashing out, and your mother feels helpless," Glotzer continued. "For your well-being, I believe you need help in a more controlled setting."

Clara might have cracked up if she hadn't felt so numb. A more controlled setting! Put her away in some nice room, then feed her those small green and yellow pills while the white coats pat her on the head with their bogus smiles? What a joke.

Had she the energy, Clara might have told the doctor about waking up each morning, seeing her reflection in the bathroom mirror, someone mutilated and monstrous. This grotesque creature staring back at her.

She would tell him she felt dead inside. That she was cutting herself, her jeans hiding a ragged mass of scars that traveled up her leg. The irony was perverse, but the compulsion to take a blade to her skin was just too strong. That she needed to feel something. That the pain jolted her from her deadened self.

Glotzer was just an incompetent fool, Clara bitterly thought. The meds he prescribed did nothing to stop the madman waiting in her nightmares. Then the knife-rape that made her scream until Rose rushed into the bedroom, holding her, wiping the sweat from her face, and telling her everything was going to be all right. Again.

What would this doctor think if she told him how she really felt? Would he be fearful knowing the rage that had overtaken her? Her need to strike, and maybe kill someone, anyone. Her girlfriends, neighbors out for a stroll. Maybe him. Even Rose. Yes, he would be afraid then.

It was later that evening Clara overheard Rose talking on the phone. She quickly recognized that the call was from Doctor Glotzer. They were talking about one of those places with a nice sounding name that hid the fact it was just another type of prison, and that Rose was considering having her locked away there.

Clara was not going to have any of that.

That night, she packed a suitcase, and in the early morning made her way to the town's terminal and took a Greyhound bus back to New York City. Clara always understood there had been no other choice. She had to return to where it all began.

CLARA

Clara exited the massive Port Authority Terminal, back in the city where her previous life had ended a year earlier. An Uber took her to a small hotel in the West Village. She registered at the front desk before tramping up the three floors to her room. Clara plopped down on a creaky bed, staring up at the ceiling with its spider web of cracks. She hadn't stayed in the room more than a few minutes when she brushed off the trip's fatigue to take to the streets.

The gray city streets were bustling as Clara made her way uptown along Seventh Avenue. She strode past the less than trendy restaurants until she ran into the crush around Times Square and the jam of tourists on line for two-fers at a Broadway ticket office. She ambled by stores with their window displays of Big Apple souvenirs, and up past 60th Street and into Central Park, filled with visitors on this sunny day. Clara wound through an entrance path before coming to a roadway, where a cyclist in his skin-tight spandex outfit nearly plowed her over, leaving the memory of his middle finger. Clara walked on toward a small construction site next to a park restaurant. A three-foot-long lead pipe had been left there by a worker. Clara wasn't quite sure why she decided to pick it up, only that she needed to.

Clara zig-zagged along the path to the northwest corner of the park, passing sparkling green lawns dotted with families and kids and people with their dogs panting to be unleashed. It was a city scene that brought to her mind the famous French painting with fancy men in top hats and women in their Sunday best, shading the sun with their parasols while relaxing at a Paris park along a river. She remembered as a kid seeing the painting in an art book and thinking how enchanting it was—to live in such an ideal world. It was nothing like the feeling she had now moving along the Central Park greens and all the happy faces.

Clara felt her head spinning and gripped the lead bar tighter as if it would steady her. A middle-aged woman approached, looking concerned, then put her hand on Clara's shoulder to see if she was okay. Clara snapped back, swinging the pipe, just missing the woman, who cried out, alarmed.

Then Clara took off, running full tilt, wielding the weapon, clearing away any park-goer that dared to step in her way—not that anyone was thinking of getting close to her. She scuttled out of the park at West 100th Street before sprinting across to Columbus Avenue. She stumbled to a stop, gasping for air, bent over, staring at the object in her hand. She had no idea why she was holding the pipe—or why she started smashing things up. It began with a car windshield, and then a storefront window, leaving the sidewalk strewn with shattered glass.

Then she was swinging the pipe wildly in the air, warding off some invisible enemy, petrifying passersby. And that's how the two cops found her as their cruiser came screeching up to the street with lights flashing. They didn't look too kindly but managed to calm Clara down and free the pipe from her grip without taking out their tasers.

Then they brought her to Bellevue.

MCBAIN

Bellevue Hospital's former reputation as the black hole for the insane was well-deserved. It was the oldest public hospital in the country, its infamy immortalized in movies and New York notoriety. Norman Mailer was brought to the place after stabbing his wife, and also Mark David Chapman after he shot and killed John Lennon. The good news: the hospital had new digs at 28th Street and First Avenue. Gone were the gated doors and boarded windows. A better staff as well, compared to the days when three nurses were accused of strangling an alcoholic to death. Back then, Bellevue was just the first stop for criminals on their way to prison or maybe a padded cell at a state institution.

Clara might very well have joined this group had this grim-faced detective not given her a break—not that Detective Phil McBain ever intended to charge her. Earlier that afternoon, he had gotten wind of a young woman—this Clara Knox—brandishing a weapon and running wild on Columbus Avenue, smashing everything in sight. He was relieved she had not included other human beings on her rampage.

McBain had rushed to her hospital room ordering a nurse to unshackle Clara from the bed railing. He then straightened her pillow, watching her sleep. The sedation had kicked in, though the drugs did nothing to stop the spasmodic shuddering that rippled across her face. Clara wore the damaged look that McBain had seen on too many victims.

So, Clara Knox was back in New York City. He had worked her case about a year earlier, torn between his pity for the young woman and his frustration for failing to capture the crazy who had viciously cut her. He understood her trauma, and Clara was deep into her suffering.

She reminded him once again of his daughter, Becky, who he hadn't seen in nearly three years. She was also struggling with her demons. The last McBain had heard, Becky was out in Portland, living on the streets. She had bolted a month after Sarah died, blaming him for messing up both their lives. And she was right about that. The detective could never escape the job—the murder and rape and all the utter depravities that had driven him into a dark hole.

And Sarah. He loved Sarah from the day he met her—she was twenty-two, blue-eyed, and loved Springsteen—so they were fated. A month after they married, he joined the force, and it was all so good in those early years. Working up the ladder, he earned his gold shield before he was thirty, and soon afterward Becky came along. McBain wasn't sure when he finally realized that the job had beaten him down. The wearing away began slowly, but by then he was in the belly of the beast with no way out. Sarah had stuck with him, his sole anchor.

And then the accident. A twenty-four-year-old drunk behind the wheel barreling headlong toward Sarah's car on the West Side Highway, full of testosterone and alcohol, with a killing machine going ninety. Sarah was dead on impact. Not a single moment left in her life to call out to him and Becky. He would have felt Sarah's love reaching him if only she had that one moment left, but she never stood a chance.

And now Becky was gone, too. She left a note that broke his heart. All she ever wanted was her dad—his love—but he was never there for her. McBain vowed to bring her home when he was done with the mean streets. That is, if she could forgive him.

McBain glanced over at Clara, also innocent and broken.

"I will find this terrible man," he told the young woman, trapped deep in the recesses of her agitated sleep.

CLARA

Clara pretended she was still asleep, listening to the two doctors crouched around her bedside buzzing about in hushed voices. They had finally come to an agreement a few days earlier about what to call her: a paranoid schizophrenic. Whatever the hell that was, she thought. More words to talk about her. More bullshit.

She could hear one of the doctors leaving the room, while the younger of the two men came over and nudged her awake. Clara pretended to stir and opened her eyes. She smiled teasingly at the doctor. She remembered him from the previous day, with the same grim look after checking out the crisscrossed scarring on her legs. He added an involuntary grunt to his observation. Clara enjoyed seeing his discomfort.

He cleared his throat, peering at her medical chart. "Clara, why did you get so violent that day on the street?" he asked, looking up from the chart.

"Isn't it obvious?" Clara said. "Just look in your notes. I must be there. Paranoid schizophrenic. Isn't that what you called me?"

Clara saw a ripple of worry cross the man's face. Then she reached over to grasp his hand and pulled it over to her breast.

The doctor, red-faced, jerked his hand away.

Clara laughed derisively. "No worries, doc. I guess I'm not your type."

The doctor scowled. "The nurse will be in shortly to check your vitals," he said stonily, backing away from her bedside.

Clara settled into her hospital room over the next few days. There were the routines and the constant hum of activity with nurses and young attendants in their pressed purple scrubs coming in and out, casting a wary eye. She was still under psychiatric observation and imagined how she came across to these people. A human tragedy, mentally deranged and physically mutilated. Were they thankful for not ending up like her? Maybe even casting a silent prayer—"There but for the grace of God go I."

Clara bitterly laughed at the thought.

The autumn sun had drifted through her window. Clara was beginning to feel some sense of calm with the drugs tamping down her agitation. But it was the nights that brought out the monster hovering in the mist. He spoke softly to her as she slept, words she could not make out. A voice without a face. He was so very close. She could feel his breath on her face. The dream so vivid. She needed to wake but could not free herself from the mist. And then she felt his hands all over her body, caressing her, invading her. She moaned from his touch and then heard him calling out a name, only it wasn't hers.

Confusing, disturbing.

She was struggling.

Needing to shed the mist.

Needing to wake.

Unable to escape the dream.

Or the monster.

Calling out to her.

Mary Jane.

That's what he kept calling her.

Mary Jane.

CLARA

Clara woke up in a sweat after another nightmarish sleep, immediately sensing someone by her bedside. Then she saw him. A male nurse in scrubs, a surgical cap and a mask that covered most of his face. Only his dark eyes were visible.

"My, you are up early this morning," the nurse said, his voice muffled under the mask. "The sun is just coming out."

Clara was not in the mood for small talk, staring suspiciously at the nurse.

"I'm getting ready for the OR, sweetheart," he said lightly. "You're lucky not to be going under the knife this morning."

Clara gasped. "What do you mean?"

The nurse laughed. "Oh, no worries. You need to relax."

"Yeah, well, I can do without the stupid humor," Clara said angrily.

The nurse shrugged. "Need to check your vitals," he said, "and here are your meds."

Clara squinted at his name tag as he leaned over. Daemon Ultrecht. She had the distinct impression that the man was smiling at her under his mask, a look that unnerved her.

"I've been checking in on you while you slept," he said. "Rough one last night, yes?"

He lifted her hand and placed two fingers on her wrist. "Ah, you are still a bit excited."

Clara felt exhausted. She had willed herself to stay awake during the night but didn't stand a chance with the drugs having the final say. Then she was back in the mist, held captive. An unseen presence calling out to her, only it wasn't *her*—Who was this…Mary Jane?

"Your gown," the nurse said. "You're soaked through." The nurse fingered the hem of Clara's patient's gown.

Clara suddenly winced. She felt a dull ache in her groin. Then she noticed blood droplets had streaked down her thigh and onto the gown and bedsheet.

Clara was certain this was not her time of the month. She reached under her gown to touch her vagina. It felt tender.

What happened?

Clara alarmed, searched for an explanation.

"This will make you feel more relaxed," the nurse said, attaching two plastic bags filled with liquid to an IV drip. "And so will this."

He handed Clara a small paper cup with two white pills.

Sitting propped up in the bed, she emptied the pills into her hand. They looked foreign to her, but she threw them into her mouth, swallowing the drugs with a sip of water. Clara saw the nurse's eyes crinkle above his mask—something funny again had struck him. He was too strange, too weird, though Clara did not try to figure it out. She suddenly felt so tired, her eyes fluttering.

It was just then that the nurse leaned over to the side of the bed. Without a word, he hoisted up her gown, leaving her partly naked and exposed. Clara was mortified, her head spinning. *"What...are...you..."*

"Shhh," the nurse whispered. With a moistened sponge, he began to gently wipe the blood from her thighs. Clara was stunned, her head swirling from the drugs, but then closed her eyes, the sponge caressing her body, now circling her inner thigh.

Clara whimpered at the nurse's touch.

What was he doing?

She thought to tell him to stop but wasn't sure she wanted him to.

"Better, yes?" he whispered in her ear.

Clara felt her body go limp. The drugs were hitting her hard now. Clara had lost her voice, slipping into a dark void before she could reply.

CLARA

Clara was still disoriented when she was roused awake later that morning. Taisha, her daytime nurse, was by her bedside. The last thing she remembered was the male nurse sponging her body. She cut off the thought, confused, not about to let on with the fortyish, no-nonsense woman.

"You're looking tuckered out, darling," Taisha said, removing an IV needle from her arm. "You should get out of bed and walk."

Clara nodded. The drugs, the dark dreams. The night nurse. Something ominous in the air. Clara desperately needed to escape from this room.

Taisha squinted at her patient, concerned. Her demeanor quickly turned serious. "What do we have here?" she asked. The nurse pointed to Clara's blood-streaked hospital gown.

Clara shrugged, embarrassed. "Guess that time," she said unsteadily.

Clara avoided Taisha's wary eyes as she lifted herself from the bed and hurriedly donned a hospital robe.

"I'll change later, Taisha. I'm off and running…well, maybe just a walk around the floor." Clara smiled weakly.

Taisha shook her head. Something was not right with her patient, and she was about to say so when Clara hastily trudged over to the door and stepped into the corridor.

The hospital was bustling with personnel tending to their duties. Clara wandered by the line of rooms, peering in at patients tied to their machines, before coming to a visitors' room. She wasn't sure why, but she opened the door to the empty space and went in. The room had little to offer except for a table with a coffeemaker and a stack of small plastic cups. Then Clara caught sight of a bookcase stacked with old paperbacks likely donated by visitors. She once loved to read and felt a flicker of that old interest as she bent down to randomly search the twin shelves. The usual complement of popular novels featuring "an epic tale of one woman's courage" and "a heart-pounding journey into the unknown."

It was a photograph on the back-jacket cover of a crime thriller that caught her attention. The picture reminded Clara of the writer, Dashiell Hammett, a favorite of her dad's. She recalled her father showing her a picture of the writer with his silver hair and black mustache. Clara remembered being struck by Hammett's serious, lean face and soulful eyes. It was a near identical likeness that she saw on the cover. A best-selling author by the name of PJ Bones.

Clara carried the book back to her room. Settling into her hospital bed, she pored through the pages, absorbed by the writer's protagonist, some private eye named Sam Rock. The man was more than capable, winning hard justice for suffering crime victims, but not before obliterating the evildoers that caused their horror. Rock punished the wicked, righting the world against those malevolent forces lurking in the shadows.

Clara had scarcely finished the book when she dashed back to the visitors' room. She lucked out coming across an almost pristine hardcover of another crime novel in the series. It was titled *Kiss and Kill*. The name PJ Bones was boldly imprinted across the top cover.

Clara leaned back on her bed, finishing the book in a single day. She was again taken in by the story. This writer understood the rage, the madness that enveloped her. That her only escape was to find and ruthlessly destroy the monster that tormented her—to right the world—and free herself. There was no other way out.

PJ Bones had written his stories thinking of her—Clara had no doubt—and she knew then what needed to be done. She recalled her literature professor telling the class that "fiction is autobiography." When the story is done, he said, "the reader sees the writer for who *he* is."

"Yes, I know who you are, PJ Bones," Clara said, making her pronouncement to the empty room. Her plan had revealed itself. Clara remembered her old self, the games she played with Billy Bruster, the power she possessed. It would take time to get her head straight, her life in order, but she needed to prepare. So, when the time was right, she would be ready. She smiled tightly, knowing what needed to be done.

Chapter 4
'My Clara at Bellevue'

Mary Jane and I were fated. No other explanation could account for how she returned to my life. It had been a year since our relationship ended—how could I ever forget her? She was my first, the one person I most cherished. I had been angry finding out she was alive, but that was more a reaction to my own ineptitude. I see it now. So, I have been given a second chance with her. Funny, the turns of life.

You can imagine my shock when the police brought Mary Jane to Bellevue Hospital that afternoon. It was as if they knew all along she needed to come back to me. All's well that ends well, and, believe me, I didn't intend to take this good luck for granted.

Not that I wasn't deserving. After all, I was a respected nurse at Bellevue, having come quite a long way in the profession since my boyhood days dissecting small forest creatures. Truly an American story. I later stepped up to nursing school, and then my early hospital experience cleaning up patients' shit and puke. I soon found the real deal in the operating room, sidling up to surgeons and their swift calls for a scalpel, forceps, clamps, and sutures. Their surgical cuts into the human body opened my imagination. I was particularly fond of open-heart surgery. I could see—and even hear—that fist-sized lump steadily pumping blood into large arteries. Quite the thing when the heart stops beating during an operation. Usually lots of commotion afterward with the surgeon and nurses scuttling about. All very eye-opening, and

I planned to make use of this knowledge. As they say, a mind is a terrible thing to waste.

Yes, I was beloved at Bellevue. Glowing praise from doctors and administrators, patients and their families. I was even given a certificate noting my compassionate nature. Just nice to be recognized. The job hardly paid the rent for my Harlem apartment, although it did have other perks. Sharp blades in various shapes and sizes were there for the taking, along with drugs and surgical supplies that came in handy. And, so, the necessities were in order.

And then came that day when the cops wheeled in Mary Jane. I could not believe my eyes when she was taken into the emergency room, strapped to a gurney, babbling and agitated. She was just raving mad using foul language I never would have approved of. Miraculously, she was back with me at the hospital and still part of the living world—a fact that stirred up old emotions and memories. How could I have been so inept then when I ran my knife along the soft fold of her throat? I recall the sensation—like skating across ice, smooth and effortless. Here she was, a year later, and it dawned on me—a greater plan was at work. Yes, Mary Jane and I were fated. No other explanation was possible, and she needed to know I was here for her.

Some precautions were necessary when I came into her room at midnight while she slept. I quietly hooked up an IV drip and then fed her the barbs. The drugs did the trick. I didn't want her to fuss while I sponge-bathed her body and whispered in her ear my plan for our future. I was certain she heard me—and felt my touch. Her moans and whimpers were sounds that danced in the air for me. She had an exquisite body with a distinctive mole on her inner thigh. I traced my finger around the beauty mark, seeing her body twitch, no doubt desperate for me to go further. Still, there was no need to rush. Our time would come soon enough.

Naturally, she didn't recognize me in my scrubs and mask when I woke her in the early morning hour. I was pleased to see the thick scar that circled her neck, a keepsake that surely reminded her of me. We grew even closer over these days and nights at the hospital. I had maneuvered the midnight shift to tend to her and was overtaken by her vulnerability as she slept. So angelic as she had been that time before. One night I spoke to her tenderly, then caressed her body. She stirred again from my touch. Then I removed her gown. No longer could there be any secrets between us.

Mary Jane was gone. It was Clara.

Three days later, Clara was discharged from the hospital. The doctors evidently surmised that nothing more could be done for their patient. I disagreed—we were only starting to bond together. I could smell Clara's intoxicating presence in the abandoned room and longed for her. I was left instead to clean up her room's detritus, coming across a thin chain with a charm of a golden bird in flight. I pocketed the necklace, with the promise I would personally return it to her. Then I noticed two hospital library books next to her bed. Crime thrillers by this big-shot author, PJ Bones. I'd bring them back later to the hospital library.

Edgar was with me then. He assured me Clara would come back into my life. You will have her again, he promised me.

"Love, like death, is eternal," I heard him say.

And I believed him.

CLARA

Clara Knox sat at a first-row corner seat at Barnes & Noble waiting for the program to begin. She could see the author, PJ Bones, standing by a side table stacked with copies of his book, getting set for his talk. Seeing him in the flesh excited her.

It had been nearly five months since her stay at Bellevue, and Clara had made good use of that time. The makeover, exercise, and Xanax helped hide her demons. She also understood her beauty, her allure, and that realization gave her confidence. There had been no problem learning more about PJ Bones, a favorite hell raiser with the tabloids and the online chatter about his drinking and womanizing and public scenes involving both. Amazon gave still another story. Bones was selling books based on his reputation, but strong hints of reader rebellion were bubbling up in lukewarm reviews. The overall gist—the tainted NYPD detective turned best-selling author had become an angry, embittered shell of his former self.

Clara was counting on that.

Clara was not entirely sure of her plan, only that she was convinced that this man would help her. She wanted his attention—that was going to be the easy part—but she needed his serious commitment. Not only would he find her monster but deliver punishment. PJ Bones would free her from the demon who consumed her.

He was the one.

She waited impatiently for the start of the event when a bulbous man with a horrendous dyed-hair fringe around his bald pate took to the microphone. The store manager was the blustering type, making a show of fiddling with a stack of books on the table. Finally, he introduced his famous guest writer.

PJ Bones then took over the mic, a tired version of his cover picture. Clara still saw his uncanny resemblance to Dashiell Hammett with his silver hair and black mustache, but Bones' lean face was more lined, his eyes less soulful and more pained. He also came up to the podium angry, his body coiled. Then, weirdly, he started by making some joke about being an international best-selling author that made the store manager wince and the audience snicker. And just then a pockmarked man shouted something out from the back row setting him off, his writer's façade crumbling into something more menacing.

Clara closely watched Bones at the podium, primed and considering his next move. For a moment, she thought the storm had passed, but then the strangest thing. The writer picked up a copy of his book from a table, staring at its jacket cover. Suddenly, he jerked back as if he'd been electrocuted. Then, flushed and furious, he leaned back into the mic, and Clara knew nothing good was about to come next.

Clara reacted instinctively, rising from her chair to face the writer. Now was the time to make herself known.

"Mr. Bones, would you mind taking a question before your reading?"

It was enough to break the tension thick in the room.

Clara could see Bones' eyes softening, his rage wilting. He seemed stunned. And she knew, as she always did, that she still had the power.

The rest was by the numbers. Waiting for his fans to clear afterward before approaching him as he sat at a small table. He was startled and flummoxed as she came up to him, asking to sign her book. She had PJ Bones without even trying. Then the getting-to-know-you-chit-chat at a local bar; her girlish coquettishness and he with his psycho-babble about older writers and younger women. She could read his mind. How undeserving he felt to have met such a wondrous woman. Clara understood his vulnerability, the anger sparked from his personal history. A life with its perpetual despair.

Then they went back to his place. It hadn't been easy for her. His sexual aggressiveness at first triggered the memory of her horrific attack. Bones needing her too desperately. Clara misjudged just how hollowed out he was, how broken. She was fearful to let him take her, but she did, convincing him by her cries of pleasure. The second time was easier. And so was the third. She was grateful that his wild stabbing had become softer and she could finally relax.

Clara moved cautiously, teasing out her dark story of being left for dead after being brutally cut open by her savage assailant. All that was true, of course, but Clara could see that Bones still failed to understand what she needed from him. He was still too caught up in the fantasy of this mysterious, beautiful woman who had miraculously come into his life. She would need to go further, telling Bones that she loved him, seeing the magic elixir of that lie on his psyche, his tough guy posturing dissolving before her eyes. He was so exposed, so vulnerable. His desperation unleashed in their frantic fucking. Clara thought that even Billy Bruster would have been cooler had she seduced him.

Clara wanted Bones even closer. She wasn't sure how, but PJ Bones would rid her of the demon that possessed her. So, she had no choice. This deceit. The Post-it with its curt goodbye would work. He would feel that blow hard. And to make sure, she added an emoji face. Smiling.

PART TWO

BONES

PJ Bones leaned back in his overstuffed chair, looking out into the darkened audience space where some thirty students sat and waited for the "special guest seminar" to begin. Sitting across from Bones on the bare stage was Professor Jack Metcalf, a near-legendary figure on the Columbia University campus. It was Metcalf who supervised a cult-like graduate writers' workshop known throughout the university. Over the years, the workshop had hosted "serious" writers as well as best-selling authors that had gone on to become household names. Bones belonged to the second group.

When Bones received the invitation from Metcalf, he wasn't sure whether he'd fit in with these ivy elites. Peter James Bones had been born blue collar, narrowly making it out of City College before becoming a cop. But he knew of Metcalf, and the guy was a straight arrow not looking to score points with his famous guest writers. Bones relaxed on the stage and waited as the student buzz in the small auditorium quieted down.

"Mr. PJ Bones," Metcalf pronounced. "Let's begin at the beginning. How did you get your start?"

"Well, I started by first getting fired from my day job. Then I needed a payday and began writing. How stupid was I to think that was a good idea?"

Students in the audience nervously laughed. Most knew the rumors of Bones' past. He had been branded as a dirty cop years ago, tied to drug dealers and unceremoniously let go from the city police department. The force had buried the investigation, but these bureaucratic secrets had a way of getting out into the public.

Bones felt at ease. He knew that the class knew, so why bother trying to be coy? In any case, Bones was not about to try to set the record straight.

"As it turned out," Bones went on, "it was the best thing that could have happened to me. Instead of dealing with bad guys and dead bodies, I could stay out of that business and sit at home and make up stories. Besides, my pay grade jumped considerably."

A young woman shot up her hand. "But your stories are all about these terrifying people, yes?"

Bones smiled wryly. "That's true, but the bad guys finally get what they deserve, one way or the other."

Bones suspected that this audience was wary of his stalwart hero and easy endings, but added, "Good to have Sam Rock on your side, yes?"

Metcalf nodded. "Yes, you have created an iconic character in your Sam Rock. A character of moral certitude. Where did he come from, PJ?"

It wasn't the first time Bones pondered that question, not that he had a clear answer. He fell back on his stock response. "I wasn't capable of writing the great American novel. I was just interested in writing a best seller. So, I thought that Sam Rock, my tough-as-nails PI, might make some money for me."

Metcalf chuckled. "But PJ, isn't Sam Rock just your alter ego? That you have created yourself in his mold?"

Bones shrugged, conceding Metcalf's point. "Yes, but he has lasted far longer than I did. I suppose we should give him credit for sticking to his guns, so to speak. . .he still is holding on."

"Holding on? To what?" Metcalf asked.

Bones looked out into the audience, eyes intently on him.

"He believes that justice will eventually prevail."

Metcalf nodded. "And you, PJ?"

Bones paused. "Let's just say I'm still thinking about it."

Bones had enjoyed the one-on-one interview with Metcalf and his group of serious, young writers looking for a way to break through. He mingled with the students afterward, their rapid-fire questions searching for the magic bullet that he'd somehow found. 'How do you find your stories, your characters?' Then the more practical. 'How do you find an agent? A publisher?' And so on, until Bones had enough, trusting he hadn't sounded like bullshit.

"Thank you, PJ."

Jack Metcalf came up to his shoulder as Bones pulled on his overcoat. "You were a hit with those folks. They appreciated your straight talk."

Bones didn't know if his host was just feeding him the standard line but hoped he had come across honestly.

The two men shook hands, and Bones turned to leave by the side auditorium door. A man, older than the other students, approached him.

"Mr. Bones, may I have a word?" he asked.

Bones held back a laugh at the guy's formality that made him sound like some schoolmarm.

"So, what's on your mind?" Bones said.

"I am an admirer of your career, quite remarkable," he said. "I am about to start mine. I am writing this story, very promising, and wouldn't mind you reading a chapter or two."

Bones was bemused at the guy's audacity. "What do you write about?" he asked curtly.

The man thinly smiled. "Human nature."

Bones narrowly eyed the man, his patience quickly fading. Something about the man's demeanor made Bones uneasy, though he couldn't put his finger on it. The guy was odd for sure—a bad wig and a spindly mustache that made his drawn face look unbalanced—but there was something else. Something lurking behind his dark eyes that seemed...ominous. As a detective, Bones had seen that look before on hoodlums he'd put away, but this guy wasn't that type. He was different though Bones wasn't about to waste his time trying to figure him out.

Bones was set to leave. "Sorry, friend, just don't have the time. Working on a new book and, you know, deadlines and all."

"That's quite all right," the man said coolly. "But mark my words. You'll be hearing my name one day. There's room for both of us, isn't there, Mr. Bones?"

The conversation had turned sideways and Bones' old instincts were back on edge. "Well, then good luck," he said warily, pushing open the auditorium door.

"See you then, Mr. Bones."

Bones took a step outside the room. As an afterthought, he turned back. "So, what *is* your name?"

"The name is 'Poe,' Mr. Bones," he said. "You know, as in Edgar Allan."

BONES AND CLARA

Bones left Columbia and walked the mile back to his West End Avenue apartment. The night air revived him, and he looked forward to seeing his lover. The last few months with Clara Knox had been astonishing—she was astonishing. He thought back. What were the odds of bumping into her downtown at McSorley's that night? He was certain that he'd seen the last of the woman—not that he still didn't obsess about her. Then seeing her at the bar, casually sipping a beer, when he came over, angry and out of control. It was all a blur now, only that she had come into his bed that night, and, this time, stayed. His gut feeling had told him something wasn't right—she was back with him, but why? After a while, he decided not to think about that question anymore.

The jaunts to McSorley's had become his nightly hangout after Clara had left him. Bones was a bad drunk, though Doc the barkeep gave him some extra latitude. His rep, however, only instigated the splashy headlines that featured the fights, the women, the mess of his life.

It had been nearly three months since those frenzied days and nights with Clara. He didn't blame her for leaving, just surprised why she'd been with him in the first place. Maybe she'd been out to notch a celebrity screw for her bucket list…but that wasn't it. She wanted him. She said she loved him. Bones believed her, at least until he saw the damn Post-it, and then that was that.

Bones was just tired of it all. It wasn't just Clara checking out on him but the whole shitty ball of wax that was his life. And he was willing to bury it all that night at

McSorley's with as much booze as necessary to get thoroughly wasted. Bones had already lifted back at least a half-dozen whiskey shots—he had lost count—before he saw her sitting there, drinking a beer at a corner table. Even the bar's dim lighting could not hide her from view. She seemed to illuminate the space, and Bones felt the old pangs surging and hitting him hard. What the fuck! His head was spinning. She hadn't noticed him, and for a moment Bones thought he'd just get the hell out of the place. Instead, he took a deep breath and then strode unsteadily over to her table.

"Clara Knox," he said, smirking, as he approached her. "So whaddaya say? Been a while, eh?"

Clara looked up from her beer and gave Bones a warm enough smile. "Wow, Peter. Yeah, it's been some time," she said brightly.

"Yeah, two months, three weeks, and six days," Bones snapped. "But who's counting?"

Clara slowly sipped her beer. "Well, things are going okay," she said finally. "Had a place in the Village, something of a hellhole. Zabar's has the best bagels, so I moved to the Upper West Side."

Clara chuckled at her joke.

Bones glowered, infuriated at the woman's nonchalant bullshit and attitude, the whiskey hitting hard and not making him any friendlier. He cut to the chase. "Yeah, I got your Post-it when you bailed out. Not a lot of information there, you know, about your future plans."

"PJ, we had a good time and all," Clara said calmly. "I didn't want a big scene or anything, so I split."

Bones wasn't into mincing words. "Kind of fucked up, if you ask me," he snarled. "You fucked *me* up!" Bones could feel the alcohol fueling his fury.

Clara sighed, her head tilted. "Well, I'm sorry about that."

She evenly eyed Bones.

"How can I make it up to you?" she said.

Bones furiously blinked his eyes. Then he slammed the table with his fist, spilling Clara's beer. "How can you make it up to me!"

The violence was enough to stop the bar in motion.

"Hey, PJ, easy man," Doc called out from behind the bar. The barkeeper wasn't about to take on another one of Bones' drunken fights.

"Yeah, Doc, no problem, I'm good," Bones said tightly.

He needed to get the hell out of the bar, away from this woman.

But then two things happened at once.

Clara leaned over and reached out to take Bones' hand. At the same time, a freelance photographer from one of the tabloids, and a regular at the bar, pulled out his camera and started shooting Bones and Clara at their corner table.

Bones jerked away from Clara and furiously pointed his finger at the man. "Get the fuck outta here before I shove that camera up your ass."

"Freedom of the press, my man." The photographer smirked and then snapped another picture. Bones made his own decision and bolted over. By the time Doc came from behind the bar to haul Bones off of him, the photographer was tending to his busted nose.

Doc got the man up to his feet and patted away some make-believe dirt off his collar. Then he handed him back his camera. "Joe, get a cab. You might check in at St. Vincent's about the nose."

The photographer fiercely turned to Bones. "You bastard. I have a surprise coming for you."

Bones took another step toward the guy, but Clara stepped in his way. "We need to leave, PJ," Clara said, then placed her hand on his shoulder.

Bones angrily shrugged her hand away. "Hey, I don't need that from you!" he barked.

Clara looked directly into his eyes. "But you do need me, don't you, PJ?" she said quietly.

"Need you? No! No fucking way!"

But Bones knew he was a liar...and so did Clara.

The next day, the *New York Post* had a featured story on its main news page, hyping Bones' "brutal assault" of the paper's photographer. The story was accompanied by a large picture with a caption—"Clara Knox hand-in-hand with the hard-bitten, best-selling writer."

A headline ran atop the story. "Beauty and the Beast."

BONES AND CLARA

PJ Bones was getting used to his second life with Clara Knox these past few months. She was, simply, a wonder, and they were making it work. Cutting back on the whiskey and some exercise had helped him shed the extra ten pounds and get back to semi-fighting shape. His mind was clearer as well, though he was having a tough grind figuring out Sam Rock's latest exploits.

He was still unsteady around Clara but decided not to give the feeling too much attention. Their sex was hot-blooded, but there was something more. Her luminous presence was inescapable. He felt passionately "in love." He held back from laughing at the idea—*who the hell was this PJ Bones, anyway?* Still, there was this mystery about Clara that unnerved him. It was her eyes that gave her away. They were elusive, looking past him into some distant thought. At those moments, he carefully kept from probing. He wasn't about to complicate their relationship. There had been enough complications in his life. Even so, the question stuck in his mind—just *who was this Clara Knox?*

Bones' agent came by his apartment that early fall afternoon. He hadn't heard from Milo Beckett in a month, which was unusual. Maybe it was *Kiss and Kill's* modest success, gone from the *Times'* best sellers list after only a week. Still, both men shared a loyalty of sorts. Bones knew Beckett could be prissy at times, but the agent had gotten him through the door when he first started out, convincing some bigwig at Random House to take a shot at this ex-cop's debut crime thriller. And it had worked out for both of them with the best sellers, the notoriety, and, of course, the millions.

Bones escorted Beckett into his study. Clara arrived a minute later with a drink tray. Bones found himself strangely ill at ease seeing her there, uninvited and then taking a nearby seat.

"So, PJ, how's our boy, Sam Rock? What are you working on?"

Beckett, as usual, got right to the point.

"Just taking some time," Bones replied evenly. "Something will come up. It always does."

It was not the response Beckett was looking for.

"You know, this is a three-book deal," he said pointedly. "We already have the advance. Seven figures. December deadline. How's that going to work out?"

"Like I said, Milo, I'm working on it," Bones said testily.

Bones was annoyed at his agent but knew he wasn't being fair. The contract was huge, and his new publisher was touting the arrival of its best-selling author and getting set for a national release of his next book.

"I have an idea."

Clara leaned forward in her chair, breaking her silence in the room. Both men turned to her. Bones sat quietly. He intuitively knew what she was about to propose.

Clara's eyes shined as she told Bones and Milo the story that Bones must write about.

BONES AND CLARA

Bones had stopped writing that afternoon when Clara slipped into the study, bright-eyed and carrying a tray with drinks. Her expression changed seeing Bones lost in thought at the desk. The only sign of movement was a screen saver flashing on his computer.

So, how is it going, detective?" she asked directly. She placed the tray with the two martinis on his desk.

Clara had pushed him hard on the storyline she'd proposed. Bones was unsettled about the idea from the start, certain it was the wrong one. The tale was too gruesome, but more the problem, it was too personal: a knife-wielding psychopath stalking his quarry, a young innocent who bore a striking resemblance to the woman who presently was preparing drinks.

Bones had grown more worried as Clara insisted he dig deeper into his killer's mindset—not that such a psychological dive would be unusual for a writer in fleshing out his characters, but Bones realized he was writing for a lone reader. Clara's deep obsession with his fictional predator crossed over into the delusional, speaking of the killer as if he had materialized in the real world—and that he would mercilessly suffer for his horrific crimes. Bones had hoped that his story might prove cathartic, a way for Clara to confront her demons. And, so, he went along. With the book finished— and the devil purged from her soul—Clara might finally be free. They might even have a life together with this ugly past behind her.

At least that's what Bones was counting on.

Bones reached for the martini, Clara's choice of drink.

"Just a writer's block, but I'll figure it out," he told her quietly.

"You always do," she said, a sharp edge of impatience evident in her voice. "What's the problem now?"

Bones saw where the conversation was going, and it was nowhere good. Clara had grown only more agitated with the slow pace of his manuscript.

"A tough case for Sam Rock, eh?" he said with a faint smile.

Clara glared, a flash of anger crossed her face, lifting her martini as if to toast the author. "But not for you, PJ Bones," she snapped. "You were the best fucking detective in New York City."

Bones looked intently at Clara. Her face was stretched tight.

"PJ, you need to make your readers understand the horror of this man," she said. "The damage that he's done...And then you will hunt him down and destroy him.""Clara..." Bones said anxiously.

"So, write your story, PJ. Find the bastard. I need you to."

Bones reached out for her hand. "OK, Clara. Just got to figure a few things out."

Clara pulled away, letting her glass fall to the floor, shattering it. The liquor puddled next to their feet. Without another word, she turned and left the study.

Bones, stunned, watched her leave. He sat slumped at his desk another few minutes, his mind reeling, before reaching under his desktop for the whiskey bottle he'd stored in the bottom drawer. He took a long pull and closed his eyes, feeling the alcohol wash over him.

It had been months since he'd taken to the bottle, but he did not have the resistance to fight the urge. He guzzled a second drink before turning back to his computer screen. Bones started to write with the alcohol kicking in hard, but he knew he was faking it.

The case of the serial killer was running stone cold for Sam Rock. The investigator just couldn't figure it out.

The very next day, the *Daily News* reported that the police were investigating the disappearance of a young man named Tre Simon, a struggling actor who had been reported missing by his parents. It was basically a non-news story, with Simon best known for his role as the once-boyfriend of the soap opera actress, the late Margot Turner. Police reported they were treating the case as a missing person stating they had found no evidence of foul play.

POE

Chapter 5
'An Afternoon at Margot Turner's Funeral'

I had some time on my hands, having been holed up for weeks with the police snooping around for the school teacher. Gone without a trace. Well, Anne Sweeny was still keeping me company of sorts, though the smell from her coffin was getting a bit much. Even Pluto was yowling, clawing at the box like the mad cat she was. My pulse was also rat-a-tatting, a dead-on signal that I was ready for something else. Someone else. Then I came across the story in the newspaper. A celebrity funeral that weekend. An event that seemed in perfect harmony with my frame of mind.

The funeral was sad. Lots of tears and that sort of thing. What can you do? The chapel was also a downer, although the set design with its rich mahogany seating and mood lighting gave the place some life. I might have made a joke there. Given the semi-star crowd attending, though, I suppose it was just the right backdrop for all this fuss.

Nevertheless, I was considering climbing into the plain wooden coffin, the centerpiece of the room, to join Margot Turner on her journey underground. I had lost all patience with the bearded rabbi pompously clubbing mourners with his bullshit lamentations. Just overkill, so to speak. He needed to shut up and get the woman buried. I was tempted to throw my one-sheet with a picture of the dearly departed at the guy but fought the urge. Maybe a sharper implement for the rabbi at some other time of my choosing.

I sat, pissed off as he spoke about "the mystery of God's plan" that took Margot Turner's life. Honestly, not much of a mystery. There had been no doubt that an undocumented food delivery guy had slammed his electric bike into Margot after running a red light on Lexington Avenue, in the process splattering poor Margot with a dinner order of General Tso's chicken and a large container of chow fun. Such is the absurdity of life, departing this earth showered with the house special from Chung Ho's Chinese Restaurant. The image struck me as perfectly ironic given the Jews' propensity for such cuisine. So, another joke. I learned about this part of the story through the social media buzz, though the rabbi opted to leave the information out of his eulogy. Too bad. I thought the detail gave Margot's death more pizazz than the usual fatal bike run-over. Anyway.

The rabbi continued to drone on about the "loving child" of Delores and Stan Schwindenheimer, and the "adoring partner" to Tre Simon, and the "devastating loss" to the entertainment world, and "to those of us who loved Margot for her starring role on television." I wasn't looking to be a killjoy, but playing a whore on "Dark Midnight Hours" wasn't exactly a Meryl Streep turn—though I do think that Margot was a very persuasive whore.

Of course, there was the political hubbub in the *New York Post* with its banner headline, 'Undoc Biker Runs Down Soap Actress.' I didn't really think it would have made any difference if the guy had his papers in order, but the front-page story got my attention and inspired me to attend the big event at the West Side Funeral Chapel. You never know when good fortune arises at such occasions. I came prepared to mourn, managing to well up some tears, then honking out my despair. I thought I was particularly convincing during the eulogy, though I probably overdid the boohooing a bit.

At one point, Margot's parents turned to see who exactly was making all the noise. I half-waved at them, adding to their confusion. They probably thought I was just another guy from their daughter's narcissistic acting circle with my tattooed "sleeve" covering both arms, black jeans, and a "Capitalism is Dead" t-shirt. I took my getup as a philosophical statement that speaks to the inherent struggle of our human existence. Yeah, I like making that crap up.

I couldn't help but notice some real-deal actor types present in the chapel. I recognized a Brad Pitt lookalike with his slicked-back dirty blond hair tied in a ponytail. I had seen his latest "action-adventure" on Netflix and thought he was pretty good with his six-pack and bulging biceps. I might have considered him for a role in my own upcoming action-adventure, but he looked like he'd be trouble on my set.

Then I saw "the right one." Tre Simon was another pretty-boy actor with a phony name and the hoity-toity airs of the artiste. I had seen his photograph in the paper, though he was much better looking in person, especially in his role as Margot Turner's distraught boyfriend. Sitting there in a corner pew, he seemed to call out to me, though his beckoning might have been a result of my vivid imagination.

Yes, he was the one. Audition over.

The poor guy was now bent over, his eyes closed, deep into his grief. Losing the love of his life. So sad.

And all this without knowing he was next in line.

Chapter 6
'Tre'

Killing Tre required some planning, so I got to work. I thought my latest disguise was inspired with the scraggly beard and Fu Manchu mustache. I had caked some filth on my pants and t-shirt, and after a few days without washing my body smell was about right for the streets.

Tre lived in a brownstone on Christopher Street in the West Village. I decided to hang by a smoke shop on his corner, splayed out on the sidewalk with a tin can for "tips." I thought I fit in nicely with the bustling street scene. Hey, I even took in a few bucks and a bag with a Big Mac and a Coke from a neighborhood do-gooder. A friendly neighborhood for sure.

I caught on to Tre's routine pretty quickly, early walks with his French poodle, the jaunts over to a nearby bakery, the weed pickups. However, something else caught my attention. Departing his brownstone most late mornings was one young man or another. They didn't look much older than eighteen. Tre was being a busy bad boy. Apparently, he had quickly gotten over the loss of Margot Turner and had found his own way to mend a broken heart.

I decided to trail him on his nightly bar rounds. He was a sloppy drunk who took his blowjobs in back bathrooms from anyone willing and able. I made the discovery one night at a local bar while taking a piss. Then there was the soundtrack, the grunts and groans coming from the next toilet stall. I deduced that Tre's period of mourning for his beloved Margot was pretty much over.

I needed to rethink my plan given the unexpected turn of events, so it was back to the drawing board the next day. I discarded my previous self with a razor and a makeover. I clipped my wig short, and pasted on stylishly long sideburns. Then I patted on some base and a bit of eyeliner to sweeten the pot, so to speak. I checked myself out in the bathroom mirror. The effect was stunning. I had shed a few years to fit in with the twenty-something demographic, and honestly, I was impressed by the new sexy me.

That night I headed to a bar on Bleecker Street that Tre typically frequented and waited, tending to my watered-down vodka. The place was styled after an English pub with lots of shiny dark wood and a dartboard. The queens were all there, loud and packed, bodies on bodies, talking and groping. After an hour, the noise was getting to me, but I stayed, switching over to beer. A leathered biker type then staggered up to introduce himself, came close in, and whispered some sweet nothing in my ear. Actually, he said he was interested in sucking my cock. Nice gesture, I suppose, but I liked to ease into my relationships. Besides, he was working way too hard on his Hell's Angel attitude. I'm sure it was my dead stare that sent him away. Along with a flash of my switchblade.

By two, I was wasted and pissed. Where the fuck was this guy? I spun off the stool and out of the bar for some air and a joint. Then I started howling. The feeling just hit me. Some street people gave me a wide berth, which was probably a good thing for them. There was this dinging in my head growing louder, and louder, and I thought of heading back into the bar to invite Mr. Hell's Angel to my place so I could cut out his tongue as a starter.

These outbursts were coming on more frequently these past months—a liability for people in my business. Emotions overpowering me. Actually, a specific emotion: rage. Now, this might seem like a case of splitting hairs given my tendencies, but my homicidal instincts were not born from hate. No, I had an intense passion for my "chosen ones." The intimacies we shared. So unspeakably beautiful. And then the total release each time it was over. Wasn't that a good thing?

How was I to make sense of this malevolent virus now entering my bloodstream? I could feel it taking over. What did that mean?

I guess Tre Simon was going to find out.

Chapter 7
'Poor Tre'

"Another for my friend," I told the barkeeper.

Poor Tre had been working on his fifth or sixth vodka straight when I came by and sat down next to him. He was having a hard time with his liquid courage.

Tre Simon turned to me, perplexed, trying to pinpoint the good-looking dude now sitting next to him.

"Do I know you?" he slurred.

"Not yet," I said, friendly-like, and smiled.

Tre squinted, trying to size me up. "Yeah, thanks," he said, pointing to his fresh drink.

I had finally hunted Tre down at one of his nightly haunts over on Perry Street. There he was by himself at the bar looking like shit warmed over. Maybe Margot was hitting him hard again, though I assumed Tre had already crossed that line, prepping for the rowdy boys coming by soon.

For the moment, I was looking to spend some quiet, quality time with Tre over drinks.

We sat at the bar a while, and I let the silence finally move him to talk.

"So, whaddaya do?" he finally asked.

"I'm in the entertainment business," I said.

"What, you an actor?"

"Not exactly. More behind the scenes."

"Fuckin' business," he mumbled. "Excuse my French. My girlfriend was an actress. Dead."

"I know. Margot Turner."

That kind of jolted him from his stupor.

"Wha…you know her? From the set?" Tre was trying to shake loose the vodka now.

"Not really," I said, leaving him to fill in the blank. He looked at me warily.

I suspected that Margot's authenticity in her role as "the whore" in "Dark Midnight Hours" came from her real-life exploits. Likely a reason for Tre's suspicions, along with his exploration of the other side.

Tre shook his head, reaching for his drink.

"Yeah," he said despondently. "She liked to screw around." Tears were starting up and running into his vodka. "But I loved her." As an afterthought, "The motherfucker spic who ran her down. I just want to kill him."

Apparently, Tre and I were like-minded chums.

I was almost feeling sorry for the guy but after an hour finally had enough of the gloomy talk. It was time. When Tre made his move to the john, I slipped some 'Special K' into his drink and waited.

He finally came back to the bar, wobbly on his feet. It wasn't going to take much to end this party.

I lifted my glass, declaring, "Death to the motherfucker!"

He smiled, slurring his agreement. "Yeah, yeah, death to the motherfucker!"

It didn't take more than a minute or two for the roofie to hit.

I shrugged at the bartender and tossed two twenties his way. I lifted Tre from his high seat, his head lolling, and half-carried him to the street. Then I flagged a cab. Twenty-five minutes later, we were at my apartment in Harlem.

I mean, was there any other way for this night to end?

Chapter 8
'This Little Piggy Went to Market'

I thought I did a handy job trussing up Tre on the hardback chair nailed to the floor, making sure his hands and legs were securely roped. I had to say that the guy's naked body was quite impressive, perking my attention. Obviously, he spent considerable time at Equinox building abs and glutes, not to mention his well-hung nature, so to speak. Likely, his strong selling point.

I waited patiently for him to come around, and then he did, hazily waking from his stupor.

"What the fuck!" he stammered, coming to grips with his present state of captivity.

"Hi, Tre," I said pleasantly, seeing no need to turn this into an adversarial conversation.

He looked at me, trying to sort me out, and then that moment of recognition. "You, the guy in the bar!" he said. "What the hell are you doing?"

The question was kind of dumb, but expected. It's interesting how denial is the first conscious reaction from my chosen. They can be stubborn when it comes to seeing the world as it is. Not normally a healthy way to lead one's life, but it was good to see reality finally seeping into Tre's consciousness. Certainly, pulling out my "tools" from a chest drawer had that immediate effect, but then Tre started up, spewing the whole "you motherfucker" thing. I found his language disrespectful and tiresome, so I tied a ball gag around his mouth. That was much better. I could hardly hear his muffled curses as I finished assembling my knife collection on a nearby table.

I undressed and stood naked beside him. I didn't want him to feel self-conscious—just us two boys. Then I went over to my closet and pulled out a pair of latex gloves. I snapped the gloves on my hands.

For all of Tre's bravado, I could see the fear leaking from his eyes and smell the stink coming from his pores. Animal stink. The terror sinking in, the grim reality of his impending future. It was always a reaction that gave me great satisfaction, though, I had to admit, the air in the room was growing thick. Anne's putrefying body arising from her coffin in the corner of the room was giving off a gaseous odor that watered my eyes. Either that or maybe I was just getting sentimental with Anne withering away.

I turned my attention back to Tre, deciding to pull the ball gag from his mouth to give him more breathing room. It was the least I could do as a medical professional.

"You don't have to do this," he said trembling, gasping for air.

I shrugged. "Of course I do," I said, turning back to my tool table.

Tre had gone silent for the moment, but then he was at it again, frantically thrashing about in the chair. What did he think? That he was going to find a way out?

Glancing at the array of implements on the table, I finally picked up a surgical clipper. I liked the weighty feel in my hand. Then I knelt down to Tre's right foot and started to massage his toes, softly singing one of my favorite childhood ditties.

"This little piggy went to market..." and then I clipped off his small toe... "this little piggy went home..." and snipped off the next... "and this little piggy had roast beef..." and the next... "and this little piggy had none..." The big toe was proving to be a challenge to cut through, but I was patient. I had to go through the piggy song more than once to work on his left foot and finish the business.

By then, Tre's screams had stopped and he had lapsed into unconsciousness. I was glad that the soundproof panels I installed were in place. No need to disturb the neighbors.

I was able to feed the guy some high-powered amphetamines to keep him awake. Stirring, his head flopped on his chest, but he finally managed to open his eyes. He stared at his toeless feet first, as if examining some alien object. I had cauterized the cuts, so not much of a bloody mess, but Tre was hardly appreciative. Then came the screeches, the howls—he might well have been set on fire— that shook the room. I thought he was being a bit overdramatic, forcing me again to stick the ball gag in his mouth. I suspected the sound panels weren't nearly enough to block out his screams.

Then Tre startled bawling, the amputation hitting him hard. I stroked his hair and fed him a pill for the pain. It would take some time though for the drug to kick in.

When he settled down an hour later, I removed the gag again. It seemed the right time for a man-to-man talk.

"I can see what Margot saw in you," I told him. "You are a beautiful man."

I had hoped the compliment would break the ice between us with all his previous racket.

Tre started in with the boohooing about his missing toes, then turned to me with his big blue pleading eyes. "What do you want from me?" he sobbed, eyeing my naked body.

I felt the need to clarify. "No, no, I'm not gay. I believe we should all choose who we love, so no judgments from me. Just live and let die, I always say."

Then I came to him and touched his shoulder. I might as well have electrocuted him, given his jerky reaction. He just needed to relax.

"No, Tre, I just love you for who you are. The real you, not this phony made-up hipster."

Tears were still streaming down his cheeks, his chest heaving, so I was pretty certain that my words were comforting him.

"You need to let me go," he rasped. "I can't be here."

I sighed. His crying and whining were getting to me. Just a needy guy, and I found myself starting to feel differently about him. And that wasn't a good thing.

No doubt Tre was sensing my change of heart.

"Look what you've done to me," he whimpered, staring down at his feet. "You are sick, motherfucker, really sick."

I didn't appreciate his unpleasant attitude or his amateur analysis. Another guy who thought he figured me out. Just like when I was a kid, with the school psych asking me about my "dark impulses" that caused me to "act out." OK, I'd had my moments, experimenting with small animals. Then the fights at school, which weren't all my fault. Then my parents taking me to some white-haired asshole, asking me all sorts of questions. Maybe I should have told him about my older cousin, Ritchie, who liked to tickle my balls, and other stuff that confused me then—but what business was that of his? Besides, the accident took care of Ritchie and my parents, so that was that.

I came back to Tre, feeling the storm rising in my head. Something bad, the feeling growing, taking over. I looked over at the guy, all wide-eyed and panting.

Didn't I try to be your friend, Tre?

Didn't I care about you?

I could tell that you are reading my mind. The way you are looking at me, trying to shake loose of your bonds. And now more of your sniveling. Pleading. Just pathetic, Tre. You're not the man I thought you were. So frightened about what is to come next. You must feel, however, that you are deserving, knowing the deceit of your existence. I cannot promise that it won't be painful, but perhaps you will learn from being punished.

I reinserted the ball gag and turned to the table and my collection of cutting edges. I picked up a small, razor-edged knife and carefully scrutinized Tre's fingers, ears, nose, eyes. I looked down to his rather prodigious cock. Then my mind turned to his hands and toeless feet. I laid aside the small blade in favor of the larger Liston knife—it struck me that it was the very same one that I used for Clara.

I placed my hand over Tre's heart. Edgar was in my ear.

"Nevermore," I told him. He needed to understand that all that once was his past life is forever lost.

And then I began again.

POE

Chapter 9
'W'

I piled what was left of Tre into a wooden box. He was still breathing though having trouble sucking in air. Just wheezing, trying to stay alive. I'm not sure why he would want to. My experience in the hospital's OR was enough to keep him alive. It was important with amputations never to sever any major arteries. Still, I wasn't entirely satisfied. I found myself too worked up and lashing out, and the results were just too sloppy. Certainly, not a professional demeanor. Too bad for Tre, who was strapped down and quite out of his mind. Understandably. I do wish though that I had been cleaner with the Liston knife.

I had plans for Tre's body parts but for the time being stored his pieces in my fridge. I would tend to these later when I returned from my cabin in Long Island.

It took me the better part of three hours along the crowded expressway and then a string of narrow unpaved roads before coming to the remote cabin. It was now little more than a worn-down shack, long abandoned except for my occasional visit. Not much was left of my old childhood home, not that I was inclined to hold on to any fond memories there. The place was isolated, surrounded by a dirt yard that butted up against the woods and a large swamp. I remember mother warning me to stay away from the swamp, though I couldn't miss seeing black vultures swooping high in the sky waiting eagerly for their prey to appear.

I pulled the Buick into the front yard, checking over at Tre in the backseat. His breathing had gotten shallower. I was hoping he'd hang on, at least for the short while. I noticed that blood and gore had blackened the bottom of his box and was thankful that the mess hadn't seeped through the thin wood and onto the car seat. I had enough to think about without contending with Tre's blood and bodily stains.

It was getting dark, and I wanted to get to work before all light was lost. I walked through the dirt yard to the back of the house where I kept a shovel and a portable lamp. The yard was still dotted with stones that marked the graves of small animals I had caught as a kid. The creatures didn't last long after my dissections, a first step to my future calling. I had inscribed each name on a stone, a proper memorial for my forest companions, but gave up the idea after a dozen experiments. Just too many funerals to contend with, so I opted for the alphabetic order. The last stone was marked with the letter 'V.'

I found a clear patch, took off my shirt, and for the next two hours dug into the hard dirt. The sun was soon gone and replaced by a full moon and a starlit sky. Long shadows from neighboring trees spiked across the yard. I sweated profusely, the physical exertion animating the inked images on my body. Their faces seemed to come alive, this, my family.

Finally, I was through with the deep dig. Then I went back to the car and hoisted Tre's box out of the back seat. He garbled something that I couldn't make out, a result of his missing tongue and teeth. That must have been frustrating for him, trying to speak. I dragged the box across the backyard and to the opening in the ground. Then I tipped it over until Tre rolled out and into the deep hole. He lay there, crumbled in the narrow space, looking upward into the black sky. I was glad that I decided not to remove both his eyes so he could take in the full moon and the stars—his last sight of the world, along with the image of me as I stood over his grave. He had kind of a sad, resigned look, and I felt the need to say a few parting words.

I recited from Edgar. "'Never to suffer would never to have been blessed.'"

I thought Edgar's wisdom might give Tre some peace, but his attitude changed quickly as I scooped up dirt with my shovel and threw it on top of him. Then his silent screams and the twisting and turning though he really wasn't capable of much movement at all.

I hummed with the task at hand, my mentor guiding me. I pitched more dirt into the hole, covering the remains of Tre's body, leaving only his face visible. He was looking up into the night sky with his one good eye, no doubt contemplating "the hideous aspect of death" that awaited him. Edgar again.

Tre's toothless mouth was open wide now, as if to take in one final breath of air. Then I shoveled a large pile of soil onto his face, obliterating it from sight. I could see him trying to shake off the dirt, but a second and third shovelful finally did the trick. I spent the better part of the next hour filling the grave, leaving a large stone on top.

I marked it with the letter 'W.'

I headed back into the cabin to stay the night. I was exhausted and planned on an early morning start back to Manhattan. My parents' bed stood to the side of the room. That was where they were sleeping when the accident occurred. And across the room next to the fireplace was where my cousin, Ritchie, had been sleeping. Everyone gone—just tragic.

I edged over to a beaten tabletop next to the stove and glanced over at a yellowed copy of the *New York Post* that I had saved from months earlier. It was still open to page three where I had left it. A banner headline blared, "Beauty and the Beast."

The story wasn't much—a photographer with his nose busted by some famous writer at a downtown bar, but I couldn't miss the half-page photograph. There she was hand in hand with the guy, vaguely familiar with his shock of silver hair and black mustache, the two looking all so lovey-dovey.

I couldn't have cared less about the fight between the two men. It was Clara—she was more beautiful than I remembered—and I could swear she was gazing through the camera lens at *me*! Was she teasing me? I peered at the image again. Her hand in his—this man. What were the two of them thinking about at that moment? Did they love each other? Were they fucking?

How could she be so faithless!

MCBAIN AND BONES

George was sprawled out on 42nd Street and thought he had scored. His "Feed the Homeless" sign wasn't attracting much attention that afternoon when a dark-haired man approached him, reached into his backpack, took out a brown paper bag, and handed it to him.

"Enjoy," the passerby told George, who was holding out the hope for some wings and fries. He nodded his thanks and tore open the bag as his benefactor walked away.

George, at once, was instantly confused. No wings or fries. What was this fake eyeball doing inside the bag? And an ear? And a nose? Jeez. Pranking the homeless. Shit, dude. Halloween wasn't even for another month, George angrily thought. He sat back down on the sidewalk, picked out the eye from the bag and examined it, the thing staring him in the face. His mind must not be working right from the drink, gripping the eyeball way too hard, mashing it in his hand. And in that instant moment of clarity, George gasped, dropping the mutilated eyeball to the sidewalk. Then he wobbled to his feet, letting loose a scream that rose from the bottom of his lungs and thundered down 42nd Street.

"Hey, brother," McBain called out as Bones came up to the 19th Precinct house. They shared a man-hug, which came naturally for the former partners and longtime friends.

"So, what's with the mystery?" Bones said. "You told me to haul my butt down here, pronto. I don't think the guys in there are planning to invite me in for some milk and cookies. Remember, I'm the bad cop."

McBain heaved a sigh. Bones was right. Cops had long memories, and no doubt his old partner's reputation was not forgotten. The department's heavy hand still roiled him. Bones had been unjustly tarred and feathered for the crap that went down. McBain knew of no other cop more faithful to his oath or more professional on the streets.

"I was called in by Cooligan," McBain said. "Our beloved captain. He's on my case."

"Didn't the son of a bitch get the memo?" Bones said. "You're about to retire. He needs to give you a break."

"Yeah, well, about a month to go, so I'm still on the job. He started yanking my chain, saying he wanted me to lead the murder investigation and see that the men weren't running around with their heads up their asses."

"Cooligan's a charmer," Bones said. "He's the guy who put the last nail in my coffin."

"Yeah, he held out, but couldn't hold off the dogs, the mayor, commissioner," McBain said, shaking his head at the memory.

"Well, maybe I should thank him, anyway," Bones replied. "I've been sleeping better since those days."

McBain smirked, then gave Bones the lowdown. "PJ, we think we got a psycho on the loose. Our asshole likes to use a knife. Real sick."

Bones nodded. "What have you got?"

"The victim is a twenty-seven-year-old. Name, Tre Simon. He had been reported missing. Then body parts started showing up a few days later scattered around the city. Gruesome stuff. Toes, hands, a foot, ears, even the victim's testicles, you get the idea. DNA just gave us a match with Simon. We haven't found the rest of him though."

"For Christ sake, Mac." Bones grimaced. "Any leads yet?"

"Well, there is this…" McBain said, hesitating. "Our boys think that the perp might be the guy who also attacked Clara. That's why I reached out to you. Thought you'd want to know."

Bones was jolted. "*What!* That was more than two years ago."

"These psychos go underground when they sense they're being closed in on," McBain said. "But once they get their first taste of blood, they don't stop."

"So what connects this guy to Clara?"

"Our bad guy was precise in handling the knife. On a hunch, I went back to Clara's file. I recalled how exacting her wound had been. It was as if she had been cut open by a surgeon."

McBain's face darkened, picturing the grisly crime scene at Clara's apartment. "I asked forensics to compare our victim's knife wounds to Clara's," he continued. "A long shot. They could not tell me for sure, but would not rule out the possibility that it was the same assailant."

"The sicko is not content with just killing," Bones said angrily. "He *likes* slicing up his victims."

"He definitely wants to show us he's around. It looks like he's now triggered. We can expect more of his butchery. No doubt he needs his bloody fill." McBain paused. "Clara was, well…lucky."

Bones frowned. "Well, don't tell her that."

"Clara is our best lead. She gave us a description of her attacker back then. A fuzzy sketch of the guy, but it's something to go on. A man in his late twenties or early thirties, bald, deep-set, dark eyes, muscular, tattoos up and down his body."

Bones narrowly eyed his friend. "So, Mac, what the hell am I doing here?"

"I'm going to need your help, Sherlock."

"You gotta be kidding." Bones exhaled. "I've been out of the trenches way too long. What do you expect me to do? Find the guy and then hit him over the head with my computer until he gives up?"

"Nah, just love your company," McBain said. He looked intently at Bones. "PJ, you were the best we had."

"And you are out of your damn mind. I make up stuff now, Mac, you might remember. Lately, I can't even get that right."

"Yeah, I heard something about you being this big-deal writer," McBain said wryly. "But Cooligan requested that I better find this maniac. Only that he wasn't nearly so polite. So, I figured you owe me—you know, for all your bullshit that I've put up with over these years."

McBain wavered a moment. "Then there is Clara."

Bones stared at McBain. "Why are you bringing her into this?"

"I think you know, PJ," McBain said. "Clara is…struggling. She's trapped in some dark place."

Bones gave his friend a hard look. "Mac, if you really want to help Clara, you want me as far away as possible. I can't think straight as it is."

McBain paused, looking intently at his friend. "PJ. You might want to stay away from your sidekick," he said quietly. Bones' heavy eyes and drawn appearance made it clear that he was back to the bottle.

"Mac, I can't get back on the streets…"

"Bones, do you have a choice? Clara came to you for help."

"Yeah. Some insane notion that I could take down her bad man. That 'Sam Rock could save the day.' How crazy is that?"

"Well, Sam and you are one and the same."

Bones bitterly laughed. "Yeah, right. Except for everything that is different."

"Listen, Bones, I need you on the case."

Bones eyed his former partner. "I guess you must—you keep calling me 'Bones.'"

McBain grinned. "Yeah, that's detective talk. No first names are allowed on the job. Or initials."

"You're a tough man, Phil McBain," Bones said.

"My detective friends call me 'Mac.'"

BONES

PJ Bones found himself lost in thought wandering through Riverside Park. The early morning air hadn't done much to clear his head. He'd woken up at dawn after an agitated sleep with Clara. It had been a bad night for her, sweat-dreams pitching her screaming from their bed. Bones had tried to calm her down but was powerless against the demon wielding a knife.

The rest of the morning had been a haze. Bones tried another shot at his book but was still chipping around the edges of the story. His sadistic killer was still on the streets…along with the real-life killer. So neither story was going well. He'd been reluctant to tell Clara that he was helping Mac on the case. That would only complicate things between them.

He had been over to Mac's place in the Bronx the previous afternoon, looking over a slew of photographs lined up on his dining room table. Most were just body parts that were magnified in the photos. Each one was once attached to Tre Simon. A DNA match conclusively identified him as the victim. Simon's corpse had yet to be found but Bones surmised that there wouldn't be much of him left.

The two men had reviewed the squad's notes. Tre Simon's bio was thin. A would-be actor, living in Greenwich Village, with bit roles in a few television programs. His claim to fame seemed to be his relationship with the late Margot Turner. McBain and Bones recalled the uproar in the press around her tragic accident. Margot, the soap opera star, run over by a delivery man—an undocumented worker—and then the political storm around the biker. Police interviews with

Tre Simon's friends seemed to attest to the general view that he was "a good guy" but having "a tough time" after Turner's death. Some coded language in the notes about his sexual "experimentation" that led to the theory at headquarters that he was killed in some random hookup. McBain's men were still checking Village bars that he'd frequented.

Bones was weary as he made his way home through the park. Clara was again clouding his thinking. She was never far from his mind, a shadowy presence lingering inside his brain. He loved this woman, but she had become more unstable, at times a stranger, and he felt helpless when that other Clara made herself known.

"Why, Mr. PJ Bones. Hello!"

Bones was shaken from his thoughts. A man wearing an ill-fitted wig and a sketchy mustache had come up from behind him.

"Yeah...Do I know you?"

The man seemed familiar, but Bones couldn't place him.

"Columbia. Your talk at the writers' seminar a month ago."

"Are you a student there?" Bones asked warily.

Bones still couldn't pin him down, and the guy didn't seem right for that university crowd.

"You don't remember. We spoke afterward. The name is Poe."

And then the memory struck Bones. This odd fellow, with the strange, phony name and affect. "Yeah, I do remember you now."

"Yes, I asked if you could take a look at my manuscript. You turned me down."

It was coming back to Bones, this weird vibe. "Sorry I couldn't help out," Bones said curtly, and turned to leave.

Poe stepped in front of him.

"Well, I just happen to have some of my manuscript with me," he said. "It's a work in progress, but you wouldn't turn me down a second time, would you? You know, author to author."

He stared at Bones with a feral grin.

Bones glared back at the man, set to pivot from being polite to emoting in his face. The guy was a pushy asshole, but he had balls. Bones gave him that. Still, something else about him didn't square.

Poe held out a clipped pile of papers.

Bones let it hang there. "Tell me what it's about," he finally said.

Poe nodded. "Yes, it has a most unusual premise. Mr. Bones, do you know what the word, 'immurement' means?"

"Afraid not. Why?"

"Quite an interesting word. Comes from the Latin, 'im' meaning 'in' and 'murus' meaning 'wall.' So, literally, 'walling in.' It's more commonly known to mean 'being entombed alive.'"

"Yeah, thanks for the lesson. The nuns never had a chance with me when it came to my Latin."

"Ah, Mr. Bones. I appreciate the limitations of your education," he said dryly. "But can you imagine finding yourself left to die, imprisoned in such a manner? Such terror that speaks to our primal fears. What would that experience be like?"

Bones wasn't sure if he was intrigued by this Poe or wanted to punch him out. There was this mix of intelligence and outright weirdness about the guy—not that Bones cared to sort it out.

"I can't say that experience is on my bucket list," Bones finally said. "Is this something that keeps you up at night, Mr. Poe?"

"Well, it's just Poe. No need for the formality. And I *have* reflected on the subject. I mean, the dead can't speak to us, so we can never know—but what that voice might tell us! The absolute terror we cannot even imagine."

Bones had enough of the nutty Edgar Allan Poe-wannabe. Could this guy be for real?

"Okay, Poe, what do you write about?" Bones said brusquely. "Get on with it."

"Yes, the story. I believe it has a unique first-person point of view. That from a killer who entombs his victims."

Bones grimaced, already regretting his decision to stick around. "Sounds lovely," he said, not bothering to hide the sarcasm.

"Just imagine, Mr. Bones. The deep intimacy that the killer shares with his victim, bearing witness as she dies inside her coffin, trapped in total darkness, such exquisite horror that eats away at her mind and then takes her body."

Bones shook his head. "Now, guy, don't you think you're taking your Edgar Allan Poe act a little too far? He's been dead for, what, two hundred years? You should let him rest in peace."

"Actually, he died October 9th, 1849," Poe said. "And you know, he once lived nearby this park in a farmhouse with his young wife, Virginia. Of course, this entire area was just a country setting then. You must know that we honor him. Edgar Allan Poe Street."

"Yeah, yeah, West 84th Street is named after him," Bones said testily. "But the wig and fake mustache? C'mon. It might work at a costume party, but you're ridiculous."

Poe faintly smiled. He despised Bones. Hated his smugness. The stupidity, disrespecting his mentor. Disrespecting him. Another one thinking him a freak. Poe thought how easy it would be to kill him then and there, but he had other plans for PJ Bones.

"No matter, Mr. Bones," Poe said acidly. "He speaks to me, and who knows, perhaps one day you will get to know him more...personally."

"Not a chance," Bones retorted. "I'm not a big fan of unhinged writers and the horror stories they concoct."

"Well, Mr. Bones, perhaps you are the one 'unhinged,' tending to your tedious days. Pretending to ignore the fate that awaits us all. That when we die, we share a home deep in the earth, consumed by the creatures beneath, only soon to be forgotten. Edgar understood that this is our common destiny—and he revealed it to us in his prophetic stories."

Bones had enough of this creep. A sinister smell seemed to radiate from the guy triggering his old cop instincts. Back then he may have taken more of interest in checking him out.

Bones just grunted and turned to leave when Poe held out his manuscript.

"Mr. Bones?" he said, grinning crookedly.

Bones eyed the offering. The man was unbearable, so he could not explain why he took the pages from his hand. Only that he felt compelled to.

Then Bones brushed past the man and walked away without another word.

CLARA

Clara was on edge. The pills meant to calm her down were only making her more jittery. She felt as if she was teetering on a high wire and about to plummet from human existence. It wasn't that she was afraid to die. In fact, death might be welcomed. It was the living world where the monsters reside.

Clara didn't know how she found herself on a subway to Washington Square Park that spring afternoon. Only that she needed to escape the madness that had seized her mind. Clara recalled the Greenwich Village park from her student days at NYU, hanging out with all sorts of street types. She was so much younger then—innocent, and a believer that people were basically good, and other similar bullshit thrown her way in her classes. She might have laughed hysterically. Clara wondered what her high-minded professors might have thought had they gotten their throats cut.

Washington Square Park was mostly cement with a fringe of green. Surprisingly, Clara was feeling better walking through the grand marble arch adorn with two statues of George Washington standing guard at the park entrance. The warm afternoon air settled over her, as she sat down at a bench near the large fountain with its open view of the park. The place felt familiar: young mothers with baby carriages, an acoustic guitar sweetly filling the air, protestors calling an end to some lesser-known autocrat, but mostly everyone looking chill. Clara was glad that she had come. This idyllic refuge gave her a brief sense of normalcy, the person she once was.

Clara pulled out a notebook and started writing. Her shrink thought that this was a good idea to help "navigate her feelings." She had mostly ignored his advice, but it was a golden Saturday afternoon at the park and that old Clara was inching to the surface. So, she took out her pad and began to write.

When she was a young girl, Clara loved to people-watch and play the mental game of imagining their lives. She glanced across to a nearby bench where a craggy old man with shoulder-length white hair was slumped over and sound asleep. A small brown paper bag sat on his stomach. Clara envisioned him as a seaman who had spent most of his life sailing around the world. When he found that there was nowhere else to go, that he had seen all that there was to see, he found that park bench, polished off the last of his Thunderbird, and decided to sleep the rest of his life away. Clara laughed to herself, jotting down the story.

Clara then decided on the young pretty blonde in cut-off jeans and tight t-shirt that revealed her deep cleavage. She had nuzzled up to her boyfriend under a nearby leafy tree. The girl reminded Clara of her former life with the glow that came from her eyes and the knowledge of how desirable she was. Her boyfriend though did not look anything like Billy Bruster. He was black with a hipster mustache and wearing a Black Lives Matter t-shirt. Presently, he was sticking his tongue in the blonde's mouth. Clara visualized their marathon fucking, a mental jump she suspected wasn't far from the truth.

Clara leaned back on the bench and stretched out the kinks in her back, growing more content with her lovely afternoon. She surveyed the park again for some other subject until she came to a man near the West 4th Street park exit. He was bald and bare-chested and glaring at her from across the park. Clearly visible was a chain of tattoos that covered his arms and body. Clara slowly rose from the bench, speechless. She had stopped breathing.

He stood there, motionless, a cold smile creasing his face. Clara was frozen in place, dropping her pad to the ground. Then she started to move, wildly swinging her arms in the air as if she were trying to blot out the image of this man.

"That's him! *That's him!*" Her shouts shattered the tranquility of the park.

Clara broke free from the shock and was suddenly in motion, sprinting toward the man, her arms pinwheeling as she barreled through park-goers. People backed off, alarmed at the sight of this frenzied woman screaming. *"The monster! Stop him! Stop him!"*

Clara stormed across to the park exit, but the man was gone. She grabbed at a woman passing by. "Did you see where he went?" The woman, petrified, just shook her head.

Clara then took off along West 4th Street, slamming into local shops to see if he was hiding. "I need to find him!" she cried out.

Then she collapsed onto the sidewalk.

A teenager on a skateboard wheeled up to her. "Lady, do you need a doctor?" he nervously asked.

Clara whipped around. *"Where is he?"* she pleaded. *"That man. He killed me!"*

Bones came home at midnight to see Clara lying on the living room couch, motionless, her arm covering her eyes. Bones wasn't sure if she was asleep but then heard her groan. He gently nudged her. "Clara, what's wrong?"

Clara slowly raised her head, a distant look in her eyes.

"PJ, he was there," she whispered, as if sharing a deadly secret.

Then Clara told him the rest. How freeing it had been sitting in Washington Square Park. She couldn't remember the last time she felt so...normal. Then she saw him, standing across the park. He seemed illuminated, his body a grotesque collage of tattoos. His black eyes on her, beckoning her to come to him. And then she did, racing through the park. Wanting nothing more than to put an end to this living nightmare. But then he was gone, a ghost that had flickered into her life before vanishing.

Bones reached out to hold her, but Clara pulled away from his touch. She did not want his pity. Was she some sort of pathetic child? Clara was repulsed by him. His weakness. She needed more from this man.

"My god, Clara, are you sure that was him?" Bones asked.

Clara gritted her teeth, wanting to smash Bones for doubting her. She could read his eyes, hear the inflection in his voice. He didn't believe a word she was saying.

"It was him!" she declared. "And then he got away."

"Did you call the police?"

"What do you think *they* would do? What have they *ever* done to find this monster?"

"I am going to call McBain now," Bones said.

"No, you won't!" she hissed. "We are going to find him, Bones…"

"Clara..."

"And then we will kill him!"

Clara then slipped off the couch and silently walked into their bedroom, closing the door behind her.

Bones stood there, stunned, confused. He didn't know what to believe—or, for that matter, who this woman was that he loved. He went over to the bedroom door, still needing to talk to her.

The door was locked.

"Clara," he called out to her. "The door, you need to unlock it."

"Bones, I want to be alone tonight," she said.

Bones stood outside the bedroom, dazed. "Clara, we will figure this out. Please open the door."

This time Clara did not bother to respond.

Inside the bedroom, Clara could hear Bones tap in a number on his cell phone and then his muffled conversation. He was speaking to McBain. Then the sound of the front door closing, and she was now alone when her cell phone rang. She looked at the glass screen alerting her to the anonymous caller. Somehow she knew who was on the other side of the call even before she swiped the phone.

Clara heard the sound of empty air.

Then…

"Clara," the caller finally said.

"Hello, scumbag," she said evenly.

"Now, now, Clara," the caller said. "Let us not be impolite."

"And what the fuck do you want?"

"Well, it was nice seeing you in the park today. You looked so happy, and also as beautiful as I remembered you. You do recall that day, I presume?"

"I hear psychos act out because they feel impotent. Nothing going on in their balls. What do you think?"

"You should not be talking so insolently, Clara. You know what happens to bad girls, don't you?"

Clara chortled into the phone. "Yes, I am very bad, insane, in fact, but you will find this out for yourself. That is before you forever burn in hell."

"Ah, you're so angry," the caller said. "We should talk this through. Come to an understanding."

"Yes, an understanding. After which, I will take out your eyes and watch you die a slow death."

"Perhaps, then, we should die together, Clara. The two of us, bound as one, and doomed for eternity."

"Yes," Clara said, then paused. "I suppose there is no other way."

BONES

PJ Bones pulled up to McBain's apartment building in the north Bronx that stood across from a small park with a tall monument of Henry Hudson. He was buzzed into the building and made his way to McBain's first-floor apartment. The detective cracked open the door in his bathrobe, bags heavy under his eyes.

"You look like hell," Bones said, stepping inside the room. "You might want to stay away from mirrors."

"OK, go ahead, break my chops at one in the morning," McBain said wearily. "So, what's going on, PJ?" The detective was in no mood for dumb chatter. "You didn't make much sense over the phone. What's this about Clara and our guy?"

Bones went through Clara's story: Washington Square Park, the tattooed "monster" she saw—or imagined she saw—and everything else that followed.

McBain fell onto a couch and pulled a pack of Marlboros from his bathrobe, kicking out a cigarette. He felt sorry for his friend. Bones loved this woman, but he also must have known that Clara was broken. Another victim that never healed.

McBain lit the cigarette, taking a deep drag. "This public stalking isn't the killer's MO," he said. "C'mon, PJ, he's not out there running half-naked around some park, taunting his victims. Clara's story makes no sense."

"Clara got a close-up and personal look at him when she was attacked," Bones said. "And she says he is the same man she saw in the park. That makes him our man, too."

"PJ, you don't even believe her story," McBain said, puffing out a cloud of white smoke. "Coming up on this guy in broad daylight, with dozens of people around. Is that believable?"

"Clara said she saw him and I believe her," Bones shot back.

McBain shrugged, taking another drag. "Okay, PJ, but you know that you are violating rule number one, two, and three in our business."

"And what is that, Mac?"

"Follow a case with your head, brother, not your damn heart."

Bones stepped back into his apartment that early morning, but Clara was already wide awake and shouting out for him. The bedroom door was open and Bones walked into the brightly lit room. Clara was sitting up in bed. Her face was rapturous.

"He called," she told Bones.

Bones stood there. "Who called?"

"PJ, who do you think? Our friend. He tried to frighten me." Clara snickered. "But he got the message. Next time his life will be in *my* hands."

Bones eased next to her in bed. "OK, Clara, we are going to get this guy," he said, hearing the doubt in his voice. "I promise."

Clara embraced him, whispering in his ear, "Thank you, my love." Then, smiling ear-to-ear, she sunk back into the bed, closing her eyes. Within a minute, she was asleep.

Bones stayed by her side, watching the soft rise and fall of her body as she slept. He had never seen Clara as peaceful.

He finally turned off the lights, exhausted and worried. McBain was right about her. Clara was so damaged. A sudden wave of desperation swept over him.

Bones quietly slipped out of the room and found his bottle in a desk drawer. The alcohol hardly took off the edge. Then he went back into the bedroom, undressed, and shut off the lamps, despairing that he wouldn't find sleep that night. A beam of light from Clara's cell phone shot into the darkness. It was coming from her night table. Bones stared at the phone before going over to the table. Clara had spoken to some anonymous caller. They had talked for almost an hour.

Bones sat down on the edge of the bed. A wave of panic hit him. He could only guess who might have been on the other side of the call.

"Oh, Clara...what are you doing?" he whispered to his lover, deep into her sleep. Not that he possibly could have imagined her answer.

MCBAIN AND BONES

Phil McBain and PJ Bones both cast an eye at the overhead television screen from their desk at police headquarters. A news flash was going live. Outside the building, Commissioner Kenneth Davis was in the middle of a scrum of reporters being questioned about the Tre Simon investigation.

"Davis has no choice," McBain said, nodding toward the screen. "Hard to keep the investigation under wraps when Simon's body parts keep showing up around town."

"Social media is having a field day," Bones said. "Our man has made the big leagues. They've crowned him 'The Butcher.'"

"Yeah, the second coming of 'Son of Sam,'" McBain said disdainfully.

"But Berkowitz had nothing on this guy," Bones replied. "He just used his .44 caliber. Those kids never knew what hit them. Our man, this 'butcher,' wants his victims to know what's in store for them."

Simon's photographs were laid out on McBain's desk, a gruesome display of severed human body parts.

"He left Simon's penis and scrotum in a bag outside of St. Patrick's," McBain said, pointing to two photos.

"Yeah, he's having his fun taunting us," Bones grimly replied.

McBain scowled. "Yeah, I don't think Tre Simon was in on the joke."

Davis was still talking to reporters before finally breaking from the pack. He was bombarded with more questions as he made his way into police headquarters.

"He's keeping quiet about our second victim," McBain said. "Forensics is still trying to identify DNA taken from a body part, a tongue. It's not Simon's. It belongs to a woman. We think it might belong to the Sweeny woman, the teacher from Queens who went missing weeks ago."

Bones frowned. "So, the guy is primed. You know he is not going to stop."

"Yeah, and we have a short window to find him before the entire case explodes in the media," McBain said. "A single murder is a good story. A serial killer on the loose in the city is a circus."

The detective also knew that a citywide panic was not going to help in his investigation. He could expect every crackpot theory and "confessed" murderer coming out from the streets and flooding headquarters.

McBain glanced over at Bones, seemingly distracted, tapping his fingers together. His anguish was palpable.

"The Simon homicide is only going to bring Clara back into the news," Bones said despondently.

"PJ, the press is not going to make the connection to Clara. She's old news and she's alive. Those jackos are more interested in dead murder victims."

Bones exhaled, shaking his head. "This is not over for her, and I don't know what's coming next. But it can't be anything good."

MCBAIN AND BONES

It had been a week since the Tre Simon case hit the city. The story was already losing traction in the local press when McBain's investigation finally got its first break: Simon had reportedly been at a gay bar in the Village the night of his disappearance. And he had not been alone.

Detective Brett Amdur briefed McBain in his office that morning.

"The bartender remembers Simon, a regular, talking to this stranger, an odd guy, heavy into makeup and attitude. The two seemed buddy-buddy enough. Then they left together. Simon was pretty wasted, according to the barkeep. But just the usual Friday night pickup, so he didn't think much of it until he read the paper that Simon had gone missing."

"Why didn't he come forward sooner?" McBain asked.

"The guy told us he didn't want to get involved. Then the reports of Simon's body parts showing up all over town became too much for him. So, he called."

"Yeah, severed bodies have a way of refocusing the mind."

Late into the evening, McBain got a second break. A call came to his desk from his contact in the city's taxi commission office. Matt Roberts, a mid-level official, had a good laugh at the detective's inquiry earlier that morning, asking if any of his guys recalled picking up two males near the Village bar the night Simon went missing. "Let's talk about a needle in a haystack," Roberts replied.

But Roberts' call to McBain was more pointed this time. "These might be your two men from the description you gave me," he said. "The cabbie recalled that one passenger was fall-down drunk and was worried that he was about to give it up all over his backseat. The other passenger told the driver to, quote, 'Get us the fuck out of here,' and gave him an address. My guy was less than pleased, but this is New York."

McBain could hear Roberts fiddling with a piece of paper. Then he read an address. It belonged to an apartment building on Frederick Douglass Boulevard in Harlem.

"Thanks, Matt," McBain said.

Roberts didn't have a chance to reply. McBain had abruptly hung up the phone, shouting a "heads-up" to his squad. Within minutes, six men armed and geared in bulletproof vests were ready to move on his order.

McBain went back to the phone and it didn't take long to contact the building's landlord. He wasn't surprised by McBain's call or who the detective was looking for. He told him about the loony in apartment 3C—that the man was big trouble with a scary attitude. He had knocked on the crazy's door after the neighbors' complaints about the clamor coming from his apartment.

"The guy looked like some tattooed Nazi inmate in one of those prison movies," he said. "I asked him to keep the noise down, but he didn't say a word, just scowled at me. He had these black eyes. Then he slammed the door in my face. Hadn't heard anything about him since, though he's two months late on his back rent."

McBain curtly thanked the landlord and hustled to join his men, who were already piled into two black SUVs. McBain snapped out orders, then radioed the 28th Precinct in Harlem for backup. He then picked up his private cell phone, hesitated, but decided to call his friend.

PJ Bones was at the computer when his phone chimed. His latest chapter was going nowhere, and Bones was grateful for the excuse to leave Sam Rock drowning in his fictional investigative mess. On the other side of the phone call was Phil McBain.

"Hey, Mac," Bones said. It had been a few days since they'd last spoken. He wanted to stay clear of the detective for now, instinctively trying to protect Clara. Bones hated that McBain was right about Clara, and about him—that he was caught in the web of her madness to think straight about her.

"Got a lead on the Simon case," McBain told him. "I'm betting that it's the same psycho that knifed Clara. I'm heading over with my men to his apartment now. Thought you might want to join me."

Bones breathed deeply. "Mac, do you think you got him?"

"Well, he got sloppy kidnapping Simon in plain sight," McBain said. "We got a beat on his apartment and we're going to grab him."

"Text me the address," Bones said. "I'm on my way."

MCBAIN AND BONES

Phil McBain raced with his team over to the apartment house on Frederick Douglass Boulevard. Uniformed cops from the 28th Precinct had already surrounded the tenement. A few moments later, he saw Bones' car rushing up, pulling next to a half-dozen cruisers catty-cornered around the building with their color flashers blinking wildly.

Bones wasn't exactly greeted with open arms.

"What's this asshole doing here?" Detective Thomas Sullivan was another lifer with a long memory. He wasn't thrilled seeing the former dirty cop.

"Hey, he's with me, Sully," McBain said. "Let it go."

Sullivan grunted. He had a tough-guy respect for his partner, but still made a mental note to have it out with him later for bringing Bones in on the case.

Bones nudged McBain to the side. "Mac, not a great idea me being here. I'm already getting in the way."

McBain was having doubts himself—maybe it was a dumb move to have Bones in on the scene. There was still bad blood from those old days, and the last thing he needed was a pissing match with his squad—but Bones was there and McBain could use him. His friend had been a damn good homicide detective before enduring all the unfair political crap that came his way. McBain also knew that Bones and Clara needed to get their lives back. Bringing down this maniac might give them a chance—not that anyone else cared, but he did. In any case, this wouldn't be the first bad decision he'd come to regret.

"Sully, get the squad ready," McBain ordered, scrutinizing the hectic scene outside the Harlem apartment building. Already, neighborhood residents had gathered around police barriers, a few agitating for a shootout.

Sullivan was back in line, coordinating duties with a sergeant from the 28th. His men would take charge of the streets.

McBain gathered his squad and gave final orders. Then he led them into the building and up a winding staircase to a third-floor apartment. 3C. There would be no subtlety in this arrest. McBain pounded on the door and shouted, "Police, open up!" He didn't wait more than two seconds before signaling one of his men carrying a battering ram to break down the door. The team rushed into the small apartment, guns out in front.

The place was pitch dark and empty—at least of any living being. A coat of dust covered the sparse furnishings. An overpowering stench hit the men as they barged into the room. A dead, rotting black cat lay against a back wall, set on by a swarm of flies.

"Goddamn!" Bones said, shielding his nose with his hand.

Sullivan went over to raise the window. Within a minute, the night heat seeped into the room, only making the heavy stink worse.

The detectives spread out to the four corners of the room. The apartment was barren of any light except for a bare bulb that cast a sinister glow. Each of the men pulled out a flashlight, and the space was immediately enveloped in beams zigzagging across the floor and walls, creating a dizzying dance of light.

"Hey, look here," Detective Amdur called out to McBain. A bloodstained chair stood in the middle of the room. Rope tatters still clung to the arms of the chair. Ribbons of dried blood had spread from the chair across the floor.

Amdur then bent down to pick something up from under the chair and brought it close to examine. He suddenly let out a sharp yelp, dropping the pointed metal chip to the floor. It had pierced his latex glove, cutting his finger.

McBain carefully picked up the small splinter of razor-sharp metal. "It looks like a tooth from a cutting saw."

"What the hell!" Amdur exclaimed.

"Christ. What went on here?" McBain said. It didn't take much detective work to sum up the bloody scene.

McBain reached into his pocket for a plastic evidence bag. He tagged the metal piece while Amdur tore off his glove to tend to his bleeding finger.

Bones called out from the other end of the room. His eyes were fixed on a long wall. The beam from his flashlight had revealed a handwritten painted message that ran across the top of the wall.

"The boundaries which divide Life from Death are at best shadowy and vague. Who shall say where the one ends, and where the other begins?"

"Look at this," Bones said, as McBain came up to his side.

Bones read the quote aloud. It was familiar, but he couldn't quite place it.

"Well," McBain said. "It looks like this is our man, all right."

"Yeah, then where is he?" Bones was still distracted by the wall's inscription.

"He won't be able to hide," McBain said. "We'll get the bastard."

Bones lurched back. The scrawl hit him at once.

"My god!" Bones said in a hushed voice. "The quote...It belongs to Edgar Allan Poe."

"Yeah, so what's the deal?" McBain said.

"Poe!"

McBain turned to Bones, confused. "So, our guy's a psycho who likes spooky writers."

"I know this man!" Bones cried out.

"What...?"

"At Columbia, I was giving a talk there when he came up to me. Then at Riverside Park one late afternoon. Creepy, arrogant bastard, in a bad wig and a lousy fake mustache. Got a bad feeling from him from the start. Wanted me to read something of his. Some book he'd been writing. Just thought he was another nut. Obsessed with Edgar Allan Poe. He even called himself 'Poe.'"

"What the hell do you mean?"

"I mean exactly that—he called himself 'Poe!'"

"Let me get this straight." McBain was perplexed. "Some guy came up to you with his book that he wanted you to read, you being the hotshot writer that you are, and he called himself *Edgar Allan Poe*?"

"No, just the name, 'Poe.' And he's that man!" Bones pointed to the wall. "Mac, it's him!"

A shout suddenly shot through the room.

"McBain, get the fuck over here."

It was Sullivan. His big Irish face was pale.

Sullivan was aiming his flashlight and peering into a wooden box that had been pushed to the side of the room. The lid of the box had been pried open.

McBain and Bones hustled up to his side.

Inside the box was a badly decomposed corpse.

A sickening, putrid smell wafted into the room. Sullivan suddenly retched, managing to hold down the heave.

"Could that be Tre Simon?" McBain murmured. He anxiously rubbed his forehead already beading with sweat.

Then he pulled out a kerchief and wrapped it around his mouth and nose.

The detectives stared at the rotting body, its decrepit face now a scowling, skeletal mask. McBain knew he would see that face again in his nightmares.

"No, the corpse is female," Sullivan said. "This might be the Sweeny woman we've been looking for."

"The woman from Queens that had vanished?" McBain asked.

"Yeah, that case was mine," Sullivan said. "The husband reported her missing while she was staying at a friend's place in the city. Then he claimed the kidnapper called him with all sorts of salacious crap about his wife, but there was nothing more. No ransom demand. No follow-up from the kidnapper. We checked out the husband, Dylan Sweeny. He cleared but was in bad shape with the wife missing and a two-year-old at home. The case went cold. She was just gone."

"Well, no way to tell if this is her," McBain said gravely.

"Yeah, we have a woman's body part downtown, a tongue," Sullivan said. "Could be hers."

McBain stooped over the box to take a closer look at the corpse.

"Let's get Tony over here," he said.

Anthony Campanella was carefully dusting black powder to the walls and furniture when Sullivan called out to him across the room.

"Looks like his prints are everywhere, his alone," Campanella told McBain as he came up to the coffin. "I guess he didn't keep much company."

Campanella, fiftyish and graying, wore the tired look of an overworked accountant—the price for earning a living examining murder victims over the past twenty-plus years. He was the squad's chief forensic investigator and good at his job.

"Well, I see here's one of his guests," Campanella said acidly, peering into the box.

He leaned in close to the decomposed body, the eyeless corpse facing him.

"So, how long?" McBain asked.

Campanella didn't need any prodding, donning a new pair of latex gloves.

"It's hard to say exactly how long she's been dead. More than a month for sure; closer to two months. She's way beyond the early stages of decomposition. That's when you'd expect to see the body bloating and a marbling discoloration of the skin, kind of like spider web patterns, but her condition is advanced. Bodily fluids have already ruptured skin surfaces. Organs, muscles, and skin are already liquefied."

"Tony, we have a lead on the victim," McBain said. "Can we see inside her mouth? Her tongue?"

"I don't think you can expect much there," Campanella said, taking out a wooden tongue depressor. He prodded open the woman's mouth.

"Nothing left, all tissue is gone, including the tongue. Skeletonizing has already set in. No facial recognition. You'll have a hard time identifying her, chief. Your best bet are dental records."

McBain nodded. He marveled at Campanella's preternatural calm during these examinations. The man might very well have been in front of a classroom lecturing on the stages of human decomposition. McBain was convinced that the man's detachment was his survival mode, distancing himself from the fact that this corpse, and so many others he'd examined, was once a vibrant, living human being with a family and a future.

McBain understood his own weakness, seeing the human being that once lived inside each murder victim. He couldn't hold back the tidal wave of anger and despair that came with every homicide investigation. His mucking about in the chronic sickness of city crime had taken its toll. Twenty-five years of this hell. He mostly had avoided daydreaming of Mexico, that looming paradise, his new life in arms reach. He needed to be reborn, but the sight of this corpse reminded him he was still headlong into the shit.

"Look at her hands, Tony," Sullivan said grimly. "They resemble...claws."

"Yes," Campanella replied. He could see her skeletal hands locked above her skull. He then glanced at the inner wooden lid with its deep scratches. "She was desperate to escape."

"She died a miserable death," McBain said, shaking his head. "Can you imagine being trapped inside this...coffin? He even carved air holes. He wanted her to suffer longer."

Campanella noticed something else, shining, and bent down to remove a gold wedding ring from her finger. Inscribed on the inner band, "DS loves AS."

"This might help you identify her, Mac," he said.

"Dylan Sweeny. Anne Sweeny," Sullivan said glumly.

McBain massaged his forehead, an old habit that did nothing to alleviate the despondency that swept over him.

The three men stood around the coffin, stunned at the savagery. Anne Sweeny. Nothing more now than a putrefied corpse, a macabre exhibit to be exhibited and probed. A spectacle of horror.

"Poe." Bones scowled, uttering the name to himself.

BONES

The two men sped back to Bones' West End Avenue apartment. McBain put on the flashers and didn't bother with the stoplights. Neither man had much to say. The horror of the afternoon cut off all small talk.

They were anxious to see what Poe had handed over to Bones that afternoon in Riverside Park.

"Clara is at home," Bones said, as they arrived at the building. "Best to keep her out of this."

Bones unlocked the door to the apartment. Clara wasn't there.

"I guess she's out for a walk," he said uneasily.

McBain heard the worry in Bones' voice, but this was not a time to talk—not with the dead body in Harlem and a madman roaming the city.

Bones had a small office in the back of the apartment. Except for his desk, chair, and computer, the lone piece of furniture was a file cabinet. No way did Bones trust any machine with his work. The cabinet stored his hard copies and all his research. Bones was sure that Poe's manuscript must be in some back file. He had thought to toss the unread pages but for some reason kept them.

Only the pages were now missing.

"The manuscript…it's gone, Mac," Bones said.

"PJ, this is important," McBain said tensely. "Could it be somewhere else?"

Bones paused but then abruptly turned to leave the office. "Come with me," he told McBain.

The two men went into Bones' bedroom. Bones opened a closet door: a small dresser meant for Clara's clothing rested in the corner space. Then he rifled through each drawer before finding a black sack tightly cinched with a thick cord. He managed to unknot the cord. A stash of papers filled Clara's bag.

Bones piled the bundle on top of his bed—news clippings from her attack along with reports from her psychologist back in Kansas. Also, a separate envelope filled with torn sheets of paper. Poe's manuscript. Pages were ripped in half, marked with a red-inked 'X' and scrawls of obscenities. Bones picked up one page marred by the word, "DIE!"

"She stole the envelope from my files," he said, shaking his head.

"Christ, this is Clara?" McBain said, examining the mutilated pages.

Bones sat down heavily on the side of the bed. "She's hurting, Mac. Bouts of hysteria; she imagines Poe stalking her."

McBain grimaced. He had seen too many Clara Knoxes before—victims that remain victims well after the trauma they suffered.

"PJ, I'm sorry...for both of you."

McBain perused the mess of crumbled, torn paper that covered the bed. Poe's nightmarish ramblings. Then he reached over, picking up a random page. It was about Anne Sweeny.

> Her screams remind me of those of a trapped animal, frantic and bucking against her fate, one that she knows is inescapable. Trapped in her coffin, the water bugs flitting across her face and neck... I open her coffin and her eyes beg me to set her free, but she must

know that there is no escape, only that
her death awaits her. Here in the dark, in
her coffin, where she will die and rot, a
fleeting memory of the beautiful woman
she once was… What did Edgar say to
me? 'The death of a beautiful woman is,
unquestionably, the most poetical topic
in the world'…

McBain let out a deep breath. "He's far gone, supremely
dangerous," he murmured.

"Yes, dangerous and delusional," Bones said. "He's
acting out his own horror stories. He *is* insane."

McBain nodded. "And he won't stop until we take him
down."

It was then that the bedroom door opened.

Clara Knox eased into the bedroom, startling both
men.

She glanced from Bones and McBain, seeing the torn
pages scattered across the bed.

"I see you found him," she said, smiling faintly.

MCBAIN

Phil McBain walked into an eighth-floor assembly room at One Police Plaza early the next morning. Police headquarters had brought together a half-dozen detective units from around the city. The place was already a beehive of activity. The Butcher case was now officially prioritized. Investigators were furiously working the streets carrying an old police sketch rendered after Clara's attack. It showed a bald man with deep-set eyes. A second sketch showed a nondescript dark-haired man with a mustache, taken from Bones' recent encounter with Poe. A warning attached to the drawings was written in stark police language:

"Wanted for Murder: suspect, 28-33 years old, over six-feet tall, multiple tattoos covering both arms and torso. Dangerous, approach with extreme caution."

McBain perused his desk calendar, what had become a daily ritual—twenty-two days and counting. He had already bought his plane ticket to Guadalajara and mapped out the forty-five-minute ride to Lake Chapala. He was pretty fluent in Spanish and loved tequila, so he figured that he was way ahead in his retirement plans. He vowed to clear the damn case, get going, and head south over the border.

McBain scrutinized the large room. A few detectives were checking out the overhead television screens. The Sweeny murder was the sensational story of the day, playing concurrently on local news stations. Reporters had tied Sweeny with the Simon murder though McBain kept details of the investigation tightly under wraps. He wasn't about to add fuel to their reports with the gruesome details—not that reporters were short on ramping up public passions with home video of a glowing Anne Sweeny playing with her infant child at the beach. Her murder had gone national with cable news reports that were accompanied by chyron headlines declaring, "The Butcher on the Rampage."

McBain closed his eyes, but he could not wipe out the mental images of Anne Sweeny's corpse found in Poe's Harlem apartment that night. The press had branded him, "The Butcher," a chilling pseudonym that needed no explanation. Did *any* name exist to describe this...madman?

For now, McBain would simply refer to him as Poe.

PART THREE

POE

Chapter 10
'Travis and Jenny'

Life is unpredictable. I mean, how could I have expected both Travis and Jenny to land right in my lap? I was cruising through JFK airport, keeping my eye out for my next companion, when Travis stepped from the curb at a Delta pickup area and waved me over.

"*Uber?* Travis, Jenny," he said as I pulled up, rolling down the passenger window.

I was freelancing that night, but I guess my black Buick got his attention. The phony Uber card in my car's windshield also helped—that and the fact that I made a good first impression in my jacket and tie.

Who knows, sometimes fate just works its magic.

I nodded back and smiled, verifying his pickup request. Then I spun out of the car to grab their luggage and pack the bags into the car trunk. "Hey, thanks," Travis said, moving aside to let Jenny get into the back seat.

The couple settled in behind a Plexiglas partition that divided us. Maybe they felt that I needed the glass for added protection from unruly passengers—after all, driving a private car for hire was dangerous business.

I could hear the two twittering away through my front speaker.

"Hey, fella, what's your name?" Travis asked as I stepped on the gas.

"The name is Poe, and nice making your acquaintance."

Both laughed.

"And nice making *your* acquaintance," Jenny said giggling.

I was so glad they were having fun mocking me, maybe even thinking I was a freak. A bit impertinent, but at that moment I had other things on my mind. I searched underneath the dash for the knob, a new upgrade I'd installed along with the glass partition. I slightly rotated the knob, hearing a slight hissing sound, so it was working fine. I didn't want to rush into our relationship, though, so I retightened the thing, cutting off the line.

"You know, we're back from our honeymoon. Cabo San Lucas."

I could see through my mirror Travis grinning. The guy was obviously still on his honeymoon high with his lithesome bride.

"Well, my congratulations," I replied. I checked out Jenny in the front mirror. "You are a lucky man."

"Yes, I am!" Travis stated exuberantly.

Jenny turned deep red, embarrassed, and softly slapped Travis on his thigh. I understood. She was taken aback by her husband's coded language that said that she was an incredible fuck. Who was I to disagree? It was hard to miss her natural beauty, wide-eyed with her blonde ponytail and snowflake skin. She had a runner's body, accentuated by black spandex tights that hugged her figure.

Travis was still into his Cabo head, nuzzling against Jenny's neck, whispering some nasty nothing, making her giggle. I decided he was another young Wall Streeter with his master-of-the-universe attitude. I'm sure he had everything: big money, big house, big cock. Jenny had hit the trifecta.

"So, where to?" I asked, interrupting their backseat foreplay.

"Greenwich," Travis said, notching his head aside from Jenny's neck. "A long trip to Connecticut, so, my man, can you hurry? And *no problema*. I'm a big tipper."

I thought how enjoyable this evening was about to become as I turned onto the Van Wyck Expressway.

The roadway had the usual crush of airport traffic with thousands of travelers returning to their trivial lives. What did they know of anything? Just like the pair in the back seat, the beautiful people home from Cabo and onto Greenwich, with their manse and green lawns, and all the bullshit niceties they felt they deserved—what was owed to them. I felt a bit giddy with the Buick picking up speed. After all, I had the power to read their future.

Then I slowly turned the knob.

It took a minute or so for the nitrous oxide to fill the back of the car. Travis was the first to notice the vent spewing the stuff. "Hey buddy!" Then the faintly sweet smell. He began shouting through the glass partition.

"Hey, buddy! *Buddy!*"

I turned on the car speaker. "Please, Travis, the name is Poe. Let's not be rude."

Then it was Jenny's turn, who stared at me through the partition, open-mouthed, as the gas seeped into the back seat. The realization had set in. She started screaming, grabbing onto the door handle, frantically trying to escape. Now, that would have been dangerous under any circumstance in a moving vehicle, but safety first—that was my motto when rejiggering the door locks to stay put.

Now it was Travis making a scene bashing against the partition and the passenger windows. The extra expense for the thick Plexiglas had paid off.

"Now, Travis, Jenny…you must relax. Soon you'll be home."

I was using my soothing voice, trying to keep a positive attitude, as the yelling and pounding went on in the back.

"And Travis, Uber doesn't take tips, so *no problema*." At least, I thought it was funny.

In a minute, the two were unconscious, with Travis splayed out on top of his new bride. I smiled at the sweet scene.

I slowly made my way to the Long Island Expressway past beach towns with old Native American names until I came to the tip of the island. The family cabin was miles off the main road and tucked away next to a dense forest and a large swamp. The place was left to rot after my parents died and foreclosed soon afterward. No buyers would dare touch this place, nothing more than a deserted, decaying shack on a dirt plot. I tried to stick around after the accident. I was ten and it was my home, even if my parents were dead. I was content being on my own with the forest creatures and my buried pets, but then they came—two men in suits—to take me away to some "children's home" with those human animals that lived there and taunted me.

I returned to the old house a few years back. Ghosts beckoned me to return twenty years after I last set foot into the place. And when I walked through the front opening— the door was long gone—I said hello to mother and father. Their apparitions wore the same cold looks on their faces that they had when I was a kid—as if I was just some stranger who lived in their home. They did their best, I suppose, making excuses for me when things went wrong at school, or with neighbors—not that I needed them to. But I could always see them thinking—how could they have given birth to this freak?

I didn't mean for them to die. Well, that was a little white lie I told myself. The stove's gas burners left on during the late night quickly filled our small cabin, so they left this earth peacefully. And what a coincidence that my older cousin, Ritchie, was over at our family place as well. Earlier that same evening, he had corralled me in the woods and whispered what a nice kid I was—not the first time. He wanted us to have a secret together, like good friends do, and he pulled down his pants, then mine, and had his fun with me again.

It was a good thing that I decided to take a walk through the woods that night. When the police came later, I'm sure I expressed the proper amount of sorrow. I even managed to tear up. Those guys gently tapped my shoulder and gave me some water—the usual comfort scam, though I saw their confusion. I mean, what was this kid doing traipsing through the dark woods so late, this at the same time the cabin's gas jets were shooting out death? They called my parents' and cousin's death a terrible accident, and, of course, I agreed with them, but I was ten and even the cops didn't think I was capable.

I was now back in my old haunt…and they say you can't go home again! The rot had spread and the place looked on the verge of collapse, but I had spent the previous year shoring it up, even adding a few features to make the place more welcoming. Let's call them home improvements. I found some peace and solitude here, a far cry from my Harlem apartment—not that I was planning to return there anyway, with the nosy neighbors and buzzy headlines about a killer on the streets. I also read in the papers the police had raided the place. I wonder how they reacted meeting up with Anne Sweeny.

In any case, some R&R at the cabin would do me good. Besides, my two new friends might enjoy a respite in this back country. The crickets' staccato chirps greeted us as we arrived in the dead of night. I walked out to the backyard, careful not to trample on the scattered stones that covered my dead creatures. Tre Simon was also buried in the corner of the yard, and I had some work ahead of me to prepare for my next two friends, but I wasn't about to rush things.

I opened the passenger doors with Travis still unconscious and spread-eagled on top of his lovely bride. Only her blonde ponytail was visible hanging off the seat. It was tough going dragging Travis out of the car by his feet. He was a big guy, so I had no choice but to hoist him by his legs, scraping him along the dirt path into the house.

I finally got Travis into the cabin, perched his body on a chair, and shackled him. No use having the guy wake up and causing trouble. I needed to get both my guests settled in quickly.

Back at the Buick, I could see Jenny starting to stir. I picked her up from the back seat and carried her into the house. She was groaning, tossing in my arms, and then her eyes jerked open wide as I approached the doorway. Our eyes locked and Jenny gasped. I smiled and felt like I was carrying my lovely bride across the threshold. I was pretty sure though that she didn't feel the same way when she started thrashing about in my arms. She even slapped my face. Silly girl. I almost dropped her, then tightened my grip. She finally shut up when I squeezed her cheeks hard. My black eyes made her see things my way.

As we made our way into the room, Jenny saw Travis, half-conscious and chained, and started to sob. "No, no!" she cried out, but I shushed her, pointing to a chair next to Travis. She obediently sat down. This *ménage à trois* had been a surprise, and I realized that I was short on shackles. I pulled a thick rope off a hook. Then I tied Jenny to the chair.

It followed with the usual getting-to-know-you question that I'd come to expect.

"What do you want?" Jenny asked right off. Her whimpering was getting louder, and she no longer was wearing that fresh from the honeymoon look. Not at all.

Then it was Travis bellowing—*"What the hell!"*—now fully roused, checking the chains that tied him to the wooden chair. He pushed back hard, but the chair was solidly nailed to the floor—one of my home improvements.

We chatted, just to break the ice after our awkward introduction. I had to say, Travis and Jenny were a disappointment—he of Wall Street (I was right!) and she a yoga instructor. I even told them about my childhood experiences at the cabin, but I could tell they were not interested. They seemed more comfortable that I wasn't just some psycho—maybe just some guy after a hefty ransom from their rich parents. Hey, maybe they were even looking forward to posting this adventure to their million followers to add to their social media cred.

I chuckled when Travis told me he thought we could be friends. He kind of stumbled around when I asked him why. Really good bullshit about how decent a guy I seemed, how I didn't mean to cause them any harm, that this was all some mistake that we could work out. So, that was fun.

The mood kind of changed a bit when I untied Jenny and told her to take her clothes off. Boy, you would have thought I was about to do something serious. Travis started bellyaching loudly and Jenny began bawling—a noisy scene. I had enough and went over to the long table where I had lined up my "tools" and picked up a blade. The heft of the knife felt comforting in my hand, as it usually did. I could see Jenny glancing over, all wide-eyed and terrified. I was glad she was having a change of heart as she got to her feet and stripped.

There was Travis again, coming to her rescue.

"Lay a hand on her and I'll fucking kill you."

I laughed. Still, I'd had enough of this master of the universe, so I stuck the knife into his left eye. I can't say it shut him up with all the ensuing noise, but it was enough to tamp down his bad attitude.

Jenny screamed before falling to her knees, blubbering. *"Oh my god, oh my god, oh my god!"*

She tried to scream again, only this time the pitch quickly dissolved into gasps. Jenny was having a hard time breathing, very much a drama queen. She then bent her head to touch the floor in some prayer pose. I found it strange. Jenny didn't seem like the religious type.

"You are insane," she murmured.

I leaned over to her and whispered in her ear. "I was never really insane, except on occasions where my heart was touched."

Ah, Edgar possessed me.

I hadn't planned on such a commotion so soon with Travis now choking on blood streaming into his mouth. He was crying out with lots of tears coming out of his good eye. Jenny crawled over to him, hugging his knees, a tender scene. So I gave them a bit of alone time before lifting her up and tying her back to the chair.

I had to admire how well she kept her body in shape. She was built like some graceful swan with her tapered legs, a pear-shaped ass, and her small, upturned tits. Real nice. I didn't have any other interest in mind. She was a married woman, and it wasn't like me to have her break her vows, but I might leave that up to her later.

I knew it was going to be difficult explaining my intentions to the couple—that I was about to guide them through an experience of great personal consequence: the moment when they were about to die. I tried to empathize with their predicament—how desperate it must be for them, holding onto life knowing they had no choice other than to accept their fate. But they were distracted, understandably.

I was pleased, however. Their story would fit nicely into my journal.

Travis and Jenny traded frightened looks. They seemed bewildered but kind of cute in their own stupid way. I did try to help out, telling them that they were two of the beautiful people, which they already knew. I assured them that I would be doing my part and that they will be doing theirs. I could tell they had no idea what I meant.

I then went over to a cot in the corner of the room for some shuteye—it had been a long day—though the two didn't make it easy for me to sleep with all their boohooing and shit.

POE

Chapter 11
'The Fireplace'

The rising sun woke me as it did when I was a kid living here in the cabin. Back then, we had a rooster that started our day. I was glad when my father finally strangled the thing, quieting the mornings. I was eager to get the day going, but first decided to take a stroll into the woods. I made my way out of the cabin past Jenny and Travis in their mumbling sleep. The tranquilizers had finally tamped down their incessant sniveling during the night.

The woods held all sorts of childhood memories and they flooded back as I snaked my way through the dense woodlands. No other families resided around these parts, so I had found my own companions. As a kid, insects and small animals became a source of wonder, and I took to them with my small knife. It was an education dissecting the creatures, seeing what parts they needed to continue life. Butterflies, for instance, did not last long without their wings. I also discovered that rabbits needed their ears and tail. As I said, an education.

We spent our summers here with father commuting to some office job he had in the city. Most times, he didn't make it back that same day. I gathered from mother's angry comments that he was with another woman, or another man. Father seemed to resent hanging out with mother and me and Sis anyway, so he wasn't missed.

Sis died in a car accident later on. That really fucked up mother's head. I supposed that was understandable since they had a real close relationship. I can't say the same for ours.

I was mostly left alone, and that was just fine, leaving me to my explorations. Summers at the cabin were much better than school with those stupid kids, pointing their fingers at me, laughing.

How things have changed. Where are those kids now? Maybe Travis and Jenny were two of them. It just seemed right having them as my guests. I had even restored the fireplace with new bricks, along with an iron ring that I inserted into the back of the firebox. Everything was in working order.

I came back inside the cabin. Jenny and Travis were groggily coming back to consciousness. They seemed confused, checking out their current circumstances, bound to a chair with me hovering about. Maybe they had blocked out the previous night, or were thinking they were waking from a bad dream, but, surprise! Here was the monster! And alive. It was quite amusing seeing Jenny yelp, her eyes darting around her own naked body, coming to grips with the reality of her nightmare.

"Good morning, sweetheart," I said trying to cheer her up.

And then there was Travis, who started moaning again, no doubt missing his eye.

I wanted to get an early jump on the busy day and headed over to the corner kitchen sink. I filled two water bottles and dropped in a roofie. The Special K was my favorite.

"No need to get dehydrated," I said, returning to my two visitors. I lifted the water bottle into Jenny's mouth and she greedily slurped down the liquid. "Thank you," she said in a whispery voice.

I gazed at her nakedness and could tell she felt my eyes roaming. She took a few short breaths and started shaking, getting excited. Jenny must have been warming up to me. I was sure that was it.

Then I turned to Travis and held up the water bottle to his one good eye. He flinched, maybe thinking that I was about to take out his other eye with the bottle. It was understandable that he'd be on edge. Then gingerly he opened his mouth and I squeezed out the water, the liquid dribbling down his chin. He no longer had that master-of-the-universe attitude.

"Feeling better?" I smiled. He stared at me looking confused—certainly a better response than the bad language he'd used the previous night.

I waited for the roofie to kick in. Jenny was already dazed, her head lolling onto her chest. Travis was also stuporous. Then I unchained him.

"I want you to come with me, Travis," I said. He could barely stand, but I managed to lead him across the room to the fireplace. He was docile enough as I forced him inside the opening. The firebox was narrow, about three-feet wide and less than six-feet high. Then I chained his arms and legs to the iron ring. Travis stared at me open-mouthed, and then his legs gave way. He would have collapsed to the floor if it wasn't for the chains holding up his crumbled, semi-conscious body.

I spent the next two hours laying rows of brick to seal the front wall of the firebox. Travis was having a tough time stringing words together, mostly spouting spurts of sounds. "Plez...don...do...thz." With each new line of bricks, he became louder, though still not making it easier for me to make sense of him. Just a breakdown in communications, but to be expected.

I finally finished bricking the firebox, standing back to admire my handiwork. Nothing worthwhile is ever accomplished without hard work. I could barely hear Travis blubbering inside his tomb.

I thought back to Edgar's poor Fortunato, waking from his drunken stupor to discover he had been entombed in a crypt, thinking it was a joke, only to slowly comprehend that he had crossed over into the darkness. And so would Travis. He seemed quiet now. I imagine that feeling would change once the roofie wore off.

I looked across the room at Jenny, unconscious, slumped in the chair. I was satisfied with how things were progressing and felt that I'd earned a breather. So, I stepped outside the cabin again and walked along the edge of the nearby swamp and into the thick woods. I looked over the grounds for the small critters that seemed so abundant when I was a kid. Maybe I'd spooked them and they never returned. If I were them, that would have made perfect sense.

I came back to the cabin later that evening, only to be met by Jenny's shrieks as I walked through the door. *"What have you done?"* she wailed. *"Dear god! What have you done?"*

Then I heard Travis's strangling noise—animal sounds coming from inside his bricked tomb. Then his pleading, promising anything, but he needed to get out. And so on and so on.

I was starting to feel a dark mood descending, the thunder growing inside my head from the racket in the room with Jenny and Travis. I was already tired of their hysterics. Their present circumstance wasn't Cabo and the honeymoon was definitely over. Better for them to see the real world and take this as a life-learning experience.

I went over to Jenny, who bucked back in her chair. She was beautiful—so terrified and desirable. I needed to touch her, but she twitched and jerked about as I ran my hand along her soft, naked body. I kneeled next to her. Maybe she thought I was about to propose marriage, and I chuckled. She was already mine.

"You know, you remind me of her," I told her.

"What, what are you saying?" Jenny was starting in again with the sobs.

"I'm saying, Jenny, that you remind me of Virginia. She was very passionate about Edgar."

"I don't know who you are talking about, mister. *Please* let us go."

"Virginia Eliza Clemm, that was her name. You know, Jenny, she was only thirteen when she and Edgar married. He was twenty-seven, so, young love, yes? Oh, one other thing. They were first cousins. Keeping it in the family, I guess. He called her 'Sissy.' He wrote in a letter, 'I see no one among the living as beautiful as my little wife.' Can you imagine such love?"

"I don't understand," she said. Then more weeping.

"I mean, look at both of us. Don't you think that we, too, might have discovered that same eternal love? But then you went ahead to marry Travis. You must know that he doesn't deserve you."

"Mister, don't hurt us anymore," she begged.

Ignoring my feelings was not going to help the situation.

"Just let us go," she went on. "We won't say anything. It was a misunderstanding. You seem like...a sensitive person."

"I am talking about Edgar's wife, Jenny," I snapped. "And you are not listening. Virginia was the love of his life.

And then she died, after years of suffering, her lungs eaten away by the consumption. Terrible way to die. She was so young, just twenty-four. How old are you, Jenny?"

"Mister, please..."

"Jenny, my name is Poe. And I am asking you how fucking old you are?"

"Okay, okay. I am twenty-three."

"So, you are just about the age Virginia was when she died. What a coincidence."

Jenny was blinking wildly, but, at last, she had stopped sniveling.

I got up from my knees, leaving her tied to the chair. I was glad to have had the talk. Jenny needed to know how I felt. I could see that she was beginning to understand. Then I went to a corner table where I kept my tools and picked out an eight-inch knife—it was the Liston and quite a special blade used for surgical amputations. It had performed efficiently on Tre Simon. I even read a fictional account of Jack the Ripper that featured the knife. I was particularly impressed by the blade's razor-sharp precision.

In any case, I didn't want to frighten Jenny—she already was having a tough day—so I concealed the knife in the back of my pants when I came up to face her. Jenny looked at me with those doe-like eyes, still imploring me to free her and Travis. I sighed, exasperated. She was beautiful, this Virginia, but she must have known that Travis's fate was literally sealed in the firebox.

Jenny was only mine, though I didn't think she quite appreciated our commitment. I reached out to take her hand, massaging her fingers. I saw her lovely face softening from my touch. She gave me a hopeful smile, maybe even thinking I had changed my mind and that all would end well for her and Travis. Her look warmed me all over.

"You must know how I feel about you, Jenny," I told her.

She looked at me wide-eyed not knowing what to say, maybe searching for the right words to express her own feelings to me.

Then I pulled the knife from behind my back and sliced off her ring finger.

I could see that she was first in shock. Not a sound, staring at the four fingers on her right hand. Then came her screams. She stopped a second only to catch her breath, and then expelled high-pitched animal howls that were truly remarkable. I didn't think any human being was capable of emoting such agony.

I scrutinized the finger in my hand, admiring the large diamond ring and gold band that encircled it. I guess Travis and Jenny's marriage was officially over—better now than later when it was bound to fall apart. Besides, Jenny was well into her new relationship with me.

The cabin was growing noisier, with a *THUMP, THUMP, THUMP* coming from the sealed fireplace—Travis again. Jenny's screams had pierced his brick tomb. He had to be using his head as a battering ram to free himself and, I guess, come to her rescue—truly a master of the universe. I liked his gumption, although he must have known that no one was being saved that night. His own death would come slowly, but for now he could only listen to Jenny's cries seeping into his darkness.

I reached over to Jenny again, taken by my love for the woman. I tried to reassure her and give her hope.

"Jenny, Jenny, shush."

Then I told her what Edgar had told me.

"'Even in the grave, all is not lost.'"

I wiped down the blood from my Liston blade. Its high-quality metal shined, with the heft of the knife comforting in my hand, but I decided that Jenny had suffered enough. It struck me that further marring this wondrous young woman just didn't appeal to me. I did not want our relationship to end this way.

Jenny was still bawling, though I think she must have felt relieved now that I'd put the knife away.

It was getting late, but I still needed to be honest with her. We needed to have a frank talk in the morning

"Rest now, Jenny," I told her lovingly, and gave her a kiss on her forehead.

She looked up at me with those tearful, doe-eyes that only made me love her more.

I wished her a good night, deciding not to overburden her at that moment.

I always thought it best to save bad news for the daylight.

POE

Chapter 12
'Taphophobia'

I woke up refreshed at dawn and came over to Jenny, slumped in her chair. She was already awake. Perhaps not surprising. There would be plenty of time to sleep later. I could hear Travis now making catlike, mew-mew noises from the fireplace. I suspected the two had some meaningful conversations during the night.

In truth, I was reluctant to let Jenny go, and my heart wasn't entirely into the day. She was sweet and beautiful and needing to be loved. I felt we'd had something special together these past days, but I had already dug the hole in the backyard and it was best not to let sentiment get in the way.

I spoke to Jenny about what was to come. She started in with the shivers and the weeping. I explained that her fear of being buried alive was natural. Back in Edgar's time, this dread of premature burial was quite common. It was given a name: 'taphophobia.' People with lingering illnesses, suffering from shallow breathing or a stroke, were put in the ground by loved ones with all good intentions, believing they were dead. Mistakes happen.

Even Edgar took notice in his stories. I was disappointed that Jenny was unfamiliar with Edgar's "The Premature Burial"—a classic—so I decided to read to her, pulling out a book of his stories that I carried with me. This, the story of a man, believed to be dead, buried in his coffin in a shallow grave.

> The grave was carelessly and loosely filled with an exceedingly porous soil; and thus some air was necessarily admitted. He heard the footsteps of the crowd overhead, and endeavored to make himself heard in turn. It was the tumult within the grounds of the cemetery, he said, which appeared to awaken him from a deep sleep, but no sooner was he awake than he became fully aware of the awful horrors of his position.

"Can you imagine being put into the ground, still alive, and the inescapable horror that awaits you?" I asked.

I relished bringing Edgar's vivid mind to life, probing the depths of our fears. I didn't see the point of repressing such thoughts. Just not good for one's mental well-being, speaking as a health professional. Jenny wasn't paying attention, now becoming hysterical. I insisted she stay calm, or I might have to punish her. She froze when I held out the knife. We had a nice talk after that...not that she had anything much to say. Just more blubbering.

"What some people will go through to make sure they are not buried alive," I continued. "George Washington himself wanted his body laid out for three days just to make sure he was properly dead before being buried. Then there was Chopin—you know, the famous composer—who asked that his heart be cut out when he died. Just a bit of insurance that he was ready for the underground. So, some interesting history."

Jenny was sobbing again, gasping for breath. I tried to comfort her.

"You have every right to feel the way you do," I told her.

She was so scared and could not stop trembling. I assumed she was looking ahead, imagining the darkness that awaited her.

"It will all be over soon," I assured her.

Then I took her by the arm and we walked together into the backyard. She was unsteady on her feet, and then she collapsed. So I carried her the rest of the way. Then I tied her feet and hands, rousing her before gently placing her into a six-foot-deep pit. I had already smoothed out the dirt to make her more comfortable. She started to stir, her eyes popping open.

"GOD! NO, NO, NO!" she cried out from the deep hole.

Jenny was obviously getting a clearer picture of her immediate future, punctuating the air with her high-pitched screams.

So, I began. I picked up the first shovel of dirt, gently letting it pour into the opening. The dirt struck Jenny like an electric bolt, and she wildly jerked inside her narrow grave. Then another shovelful and another. I kept piling dirt into the hole and she became more crazed, thrashing about, looking quite pathetic. She reminded me of those forest critters I buried alive long ago when I was a kid, also afraid of accepting their fate. Now they were about to be Jenny's neighbors.

It was a pity giving up Jenny to the earth, though she was a fighter. Even as she choked on the earth, she fought for breath. The effort only made her choke more violently with the dirt sucked into her throat and lungs. I really did not see the point. Better to suffocate quickly than to needlessly suffer. But Jenny was determined to live, like those others. Still, I found her feeble struggles quite heartrending.

It took a bit more time for Jenny to finally calm down, the weight of the soil finally keeping her body still. She let out a long sob just before I shoveled a large mound that blanketed her face. I had saved that part of her burial for last, wanting to gaze upon her lovely, sad face until the very end. Finally, she was silent, though I noticed the earth quivering above her body for a few moments. I suppose Jenny was still struggling under the ground to stay alive.

I made my way to the cabin about an hour later. Jenny was properly at rest. Of course, she deserved a stone, so I found a rock and marked it as 'X' to join the others. But I was feeling strangely tender at losing Jenny. She had that effect on me. After all, I'm only human.

I went inside the cabin and was immediately aware of a sharp, staccato sound coming from the fireplace—Travis, chained inside his tomb, tap-tapping his head relentlessly against the brick wall. I sensed that he was missing Jenny, too.

Chapter 13
'Home'

I felt my heart swell strolling near the cabin, seeing the majesty of God's work that night. It almost made me want to believe in Him. My eyes drifted to the incredible dome of stars that covered the night sky. I could see the Big Dipper and the Gemini Twins and a few other constellations that I couldn't remember. Ever since I was a kid, it was just a fun mind-game connecting the dots of light. My zodiac sign was Aquarius, so I was "imaginative" and "uncompromising"—not that I believed in that nonsense, but I had to admit the description was right on.

I avoided trampling over the small stones that marked my animal cemetery out of respect for the dead. Each one brought back childhood memories experimenting with these critters that I'd caught in the woods.

From the cabin, I could also see through the woods to the large swamp in the distance. Mother had tried to frighten me away from the place, warning me about poisonous snakes, vultures, and other dangerous creatures—not that I was listening. At night, I made my way to the wetlands, taking in the night shadows and the swamp noises that surrounded me. The murky waters were my home away from home.

I now went over to the edge of my dirt backyard. Here were larger stones. Underneath the ground was Tre Simon, or what had been left of him. Nearby was Jenny Graham. The soil around her grave was still freshly tilled from two days earlier. I still felt heavy-hearted that she was deep in the ground, though it made no sense looking backward. Jenny was well dead by now, and I needed to move on. And, besides, Travis was next.

I was patient having to endure his ravings during the last days, but finally, the noise and banging subsided. Then I tore down the bricked tomb to retrieve his body, only to find that he was still alive, twitching and mumbling incoherently.

I admit to feeling a twinge of jealousy and even hatred toward the man. Travis never did deserve Jenny—some fucking master of the universe he turned out to be.

"She is deep in the earth now," I told him afterward. "I imagine though the worms are enjoying themselves. Jenny must be quite delicious."

His moaning was pitiful.

It wasn't kind of me going on like that. Travis was having a hard enough time, but we weren't quite through yet. I began resealing the firebox, one layer of brick after the next. The darkness was closing in around him once more. And his howling started in again.

MCBAIN

The missing persons' report sat on Phil McBain's desk. Such reports were never good news. Typically, they were about some old man with dementia wandering the streets lost, or a confused runaway who winds up on dope or tricking. Most troubling were the innocents abducted in plain sight. Those almost never ended well. This report though was even more disturbing for McBain, knowing what he knew with a serial killer on the loose.

The facts were blunt. Jenny and Travis Graham of Greenwich, Connecticut, had vanished without a trace a day earlier. Airport logs showed that they had boarded Delta flight 732 from Cabo San Lucas and arrived at John F. Kennedy Airport in New York at 9:21 pm that Tuesday. They had flown first-class after a ten-day honeymoon at the Esperanza Resort, where they stayed in the five-thousand-dollar-per-night luxury villa. Records showed that their luggage was retrieved and inspected at customs. They were last sighted through a security camera leaving the airport shortly afterward.

The report noted that Travis Graham is the son of Benedict Graham, a well-known Connecticut billionaire, who made his fortune investing in foreclosed business properties. Jenny Anderson is the daughter of Lawrence and Marjorie Anderson, socialites and prominent donors to the Metropolitan Museum of Art and the New York City Ballet. Jenny and Travis Graham were very much the glamour couple.

It didn't take long before McBain's phone was ringing. On the other end was Trevor Cooligan, his commanding officer.

"Mac, we need to talk," Cooligan said brusquely.

The chief was never long on conversation, which McBain appreciated. He was in no mood for bullshit and his commander was not one to hoist the stuff.

"The missing Connecticut couple, right?" McBain replied.

"Yeah, looks like they were taken."

"Isn't that Connecticut's jurisdiction?"

"Looks like a snatch from JFK. Headquarters wants your team in on the case. FBI is on it, too."

"Any cameras to help us out?"

"That might be our only good news," Cooligan said. "We have a black Buick at their pickup spot outside the airport terminal. Not much of a visual. The photo is from a security camera. No plates or much of anything. Also, we already contacted Uber and other car services. No luck."

"What about the driver?"

"More of the same. A gray, blurry photo of the driver. Dark-haired, mustache, in a jacket and tie, but that's it."

"Chief…this might be our man."

McBain could hear Cooligan exhale into the phone.

"Damnit, this isn't going to end well," Cooligan said tersely. "I'm sending you this photo now. And Mac, Benedict Graham is kicking up the shit-storm of the century. Can't blame him. It's his son and daughter-in-law, but it's our asses on the line."

If his investigation wasn't already complicated, McBain knew that Benedict Graham was a man with deep pockets tied to local politicos. His reputation preceded him, one that never would be confused with Mother Theresa's—not that his billions or connections or anything else would do him much good if Poe was involved.

McBain checked his official email and clicked into Cooligan's attachment. A grainy image appeared of a man standing outside the driver's side of his car, his right hand in the air, gesturing to someone off-camera. No doubt that he was calling out to Travis and Jenny Graham, beckoning them to come with him.

A picture of the devil luring the couple into hell, McBain grimly thought.

BONES

A well-dressed man, his face oddly skewed by his ill-fitted wig and wispy mustache, came up to the front desk at the West End Avenue apartment building that morning. He was courteous enough as he held up a brown manila envelope, inquiring whether this was the residence of PJ Bones in apartment 1415.

Ron, the doorman, had to correct the man. "Yes, Mr. Bones lives here, but you must mean apartment 1711."

The man opened a small notebook, peered at a page, and nodded. "Ah, yes, that is right, here it is. 1711."

Ron took the package.

"Thank you, my friend," the man said. Then he exited the building.

Ron went to his station's phone and punched in the apartment number code. "A package, Mr. Bones."

"Thank you, Ron. I wasn't expecting anything. Can you tell me who it's from?"

The doorman checked out the envelope and saw no return address. "Well, I can't say, but this gentleman said it was for you. He seemed confused though about your apartment number. I straightened that out for him."

Bones stiffened. Ron was generally more careful. He should have known better. He had no doubt: Poe had tracked him down—and Clara.

Five minutes later came a knock on the door. Mel, a building staffer, held out the envelope for Bones, and then wished him a fine day as he turned to leave.

"Thanks, Mel," Bones said edgily, knowing that this day was going to be anything but fine.

Bones gingerly held the package as if it contained a bomb primed to explode. He pulled a letter opener from his desk and sliced it open. He saw the slender manuscript, wishing it away.

Bones glanced at the first page. Poe writes in the first-person. It is an intimate account, compelling him to bear witness to his insanity. It begins with the funeral of the young actress, Margot Turner, then Poe's stalking of Tre Simon near his Village brownstone. Later, he writes about seeing him at a bar, where he spikes Tre's drink and brings him back to his Harlem apartment. And so begins a grisly night that feeds Poe's maniacal addiction. Bones closed his eyes, failing to keep a repressed memory from flooding back. The chair where Tre Simon had been mutilated. The bloodstains spreading like fingers across the floor.

"I could see the fear leaking from his eyes and smell the stink coming from his pores,'" Poe writes in the manuscript. "Animal stink. The terror sinking in, the reality of his impending death..."

Bones tossed the pages to the floor. He could no longer bear to touch this obscenity when his phone started buzzing. McBain was on the other side. He didn't bother with a greeting.

"PJ, we got a delivery at the precinct," McBain said bluntly. "A finger. It once belonged to Jenny Graham."

MCBAIN AND BONES

The streets around One Police Plaza were clogged with television vans and reporters as Bones hurried by. He recognized a few of the on-air news personalities. Two street guys were acting out as asses behind reporters going live on-air with the grim news about Travis and Jenny Graham.

The previous day, McBain had given him an entry pass to police headquarters. "This crazy is 'Bad Guy Number One' on our most wanted list, so you're unofficially deputized, cowboy," he said, adding a caution. "And, Bones, avoid the guys on the second floor. They are unleashed now."

Bones understood. The press room—it was called 'the Shack'—was a beehive of activity that morning. The story of a savage serial killer was out in the open and already teeming with sensational media chatter. The coverage was only outdone by Travis and Jenny Graham's army of Instagram followers in a state of collective frenzy in streams of online posts.

Bones entered headquarters and took the elevator to the eighth-floor Real Time Crime Center. It seemed a strange name to call the large computer network used for major investigations. He caught sight of McBain through the window of the detective's small office. McBain was on his phone, snapping orders, and in no mood for small talk as Bones came through the door.

"This is a full-court press," McBain told Bones, slamming down the phone. "We haven't found any bodies yet, but we're treating the Grahams' disappearance as a double homicide investigation."

Bones speculated that Jenny's amputated finger made that an easy call. A large photo of the digit took up the center of McBain's desk. Two bloodied rings were still attached to the finger.

"More of the Butcher's sick handiwork," McBain said angrily.

The detective sat down heavily in his desk chair. "We're still picking up pieces of Tre Simon," he said gruffly.

"Yeah, no mystery there," said Bones. "Poe is on a rampage. This blood kinship he feels with the dead author. Playing out his own horror stories...I pity the Grahams."

Bones glanced at McBain, taking note of his friend's pronounced facial twitch, a consequence of his years on the job tracking down these psychopaths. The Butcher case had not made his life any easier.

"The mayor and his benefactor, Benedict Graham, have declared war, and every precinct chief is on notice," McBain said. "Either this maniac is found, and soon, or heads will roll."

Bones had seen Graham, a hard-boiled guy, on television a few days earlier being interviewed by reporters after his son and daughter-in-law had gone missing. Graham said that he would pay whatever ransom demands were made by the kidnapper, and pleaded for the couple's safe return. Bones assumed that Graham had a far different attitude after the Butcher's package with Jenny's finger.

"Graham is out for blood, and I can't blame him," McBain said. "The word is that he told Commissioner Davis that he and his men would like to assist police in 'interrogating' the man once he was found and arrested. Davis, though, is a straight arrow. Can't see him greenlighting vigilantism even with Graham's clout."

Bones shrugged. It wouldn't be such a bad idea giving Benedict Graham and his boys some bonding time with Poe.

It was then that the police commissioner walked past McBain's office into the adjoining anteroom. Some thirty detectives were already crowded around waiting for the scheduled meeting. McBain led Bones to the back of the room, avoiding the side glances thrown in their direction. The day was complicated enough without bringing back old histories.

Kenneth Davis was already red-faced, his infamous hair-trigger temper primed and set to let loose. No one in the room had any intention of giving him lip.

"We got a break. We know who this guy is from his prints found at his Harlem apartment. His name is Daemon Ultrecht. Thirty-two-years-old. Troubled history. Rap sheet, mostly petty crime when he was a teenager. Minor theft, but also some weird shit. Killed a neighbor's pet dog when he was nine. Both parents and a cousin died in a gas leak accident at their home on Long Island. It seemed that little Daemon was out and about when the accident occurred. Reports called the deaths suspicious, but there was no evidence to point to the kid. He was taken to a children's shelter outside the city, ten years old at the time, and became a state ward. At thirteen, sentenced to two months in juvie after attacking another juvenile at the facility. Slashed him badly with a cutter. Psychiatric eval not exactly a glowing report card—hearing voices, speaking to unseen presences, dark fantasies—what you'd expect from an aspiring psychopath. Not that we can lock up people for what they imagine. A clean record since. Not even a traffic ticket. The guy even got his degree in nursing from some online college. Then he was hired at Bellevue. The hospital had no problems. Doctors and staff liked the guy. His annual report described him as 'kind' and 'empathetic' with patients."

"Didn't they say that about Bundy?" Don Schecter, a newly minted detective, murmured.

One of Davis' assistants passed along a blurry photograph of a sixteen-year-old Ultrecht. The picture showed a placid-face teenager staring dully into the camera. A large nose ring looped around his nostrils. His head shaven. His right arm was covered with tattoos, with images of distorted faces and scripted letters that were barely legible in the photo. Clearly vivid though was a tattoo of a large bird with deep-black plumage that formed around Ultrecht's left shoulder and covered the top of his arm.

"Jesus! Do you know what this is?" Bones said to McBain, pointing to the photo.

McBain took a closer look. "What, a crow?"

Bones shook his head. "It's a raven, Mac."

On the street outside headquarters, Bones and McBain pushed past the crush of media types, restlessly waiting for Davis' press conference. The two men got into Bones' car for the drive uptown

"Mac, the guy thinks he's this creature, this raven."

"Great, PJ. I'm glad we nailed down his psychological profile. I was worried about finding just the right name to call this maniac. Actually, I settled on maniac."

"No, you don't understand. He sees himself differently."

"Yeah, I know. Sometimes we refer to those people as insane."

"Mac. He's convinced he holds extraordinary power. I remember the poem from college. The raven is a mythical creature, a talking bird that can decide life and death."

McBain snorted. "I must invite this guy to my next Christmas party. A fun guy, though I will definitely ask him to leave home any sharp objects."

"Well, at least we know the person we are dealing with."

"And who is that, PJ? We have a name. A man with a tattoo of a raven on his arm. He kills people indiscriminately and viciously. Other than that, we have no idea who the hell he is or, for that matter, what he is. Perhaps he is closer to being a raven than an actual human being. Aren't they flesh-eating animals?"

Bones nodded. "Yes, ravens are carrion birds. They eat dead and rotting flesh."

"Even human flesh?"

"Yes, even human flesh."

"Yeah, well, then that is our man"

POE

Chapter 14
'A Name to Remember'

I wasn't all that surprised by the hullabaloo in the media about
"the serial killer on the loose." Quite a scary guy. I see that the
police had yet to disclose all the grisly details—a shame—but
there's no stopping the newspaper headlines or wild online
prattle that was not far from the truth. Well, we all love a good
murder mystery, especially one involving a psychopath that
pops up like some boogeyman at Halloween. And I do fit in.

The all-points bulletin has made me into something of
a celebrated killer and how entertaining seeing the chaos
surrounding my notoriety, the NYPD running around, all
panicky, getting bombarded with calls from those "good
citizens." Apparently, I am hiding around every street corner
of the city ready to pounce upon some poor victim. Really a
poor picture since I carefully select my chosen ones.

Not to be overly critical, but I am surprised at the lack
of professionalism in the case. Perhaps it is my narcissism
talking, but the police sketches of some thirtyish man sporting
wavy dark hair and a mustache were elementary school work.
I imagine the description could fit any one of the thousands
of men in the city. Such ignominy can be infuriating, but I try
not to be over-sensitive.

Still, I found my public persona way too shallow, failing
to reveal to the world the true me. I think back to those kids
at the children's home. They, too, did not understand me. I
was someone not worth the time of day. Invisible and
nameless. Except for the times when I was easy prey for their

abuse and ridicule. Would they have mocked me if they knew then what they know now? No, they would be very afraid.

Now I have a name they will all remember.

BONES

Bones was at his desk trying to break out of his writer's block. His story had gotten too complicated. Sam Rock was lost in his investigation; the trail to the killer had grown cold.

He leaned over his desk, his forehead resting on the computer keyboard. The day's work hadn't amounted to much of anything. He didn't believe a word of his hackneyed tripe. A world in which the moral order is made right again. One in which the hero rises triumphantly. His readers were invested in Sam Rock. He was their hope ensuring they could sleep safely ensconced in their beds. How could he fail to satisfy such delusions?

That is why Clara came to him. Believing in him—that he would find the man who mutilated her. The monster who came to her door, then stayed inside her mind. He could put an end to this evil, and, finally, rescue her from his grip.

It made no sense to Bones—only that it did to Clara.

Clara's cell phone rang, the chimes breaking the silence in the apartment. Bones heard the sound coming from the bedroom, then Clara picking up the call. At once, he was on edge. Bones brooded over who might be on the other side of the phone. Clara knew no one in the city. She also had long cut off contact with her mother in Willow Brook and anyone else there.

Bones got up from his desk to check in on her, but by then Clara had hung up the phone and was in the bathroom.

Bones came up to the open bathroom door. Clara was putting on some lipstick and makeup. "Hey, you must have a date." He hoped the joke landed but heard the edge in his voice.

"Oh, yeah, a date," she said sardonically. "With Heidi, you know, the one at my session."

Bones recalled Clara's weekly meeting downtown for assault victims, but had no recollection of Heidi. "Don't recall you mentioning her," he said.

"Oh, yes you do, PJ. She has had a tough time after the rape and all. We women need to stick together, yes?"

"Yes, of course. So, where are you headed?"

"I thought we'd catch up at the Saloon. Won't be more than a few hours."

"C'mon, I'll give you a lift," Bones said. "I need a break anyway. The book is going nowhere."

"PJ, I'm a big girl," Clara chided. "I can get there and back. Besides, you've got work to do with your killer."

Clara turned to Bones, softening. "Then what about dinner at Pasquale? And after we come back...You look like a man who needs to get laid."

Bones chuckled. A glimpse of the Clara he first met. "You always were a keen observer of humanity."

"Nah. I just know a horny man when I see him."

Then Clara went over to give Bones a long, lustful kiss.

Bones, surprised, puffed out a breath. "Jeez. Maybe you can give this Heidi a call and tell her you suddenly came down with, uh, smallpox. It's making a comeback, you know."

This time Clara laughed, slapping Bones on the chest. "Forget Pasquale. Just be hungry when I get back, that's all."

Bones grinned. It had been a while since he saw this woman. Was it possible she was on her way back to him? Lord, say it is so, he thought.

Clara smiled, letting go of Bones and picking up her coat and purse. She turned at the front door, gave a short wave, and smiled again, though not quite as brightly as before. Then she left the apartment.

CLARA

The late afternoon was clouding up with a storm brewing as Clara left Bones' apartment building and walked the one block west to Riverside Park. She hadn't been out into the park more than a few times since moving in with him, but she still found the long strip that followed the city along the Hudson River a tranquil getaway. The usual inhabitants were tending to the gardens, along with the dog walkers, cyclists, and everyone else. No one seemed in any hurry, despite the change in weather. Clara found an empty bench that faced the river and waited for him to appear.

He came up quietly a few minutes later, leaning next to her as if he had been there all this time. "Waiting long?" he asked affably.

"I have been waiting a long time," Clara said. "Years, in fact."

"Well, I'm glad that we are finally able to meet and talk. You also have been in my thoughts. You know, ever since our last association."

"Yes. I remember very well. I don't think that is something I will ever forget."

"You know, it was an act of love, and I needed to have you."

"And what now?"

"You have that power—to make men want you—and I still think of you."

Clara smiled tightly. "And I you," she said. "You are in every minute of my day and night."

"So, we are both obsessed," he said.

"Actually, you are something more," Clara replied. "You haunt me."

"I understand. I am everywhere for you," he said, nodding. "I, too, have the power."

"Yes, but you know that we cannot survive this way."

"That is true. You and I must resolve this...madness."

"Whatever the word. Only that it can't go on."

And with that, he reached over to touch Clara's cheek.

Clara fixed her gaze on him, taking his hand, and pressing it to her lips.

BONES

Clara was gone late into the evening and each passing hour only fed Bones sense of dread. He bent down to a bottom desk drawer and pulled out a bottle. He was back to his whiskey. He had given up that fight. The drink still did nothing to stop his current anxiety nor the past from hurtling into his consciousness. His alcoholic father. The abuse he had showered upon his mother. The bruises that blotted her arm that she tried to hide underneath her dress sleeve. PJ had seen them anyway, running into his bedroom, bursting into tears, hating his father, loving his mother, torn into halves.

And then, years later, the phone call from the woman his father had left his mother for. She told him what had happened. His dad had been in the South Tower after the plane had struck. He'd been trapped with all the others, finally deciding it was better to jump from the seventy-fifth floor than to die in the inferno. The woman sounded like a kind and sympathetic person, but Bones wasn't sure if her feeling had to do with his father's death, or because she perfectly understood what he and his mother had to endure over the years at his hands.

Not that Liam Bones would ever leave him in peace.

Bones knocked back another drink and closed his eyes, the alcohol fogging his mind. He was back with his father again at the tall building, standing next to a window ledge— the two of them trapped in the flames and smoke, looking down at the world from high above the hard streets. They were always there together in the quietness, free from the chaos surrounding them—father and son silently peering out the broken window, gazing into the open space high above the city. Both of them understanding what Liam Bones needed to do—for the first time in his life taking control of his own life. And so he stepped forward past the window ledge and into the air. Bones could only watch as his father plunged into space, wondering what he must be thinking in those few flashing seconds of flight from the seventy-fifth floor with the earth coming up to crush him. Was Liam thinking of his son, having any regret for not loving him more? Might he possibly have wished for a second chance, to finally be a father to his boy?

Bones took another drink, realizing that he was now at the same age Liam Bones was that September morning. He was grateful that the drink was hitting him hard.

Bones was asleep at his desk when he was roused by sounds coming from outside the apartment. Someone jiggling keys into the door lock. Clara walked into the apartment, soaked from the storm.

Bones rubbed his eyes, struggling to shake off the whiskey.

"My god, Clara!"

Bones swayed off his chair and staggered over to her.

Clara just smiled.

She looked radiant—her apple-red cheeks wet and shining; a glow in her green eyes. For that moment, she reminded Bones of the Irish lovely who had first taken his heart.

Then spontaneously she bounded into his arms, her hands locked around the back of his neck, drawing him toward her lips. She was hungry for him, ravenous. Then she stripped off her wet clothes, tossing them into a pile, rifling at Bones' shirt and pants until he, too, was naked. She pulled

Bones down to the living room rug and told him she was about to have her way with him.

CLARA

Clara searched Riverside Park a week later thinking she might find Poe again—that *he* would find *her* again. His calls had stopped, and she didn't like that. Of course, Clara wasn't about to tell Bones about their previous rendezvous in the park. She no longer needed PJ to find Poe. Poe had found her. They had found each other.

Their secret encounter was nothing like that afternoon at Washington Square Park when he was just standing there, statue-like, radiating across the park. She could not believe her eyes—he was as menacing as he was in her nightmares. His gleaming bald head and black eyes. His beast's body pierced with horrifying tattooed faces. Clara chasing after him. Frenzied. The faces of park-goers, the peace of their afternoon upended, recoiling from this madwoman frantically racing past them. They had no clue about the maniac in their midst. She was the one seen as dangerous—a raving lunatic crying out.

Afterward the calls began. Clara was startled, but then he was on the phone, his voice shadowed by a slight echo as if he might be speaking from a cave. She stared at the spam contact on her phone. He was now in her ear. Calm, a lover reassuring his mate. He said that he loved her, the same words he uttered that afternoon before cutting her neck.

She ranted when he first called. He was a scumbag that would burn in hell. She was the one out to kill *him*. His laugh was the last thing she heard before she punched out the phone. His calls then came more regularly. Clara grew more obsessed, *needing* him to call. And she listened carefully when he spoke about their future.

He recounted how enraged he'd been finding her alive after the knife attack, but that he no longer wanted her dead—they were entwined forever.

"We are one and the same," he said. "Ordinary life in its shades of gray is nothing more than a soulless existence. You need me to escape that world, don't you? I am your life-giver."

"That's not what I remember when you cut my throat," Clara told him.

"Fate works in mysterious ways." Poe chuckled. "You survived only to discover your life—with me. One of life's inexplicable ironies, yes?"

Clara hesitated, a stillness coming over her.

"I suppose you are right, Poe," she said flatly. "We *are* one and the same."

Clara had agreed to meet up with him that late afternoon after he last called—there, at Riverside Park, sharing a bench with him, overlooking the Hudson. Perhaps passersby thought they were two lovers, maybe envious of this beautiful woman and her rather intriguing beau. There would see an aggressiveness about her, almost a courtly manner about him. They looked so coupled, a hair's breadth from each other, and most likely sharing the most secret of intimacies. And those onlookers would be right.

Afterward, Clara came back to the apartment in a rainstorm. Bones looked ragged as he came to the door reeking of his whiskey. No doubt he had a rough night wondering where she had been, certain she wasn't at a support meeting with someone called Heidi.

Clara felt his desperation, sweeping into his arms and then taking him into the bedroom. Bones could never resist her. She understood most plainly her dominance, wildly tearing at his body, unleashed in her sexual frenzy, and thinking of Poe.

Clara was not about to confide in PJ. She remembered his pitiful response when she told him of the encounter with her "killer" in Washington Square Park. Bones had been fearful—of her—not believing a word she had said. He placated her like a child. Maybe even considered bringing in doctors with their own suspicious eyes and cryptic language to help them make sense of her. As if any words could describe the fury compressed inside every fiber of her being.

Clara was on her own, though she might still need him. In fact, she was sure that Bones was necessary if she were to move ahead with her plan. But she'd need to move cautiously. So, that night—locking him out of their bedroom, then pretending that she was asleep when he came back from seeing McBain. He'd spotted her phone light beaming at her bedside—just as she'd left it, beckoning him, and knowing he could not resist seeing the call. From some unidentified caller.

Clara was pleased with her performance—she had always been a fine actress—and heard Bones' troubled voice by her bedside. But he had no idea. He could never see the truth. That she was very much in control.

BONES

The cell phone chime rescued Bones who was staring at a blank computer screen and glad for the excuse to break away from his writer's block. He had expected the call from Clara, who said she was going for a jog in Central Park. Something about getting her mind and body back in shape. He was still gripped by everything about her, her scent, her sexual voraciousness. Even her madness. Everything about her overpowered him.

Bones checked his phone. The number was not from Clara but some random caller.

He tapped into the call.

"Yeah," Bones said.

"Hello, PJ," the caller said. "You must remember me."

Poe.

Bones squeezed the phone. "Yes. I do. You're the sick bastard we're looking for."

"Now, now, PJ," Poe said. "This is no way to treat a colleague. By the way, what did you think of my manuscript? Your doorman was kind enough to accept it and told me he'd get it to you. Apartment 1711, yes? I thought it was a stronger story. Tre was so...vivid—more than the previous one about poor Sweeny, the school teacher. You know, the woman you found in her coffin when you searched my Harlem flat. I imagine she was in quite a state by that time. Also, I have been diligently working on my latest chapters. Quite sad actually with Jenny, though Travis was a pleasure to kill."

Bones seethed. "We are going to find you and you can look forward to spending the rest of your worthless life rotting in your own caged box."

"Aw, PJ, no need to get yourself in a tizzy. I mean, we are almost friends, having shared the same woman. That, of course, is Miss Clara Knox. Just an extraordinary woman."

Bones was momentarily stunned hearing Clara's name. "Poe, you're nothing more than a murderous freak," he snapped. "Of course, you must know that by now."

Bones thought the call went dead.

Then Poe was back.

"Well, I just decided to catch up now that we are both famous," he said. "We should chat, PJ. You know, person to person—just two writers sharing some war stories."

"Good idea. So, how about downtown, say at One Police Plaza," Bones said. "I'll have some of the guys there even throw you a little party. You know, cake, ice cream and handcuffs."

"Ah, PJ. Just hate parties, at least the ones that I don't host. I have this little out-of-the-way place. I'll get you out there. And, PJ, let's just make this our thing. I hate party-crashers. It would be a shame to ruin the evening."

"Sure, Poe. You and me then," Bones said.

"Oh, also, regards to Clara. We had a nice intimate chat the last time we saw each other."

"Yeah, you have a way with women, cutting their throats. You're a big man. Having trouble getting it up, are you?"

"PJ, you can do better than such adolescent insults. And, oh, that was old history with Clara at her apartment. So long ago. I'm talking about recently. You know, Clara and I, in Riverside Park, last Monday. It was her idea, and I was flattered by her company."

Bones stared into the phone. What was that?

"Oops, cat out of the bag," Poe said coldly. "So sorry, but I thought she would have told you about us. I must say that she was even more magnificent than I remembered."

Poe snickered. "Will be in touch, PJ. Do come over to my place." And then he hung up.

Bones held the cell phone in front of him as if it were a strange object. What was this? Clara meeting up with Poe at the park? The man who tried to kill her, had traumatized her—together? Impossible. Poe was psychotic, goading him. Yet...the previous Monday...that night, so intensely vivid. Clara had come home late that evening, drenched from a downpour but radiant and wild. Her sexual fury had overwhelmed him.

Clara and Poe? How could he make any sense of this *insanity?*

Bones sat at his desk, dazed, when the cell phone buzzed with a brief text message from an unknown caller—a set of numbers, a GPS location.

Bones closed his eyes, letting the stillness wash over him. Then he went to his desk drawer, pulled out his old Glock, a clip, and a carton of bullets. He loaded the magazine slowly and snapped it into the semi-automatic pistol. Then he called McBain.

"Hey, PJ, you are out of your fucking mind! No way you're going to meet up with this crazy."

"He seemed like the friendly type on the phone," Bones said acidly. "Besides, I am not passing up his invitation."

"Listen, I got the cavalry here. Give me his location, then I'll get the guns. Let's do this the right way."

"Mac, you know he will have eyes on me from the moment I'm in sight. This is the chance to bring him down.

Hey, I was undercover with the department. Did well enough. You might remember."

"Yeah, I do. You were young and strong and good at what you did. Now you're old and slow and you are going to get yourself killed. Besides, you haven't shot a gun in twenty years. Seriously, PJ, this is a fool's move. Getting yourself messed up is only going to wreck my day. If you're going, I'm coming."

"Mac, we can't have your boys barging in. I know this man. He is sick but deadly smart. I need to find him. Besides, this has become…personal."

"Why, because of Clara?" McBain said. "She's old news to him. He's graduated to slicing and dicing."

"Afraid not," Bones replied, hesitating. "He's back in the picture with her."

"What the *hell* are you talking about now?" McBain asked sharply.

"It means that something is happening that is so fucking strange that I can't wrap my mind around it. So, I'm going after him."

McBain was having enough of Bones. "Hey, let's cut the crap. You called because you need backup. Well, I'm your backup, like old times. And if our guy has an objection, I am sure we will respectfully work it out. That is, after we administer some justice and crush his testicles."

Bones nodded into the phone and grunted. "Yeah, Mac, I *am* going to need you."

"Hey, maybe we'll even get lucky, and he'll give us a reason to kill him," McBain said.

"Do we need another reason?" Bones asked.

"Yeah, I think we have enough of them."

MCBAIN AND BONES

The GPS was having problems computing Poe's coordinates. Bones and McBain found themselves directionless in these low-lying wetlands on the remote edge of eastern Long Island. They doubted whether anyone could possibly have inhabited this part of the island. The land had been routed by floods, deserted, and taken over by biting flies, snakes and vultures.

Getting off the expressway, Bones weaved along hard dirt paths pockmarked with divots and stones that rattled the insides of their car. He followed a backroad that took them deeper into the island before coming to a hundred-year-old cemetery, the only visible marker of previous human existence.

"Where the hell are we?" McBain called out.

The GPS was useless as Bones continued to slowly navigate the beaten road that hugged a large swamp bordered by a thick forest, a part of the island long forgotten.

Suddenly, McBain shouted.

"PJ! Straight ahead!"

McBain pointed to a dilapidated cabin, barely visible, about fifty yards in front of them.

Bones braked the car, pulling off the road behind a large boulder. He squinted, unsure what he was looking at.

"Could that be Poe's place?" Bones asked. "It looks abandoned. Not any different than the cemetery we passed. No one could live in that place."

"Well, seems just perfect for our guy," McBain said. "Let's wait here for backup from the city. I'm calling it in."

"Mac, if he sees our guys, he will run," Bones said tersely. "Time to nail this fucker."

"This is stupid-stupid, PJ. You don't know what he's up to. Actually, we do know, only that it is nothing good."

"Well, I suppose we're about to find out."

"Brother, this is a mistake. No time to play cowboy."

"I'm not giving this bastard another minute to breathe fresh air."

McBain frowned. His partner was reckless, acting out like some impulsive rookie. Storming the place was dangerous, but Bones was giving him no choice. He checked out his Glock, grunting his readiness.

Bones nodded, then pulled the car deeper off the road and out of sight from anyone in the house watching and waiting for visitors.

"We get out here and make our way through the trees," McBain ordered. "Guns out, safety off. And listen, PJ, when we see this guy and he even looks cross-eyed at us, we shoot first and give him his Miranda Rights later."

Bones was not looking to argue.

McBain and Bones crossed over into the woods where their world suddenly turned dark under the canopy of tall trees. It was not going to be an easy trek through the forested wetland. The two men were forced to holster their guns to fight through the thicket that blocked their path. They were already perspiring heavily but finally in sight of the cabin that stood in the middle of a large dirt field. The place was badly battered, scarred by the elements, with square black holes marking where a door and windows once existed. It was nothing more than a broken-down shack, seemingly weary of its own existence. Not a person was in sight.

"Looks like we struck out here, Mac," Bones said glumly.

McBain was about to agree—but then he saw him.

"There!" McBain shouted.

A bald, tattooed man had bolted from the cabin's back door and was running through the dirt yard, past some trees, and into the swamplands.

Poe.

"We split up, PJ!" McBain said. He pulled out his gun and pointed to the woods that ran parallel to the swamp. "I'm straight ahead. You outflank him through the trees."

"Hey, Mac, careful," Bones replied. "I saw something in his hand."

"Yeah, I saw it too, but he is a very dead man if he turns on me. Now go!"

Bones took off through the woods.

McBain plodded through the tall, wet grass and sodden terrain, slapping at a swarm of insects that were starting to feast on his sweaty face. Then he caught sight of Poe on the opposite side of the swamp. He was standing on the edge of a powdery flat of land that reached across the swamp. . . *a sandbar*. Where did *that* come from?

For an instant, McBain was mystified seeing this long stretch of sand wedged into the swamp waters. But his attention quickly turned—Poe was now watching *him*. And then he was gone, dashing into the surrounding woods.

It was only a moment later when McBain heard a painful groan and then a sharp cry.

Bones shouting out from the woodlands.

McBain stepped onto the sandbar and raced across the dense surface toward the desperate sounds. He abruptly stopped. Poe had now reappeared on the swamp bank. Directly in front of him was Bones, on his knees, hunched over and dazed.

McBain pulled out his Glock.

"Poe, it's over," he stated.

"Now, detective, it's rude of you to crash into my consultation with Mr. Bones, though I must say I had the feeling you might make an appearance."

McBain cautiously made his way on the sandbar, his gun out front, his eyes fixed on the bare-chested Poe fifteen yards away. Tattoos covered his torso and arms; bizarre wild images of faces and inscriptions, a horror collage that joined with the man's feral face and glistening skull.

McBain eyed Poe's taser pointed at Bones. He could see that Poe had already fired the weapon. Bones was still shuddering from an electrical dart. McBain was tempted to take a headshot to put an end to the psycho, but Poe had propped Bones in front of him. He was shielded, so the shot was risky. Poe then raised the taser to Bones' throat. A second tase would be lethal.

"Listen, we can make this easy or hard," McBain snapped. "Drop the weapon. Step away from Bones. On your knees with hands on the back of your neck. Easy enough."

McBain took a few steps closer, his feet now trudging through the heavy sand until he was forced to stop. He found himself sinking into the muck and unable to move.

The detective stared down at his feet buried under the thick mire. "What the hell?" he called out.

"Actually, quicksand is not indigenous to the area," Poe said, smiling. "It requires the right composition of sand and water. It took me quite a while to construct—certainly more challenging than the animal traps I built as a kid. But, hey, look at you, here in the middle of a swamp. It worked out, don't you think?"

Poe raucously laughed.

McBain frantically tried to free his feet, but the effort only pulled him deeper into the sinking hole. The quicksand was now up to his ankles, then, within seconds, rising past his calves. He felt himself only slipping further down with each move he tried to make.

"Jesus Christ!" McBain grimaced.

"Now, Detective McBain," Poe said. "It's best not to thrash about. You'll only sink more quickly, though you would only be delaying the inevitable."

Bones had barely recovered, sensing Poe behind him. Then he saw Mac. He had no time to think. In one motion, he swiveled on his knees and hurled himself upward into Poe, knocking him to the ground. Both men were momentarily dazed.

Poe seethed as he got to his feet. "Now, Bones, little good that is going to do you or your friend."

Then Poe lifted his taser for the second time that afternoon and shot two dart-like electrodes into Bones' stomach. The fifty-thousand volts of electricity kicked Bones into convulsions, the electrical pitchfork repeatedly stabbing his body.

Suddenly, a gunshot rang out and Poe went down.

McBain finally had Poe in his sights, winging him in his shoulder.

Poe screamed.

McBain took aim again and fired, missing Poe. The detective could not find a foothold to steady his weapon. Every motion sank him deeper into the quicksand. He was now trapped up to his waist.

Poe writhed in agony next to a semi-conscious Bones. The bullet had pierced through his shoulder. Blood poured from his tattooed raven. Furious, Poe got to his feet, reloaded his taser, and this time targeted McBain. He fired, the long electrical wire snaking through the air and snapping into McBain's neck. The detective's body went into spasms as if he were a grotesque, uncontrolled puppet tethered to a string.

The convulsions finally stopped with McBain gasping for breath.

"You motherfucker," McBain said wearily. His gun was gone, lost under the wet sand.

Poe grasped his bleeding shoulder, his face twisted in rage.

"Die, McBain!" he hissed. "And know that your death will come slowly. Oh, you will be pulled deeper into your grave yet not sucked under. Your death will be worse. Much worse. Soon enough, you will be entombed up to your neck. You will not be able to move a muscle. Certainly, you must be feeling trapped by now. I can already see the anxiety beading up on your face. Understandable, detective."

Poe chortled gleefully.

"All that intense pressure enveloping you. You do feel it, don't you? Crushing your muscles and nerves, wreaking havoc on your body. The small creatures here will certainly enjoy snacking on your face—that is before the vultures come, first chewing out your eyes. A delicacy for them. By then, you might be fortunate to be dead meat, carrion, for them. Better that than being eaten alive by those black scavengers. I would not wish that fate on my worst enemy."

And Poe roared again with cold laughter.

McBain stared silently at Poe. He could hardly breathe; the heavy sands were rising past his chest, squeezing his lungs. Now heart palpitations were kicking in, and he could feel blood spiking into his brain. His body calling out to stay alive. But there was no use fighting back.

The detective sighed, settling into the quicksand and the dark destiny that awaited him, suddenly feeling an overwhelming weight of sorrow. How he missed his wife, Sarah. And there was Becky. He loved his daughter but had failed her. He saw her desperation, running up to him each time he came home from the job, her eyes pleading for his love, only that he could never escape the madness of the streets, becoming a stranger to his own family. Sarah. Becky. They deserved so much better from him.

He closed his eyes, the thick sands at his neck, making peace with his fate. McBain wasn't religious, but he mouthed a few words, asking for forgiveness from any god who would listen.

BONES

Bones lay crumbled on the muddy bank where Poe had left him. He was on the edge of consciousness yet still aware of the vibrations around him. Flies tested his body, swarming then backing off as he mustered just enough energy to feebly swat them away. They were not easily dissuaded, making a second then third run at him, attacking his face and neck. Bones jerked wildly from their feeding frenzy, suddenly feeling his flesh erupting into blood-filled welts. He was no better than a living cadaver to be probed and preyed upon. The only other sensory awakening came from the intense pains that ramped through his body. The result of Poe's taser.

In the blurred recesses of his mind, Bones knew he had to move from this place or die with the swamp creatures circling. He began to crawl along the fetid terrain until he came to the sandbar. There he saw McBain, or that part of him that was still visible. McBain's head rose above the sand, the grotesque remains of the person that had been a brother to him. Another victim of Poe's. Cruelty that was unbearable.

McBain's dead eyes were wide open, staring blindly into the sky past his earthly existence. His face seemed obscenely contorted, perhaps a dying last effort to yank himself free from the crushing sand. Vultures now danced around his head, viciously pecking at his face. His eyes were missing. One predator had ripped off an ear and was devouring the fleshy piece.

"You came so close, Mac, leaving all this insanity behind," Bones murmured. "You deserved Mexico, not this. Not this."

Bones wept. He could not remember the last time he cried. The misery of his shitty life becoming clear in the swamp. A fitting place to bring back his father, who abandoned him when he was a child before leaving him for good in his death flight off the tall tower. Then the NYPD that stabbed him in the back to protect its own sordid reputation. The bad marriages, the booze, the despondency. He was nothing more than an imposter, hiding inside his novels, taking on the pretense of a tough guy. What a load of delusional crap that was. And Clara. The pain and passion he felt for her. Clara was the reason he had come to this hideous place—to destroy Poe, the man who so badly damaged her. But she was not to blame for this horror. This was his own undoing, his own madness. Mac had seen his obsession with Poe and tried to warn him. Now Mac was dead. And he was the one alive. How could this be fair?

Bones steadied himself and then stepped onto the sandbar. Some impulse drove him to Mac, to tell him he was sorry. More madness. He started to crawl on his stomach along the dense sand when he felt the surface starting to give. Soon he would be sinking into the mire. He rested on the spot, weighing whether to embrace McBain's fate. Maybe this was the time to let it all go, to settle into the ooze and call it a day. Maybe Mac was the lucky one.

Bones turned over on his back, the quicksand starting to wall his body. Within seconds, the choice to live or die would not be his to make. Bones exhaled, shaking away the deep despair that had cut so deeply. Instead, an all-consuming rage permeated his senses. He was unwilling to die on Poe's terms. He could not let go of his own life when this monster still prowled the living. He could not let this evil prevail. Poe needed to be gone from the earth.

Bones tried to pivot back onto his knees but his feet were already mortared under the sand. Suddenly, he was breathing harder, anxiety rising, his body starting to edge into shock as he felt himself slipping deeper into the quicksand. Bones wiggled his feet inside the shoes. If he could free his feet, he stood a chance. With one push, he yanked both feet out of the shoes and to the surface. Bones took in a deep breath, then began to crawl on his stomach, inching his way off the sandbar and stumbling onto the muddy bank of the swamp.

The exertion set off spasms, his body still suffering from the taser's electrical darts. He waited a few minutes to ease the agony. Then he pulled out his cell phone and called One Police Plaza.

"Sergeant Johnson," the desk sergeant said tersely.

And then the connection went dead.

Bones called again but could hear his cell phone fighting to stay connected.

"This is Johnson. Who is this?"

"Officer down, Sergeant Johnson! Officer down!" Bones shouted into the phone. "Phil McBain. He's dead!"

"Who are you? Where are you?"

Bones again started to respond, then was cut off again.

He punched in the number a third time.

Johnson grabbed the call an instant later.

"Who the hell *are* you?" the sergeant said angrily. A 999 call— "police officer down"— wasn't anything to fuck around with.

"Peter James Bones. Target my GPS—and find us," Bones snapped. "Get to Detective Thomas Sullivan. He will know who I am and who I am with."

Then Bones explained what else will be necessary.

Extricating McBain would not be easy.

BONES

Bones made his way into Poe's cabin to wait for the NYPD. No doubt a long line of police vehicles were already speeding to the place. Then there would be the grisly task of retrieving Mac's body and the sweep of the house and grounds.

Bones felt a chill in the dank and decayed space. Poe's childhood home. A foul odor reeled his senses. Bones could not make out where the putrid smell was coming from, taking a handkerchief to his nose and mouth, an effort that did little to filter out the stink.

Sunlight trickled through the empty windows and reflected off dust motes that hung in the air and coated an old desk that stood in the middle of the room. An ancient computer and keyboard took up much of the entire desktop. Bones was tempted to start up the computer—more of Poe's psychotic ramblings would likely be found inside that machine—but thought better not to mess around and complicate things for forensics.

Bones scrutinized the rest of the room. A beat-up mattress had been shoved into a corner next to a rusted kitchen sink. A faucet drip beat like the second hand of a clock. He found the sound grating, more of Poe's pokes into his brain. It was then that Bones noticed a small wooden case holding about a dozen books. He went over to scour the titles and, not surprisingly, found the collected works of Edgar Allan Poe. And a dozen books by PJ Bones.

Bones might have known. Poe stalking him. There was that time at Columbia, then on the streets, and at his apartment building. Yet seeing his books in Poe's house seemed even more insidious. Poe trying to understand *him*. He could have easily killed him in the swamp but let him live. Why? Was this just another one of Poe's sadistic games? To keep him alive to see his world shatter? To see Mac dead in the swamp? And Clara Knox—was Poe somehow back in her life? Was she a part of Poe's? Bones' mind swirled.

It was then that he spotted two hardback chairs in the corner of the room. Chains and frayed rope hung from the armrests. Bones remembered Poe's Harlem apartment. That was where Tre Simon was killed. Tied to a chair. And cut to pieces. He knew in his gut that Travis and Jenny Graham were held captive here, tortured, and killed. Bones closed his eyes to shut out pictures that flashed through his mind, but the drip-drip of the sink's water faucet made that mental escape impossible.

Bones slowly breathed, drawing on an old meditation technique he learned on the job, and felt himself calming down. It was then he spotted something next to one of the chairs. At first, he thought it was an almond shape piece of shiny, red plastic. He picked it up, instinctively rubbing the thing between his fingers, wiping off the grit. He hesitated a moment, then yelled out, pitching the piece to the floor—a fingernail. Bones had no doubt that it once was attached to Jenny Graham's finger.

Bones lurched over to the sink, just holding back a surge of bile. He'd had a tougher stomach when he was a detective but was no longer that guy. He opened the faucet, took a handful of brackish water, and wiped his face. It did little to tamp down the punishing trauma of the afternoon.

Poe's cabin was nothing more than a house of horrors, a place of death. Bones needed to leave this place. He headed toward the door only to stumble over some loose red bricks scattered around a broken-down fireplace. Bones could not help but notice its odd construction—a tall, brick wall had been built sealing off the inner firebox. Bones did not know why but he decided to pick up a sledgehammer that had been haphazardly tossed to the floor. Then he started breaking down the standing wall. With each strike, another slab caved in, filling the room with mortar dust. A rancid stench from inside the firebox began to flood the room, thickening with each blow.

Slowly, the corpse of Travis Graham came into Bones view. The body was buckled over to its side, chained to an iron ring. A single bulging dead eye stared at Bones. A second eye had been slit open and hanging out of its socket. The terror written on Travis's decomposing face was unmistakable, but it was his ear-to-ear twisted grin that was most horrific.

Bones fell backward at the sight, struggling to catch his breath.

He finally steadied, looking back into the firebox at the corpse. Bones imagined Travis in his death throes, knowing that nothing in his life had prepared him for that moment. Travis' privileged past was meaningless. Not his youth or riches. Not Jenny. There was just this darkness in which he was imprisoned and where he would die alone. Only this.

Less than two hours later, a phalanx of police vehicles, lights flashing, came racing up to the cabin. Detective Thomas Sullivan bolted out of the lead car as it came to a stop. Bones did not bother to greet him.

"Over there," Bones said, pointing to the sandbar. "And in there." The cabin.

Both men silently made their way across Poe's dirt property through the woods until they came to the edge of the swamp and the sandbar. Bones held out a hand to stop Sullivan.

"There he is," Bones said quietly. About twenty yards out on the sand, McBain's head was barely visible. A half-dozen vultures bounded about his head, tearing at his face…what was left of it.

Sullivan squinted, not sure what he was looking at.

"What the hell is going on here, Bones?" he said angrily. "Where is Phil McBain?"

"That's Phil." Bones said, pointing out to the sandbar. "There's quicksand. Your men will need to be careful to retrieve his body."

"Jesus H. Christ."

The burly Irishman, his hand on his forehead, sagged at the sight of his partner.

"Daemon Ultrecht is still alive," Bones said flatly. "We recover Phil and then we go find him."

Sullivan furiously turned to Bones. He made no attempt to hide his contempt.

"So, Bones, why the hell are *you* alive?" Sullivan seethed. "Why didn't Ultrecht put you away, too?"

Bones had already struggled with the same question. Why *was* he alive? Poe could have easily finished him off.

"If you ask me," Sullivan went on, "the wrong man is dead."

Bones was in no mood. "Shut the fuck up, detective."

Sullivan leaned into Bones' face, fists clenched. "We're not through, asshole," he snarled.

"Listen, Sullivan. We've got a murdered cop. And the crime scene inside that cabin will mess with your mind. Don't you think you have enough on your hands without this bullshit?"

Sullivan snorted and took a step back. "Yeah, right. Why waste my time with a douchebag dirty cop? Never could figure out what McBain saw in you, anyway."

"Well, don't trouble yourself," Bones said. "Let's get to Mac. It's not going to be easy getting him out of there."

Sullivan nodded. "Then we need to finish this."

"Hey, enough crap," Bones snapped.

"Not you, douchebag." Sullivan grunted. "Ultrecht. We're going to kill the motherfucker."

PART FOUR

Chapter 15
'The Butcher'

Well, I deservedly made the big time. The police are apoplectic with all their name-calling. I am a "psychotic killer," "cop-killer," "homicidal maniac." Boring, boring. The media at least are trying harder. So, I have been anointed "The Butcher," still a bit disappointing, this lack of imagination. I mean, "The Butcher." Awfully generic and just not up to par with the type of media sensationalism that brought Americans the "Night Stalker," "Angel of Death," and the "Love Slave Killers." I could go on.

I did find watching the televised police press conference on my phone most entertaining. I guess there were some hard feelings after all the excitement at the cabin and then seeing poor McBain, eyeless and all. Some dick named Sullivan was especially angry. He might well have been foaming at the mouth, making all sorts of threatening noises, going on about a manhunt, assuring the world that the cop-killer would be found and duly punished. No doubt he wanted to put a bullet in my head. I thought he was making a fool of himself, sounding so helpless. I understood. It had been a rough day.

Then there was Benedict Graham coming out of police headquarters all flushed and spitting anger toward reporters surrounding him. I imagine he'd just heard about his dead son, maybe saw a few pictures of the corpse chained in the fireplace. And then Jenny, brought up from underground. Another vow of revenge—he would "stop at nothing" to find their killer. Benedict Graham didn't seem like the forgiving type, and I suspect he dreamt of what slow torture he could offer me.

I was half-expecting to see PJ Bones in the news reports, but not a whiff of the guy. I guess he was still upset seeing his good friend as he did. Just a head in the sand. I assumed I had done Bones a solid, letting him live. I was having second thoughts about that myself. I'd been tempted to toss him into the quicksand to join his friend but decided to let him live— for the time being at least. I could cut the breath out of him later after our squabble was over. I liked this competition for Clara. She told me that she'd believed Bones could help her find me. Really, there was no need. It's funny how life works out.

I was okay for now with a few thousand dollars in cash after I'd emptied my bank account. Then I retrieved my Buick from an abandoned lot where I had hid the car and skedaddled out of New York, heading west over the George Washington Bridge.

No doubt the entire NYPD would soon be on my tail. Rumor had it that the department was predisposed against cop-killers—not that they would appreciate my joke. The chase was on.

I went as far as Wilkes-Barre, PA, coming up to some dump a mile outside the city called the Old Wagon Wheel Motel. The shithole's attraction: a large broken wagon wheel that sat on a patch of dead grass underneath a neon-lit vacancy sign. My room was decorated with a faded picture of Indians on the warpath. The only things missing were a few scalps to round out the ambiance. I imagine the place was going for a Disney theme park feel.

I did catch the eye of the big-breasted motel manager, who was giving me the up and down. At first, I suspected she might have recognized me from my "wanted" poster, this despite my newly grown goatee and Ray-Ban shades. But that wasn't it. Nothing was subtle about her message. I got the impression she was imagining my cock inside of her mouth when she started licking her lips. All the excitement of the day had stirred me up, so I'd consider the offer later. I needed some release time, after all.

I unpacked a new burner and spent the next hour tracking my exploits on the phone. "The Butcher" had exploded all over social media. Lots of gossip though that I didn't appreciate. All the psychobabble about my "relationship" with mother and father and then their tragic demise. And loose talk about my "creepy" childhood at the cabin and early interest in cutting up small forest creatures. It was disheartening to find out that the cops had dug up my backyard and animal burial sites. Let the dead rest in peace, I say.

I was gratified with the more colorful coverage that compared my "case" to serial murder mysteries on Netflix. "The Butcher" was being spoken about with the same reverence as the "slasher," and the "ripper." Not that I was vying for such acclaim, but the public acknowledgment was certainly warranted.

Just then, someone knocked on the door, prompting me to pull out my taser. I went over to the window and peeked through the cheap curtain. The motel manager was standing outside with a sly grin on her face.

I put away the taser and opened the door. The woman had a bottle of cheap red wine in her hand and reeked of three packs a day. I got a closer look at her now. She had painted her wide face with heavy makeup and bright red lipstick giving her a clownish look.

"I thought I'd welcome you to the Old Wagon Wheel Motel," she said, with her tits bulging out of her low-cut shirt. "We like to make our guests feel right at home here."

I had a sudden yearning for Clara Knox, but she would have to wait.

I sighed, staring at this grotesque woman in front of me. She waved the wine bottle at me.

"Come on in," I finally said.

BONES

PJ Bones could see that Becky was relieved when all the official outpouring for her father finally ended. Quite a show. Hundreds of cops lined the route of the cortege that led to Woodlawn Cemetery in the Bronx. All were dressed in their blues and spit-polished shoes in honor of one of their own. Mac would have disdained the attention but surely love the bagpipes that reminded him of his ancestral home in Derry. Bones had managed to keep his composure for most of the day until the bagpipes did him in, and he silently shed tears for his lost friend.

Becky carried her dad's mien that morning, a cool detachment that McBain had perfected. She almost seemed a bystander to the day's ceremonial events.

An hour after all the dignitaries had left, Bones and Becky still stood next to the plot of freshly dug dirt adorned with flowers and a photograph of a young Phil McBain in uniform. Bones remembered the day Becky was born, coming around the same time McBain was awarded his gold shield. Mac with the cigars, red-faced with drink and joy for his newborn, Rebecca Rose.

Bones knew her story, living on the streets of Portland. He hadn't seen her in nearly three years. She looked older, more hardened, beaten down by her demons. And now an orphan at 20.

"He wanted to make it up to you, Becky," Bones said softly.

"Yeah, I guess that's not in the cards."

"He loved you very much."

"Please, Bones. The badge was his life. I was just an acquaintance. So was my mom."

Bones did not see the point to argue.

"But a damn fine cop he was!" he stated. Bones felt the need to have these words in the air. "You should be proud of your dad."

"Bones, I heard enough eulogies today. I loved my father…but, you know, I can't remember once when he held me without feeling his sadness. He would come home each night and never say a word about his day. I saw it all in his eyes. I wanted his love, but he was always somewhere else in his mind, out on the bad streets." Becky paused. "And then there was mom. Drunk bastard killed her. He might as well have killed my dad, too."

Bones would never forget that awful day. But there was Mac back at work just a day after Sarah's funeral. He never could bring himself to talk about the accident.

"Becky, how are you doing out in Portland?" Bones asked.

"All right, I guess. I'm in rehab again. Not easy dealing with that monkey, but I'll get by."

"I'm sorry about that," Bones said gently.

Mac had told him about Becky's addiction. She was deep into the smack. He first tried to help her, but she didn't want anything to do with him.

Becky tightly smiled. "You were dad's best friend, Bones. His brother. He loved you."

Bones felt tears welling up. "Becky, if I can help…"

"Bones, I'm flying back to Portland, tonight. I probably won't be seeing you again, but you can do something for me….When you find this horrible man, make him suffer for what he did to my daddy."

Bones blinked hard and nodded.

TOMBS

Tory Tombs, forty-five years old, loud, divorced, and a deadbeat dad, was convinced he had a good one for his Thursday night internet radio show coming from his house trailer outside of Yonkers.

"Well, folks, it's Tory Tombs welcoming you live to 'Tombs' Talk.' And who doesn't like to talk about serial killers? I mean, folks, these vermin are dangerous and walking the streets right now. Maybe right here in Yonkers. Maybe he's your next-door neighbor. Did you hear about that psycho down in New York? Big news. Cutting up his victims. Burying them alive. Pardon my French, but we know these assholes are sick. My question tonight for you all—why do some women like to hook up with these men? Insane, right— especially when so many of us good-looking guys are already around?"

Tory let out his signature booming laugh. He was certain that his audience appreciated his cool handle as host.

It had been tough going getting his "Tombs' Talk" off the ground, though Tory was upbeat, seeing another dozen set of ears on his show since its debut three months earlier. His "ratings" were now up to 134 listeners. Not quite enough to convince Larry Inglewood to advertise his used car business on his show, but Tory thought he might be getting closer to snaring the sponsor by changing his "stage name" from Vlordish Stanislaw to Tory Tombs, no doubt giving the show more panache. The alliterative style with a hint of the spooky was a stroke of genius. At least he thought so.

"So, friends, tonight we have a wild one: 'The Serial Killers Women Love to Love.' And who better to talk about the subject than our special guest, Dr. Mitchell Siskin, a leading criminal psychologist who has spent the past thirty years studying such deranged women and their sexual obsession with these killers. He's here to share his expertise, but first, let's get started with a call-in from you listeners."

Tory saw his computer screen light up with a half-dozen callers. He had struck gold with the night's topic and mentally patted himself on the back. Sex, women, killers—I mean, how great was that?

Tory tapped at a button on his computer.

"Tory, I have a confession," Gloria from Dobbs Ferry was shouting into the show. "When I was a much younger woman, I sent Ted Bundy fifteen dollars and a note declaring my love for him. He was so handsome and charismatic—you know his trial was even on television and he looked like a movie star—I just fell hard for him."

"I guess that it didn't work out all too well for you, Gloria, with Bundy's thirty-six murders and all." Tory applauded himself again for having boned up on serial killer factoids before going on air. "It also looks like you had competition. Didn't he get bags of mail with love letters and photographs from his groupies before they fried him?"

"Well, Carole Ann Boone lucked out, she did," Gloria said testily. "They got hitched during his trial—inside the courtroom! He was acting as his own lawyer and then popped the question to her on the stand—she was there as his character witness. According to Florida law, they were legally married! Wouldya believe? Didn't help much at the trial. The jury still convicted him for kidnapping and killing a twelve-year-old."

"Well, I'm sure you look back now to see how young and foolish you were at the time."

"Not really," Gloria went on. "He reminded me of JFK."

"Thank you, Gloria from Dobbs Ferry. Gotta go." Tory cut her off before she could say another word, then announced, "Folks, I want to bring on Dr. Mitchell Siskin as my special guest tonight to talk to you. If anyone can understand such women as Gloria, it's you, Dr. Siskin."

"Thanks for inviting me, Tory," Siskin said.

"So doc, let's get to it. How could anyone fall for a Ted Bundy?"

"Tory, it's far more common than you or your audience might believe. These serial killers draw in these women who don't quite get how dangerous these men are. Afton Burton— she called herself 'Star'—she was this rather beautiful twenty-six-year-old woman who became Charles Manson's fiancé. For god's sake—he was eighty years old at the time. Then she ran around television shows declaring her love for her man along with a website asking supporters to demand Manson's release from prison."

"Are these people just off the wall or what, doc?" Tory asked.

"Well, we have a clinical term for such people. It's called 'hybristophilia.' This is when someone has a sexually obsessive attraction to people who commit violent crimes like rape and murder. Such women are seemingly enthralled by the danger these killers evoke—their "nature of evil," as it's referred to— but they are playing with fire. These men are a different species than the rest of us."

Tory was getting revved up by the talk. "I saw a movie about Richard Ramirez, the 'Night Stalker' guy. He brutally killed over a dozen women and girls, one as young as nine!"

"Yes, he was a classic psychopath," Siskin said. "But that didn't stop his fans and 'sympathizers' from writing him

adoring letters and even paying him visits at San Quentin State
Prison. A woman by the name of Doreen Lioy—she was a
magazine editor—first wrote Ramirez a birthday card, then
more than seventy love letters during his incarceration. She
told an interviewer that it was Ramirez's mugshot she saw on
television that first 'captivated' her. It was something in his
eyes, she said. A courtship followed and they were married at
San Quentin, with Lioy stating that she would commit suicide
if Ramirez was executed. He died before they could finally
strap him in, but their romance and marriage was over by
then."

Tory interrupted the lecture, growing annoyed that the
doctor was dominating his air time. "Well, Dr. Siskin, my
computer is going wild. Let's take a call."

"Hey, doc, Tory," said Mel from the Bronx. "Don't
you think that we should just go ahead and castrate these
animals? That would be enough to calm down those stupid
bitches just looking to get laid by some fucking moron."

Tory hit another button.

"You're on caller, with Tory Tombs and Dr. Mitchell
Siskin."

A slow, deep voice responded.

"Hello, doctor," the caller said. "I am fascinated by
your insights and this 'hybristophilia.' I am also interested in
these women and their obsession with such serial killers.
Perhaps you might consider that this woman has no choice.
She is spellbound by her lover. So much so that she is willing
to abandon so-called 'normal' impulses that might rebuff this
man for what he has done, for who he is. The fact that his
very power compels her to seek him out. She cannot resist."

"Such feelings are seriously delusional," Dr. Siskin
stated. "These killers are pathologically sick and incapable of

loving another human being, yet perfectly capable of taking an innocent life."

"Doctor, what if you are incorrect?" the caller asserted. "Killers possess unbounded emotions even more so than your *normal* person. They are, by nature, intense individuals with feelings—yes, even love for their victims—that fire their ferocity. Is it any wonder that a woman might also then crave that intensity? The need to feel alive in his presence?"

"Well, this sounds to me much like undiagnosed claptrap."

Siskin found himself annoyed at this caller's amateur psychoanalysis. "You cannot possibly be in the field yourself?" he asked indignantly.

"Well, yes, but from a slightly different perspective. Let's say, a more personal view."

"Then these unfounded speculations are merely your own, I presume?"

"Well, I do have a certain experience, doctor, 'in the field,' as you might say."

"What do you *mean*?" Siskin asked brusquely.

"I kill people."

A two-second beat of dead air was followed by Tory Tombs' raucous laugh. "Ah, thank you, caller. Good one. And I appreciate your sense of humor. At least we agree that something needs to be done about those damn psychos. They're close to home. This one sicko is on a killing spree over in New York City."

Tombs waited for a response.

"Caller?" Tombs asked. "I guess he hung up, doctor."

"Yes, well, I think he is quite confused..."

"I am still here, Dr. Siskin," the caller said coldly. "And Mr. Tombs, the word is 'psychopath'—they are psychopaths, not 'psychos.' Also, you might tone down the 'sicko' remarks. Far too disparaging and insulting."

Tory forced a chuckle though listeners could hear his voice waver. "Okay, okay, mister serial killer. Do you have a name?"

More seconds of silent air.

"You can call me Poe," the caller finally responded.

"Poe? *Poe?*" This time it was Siskin who responded. "Like Edgar Allan Poe?"

"Yes, doctor. Like Edgar Allan Poe. We are somewhat related—by blood, as you might say."

Tory Tombs was at a loss for words, one of the few times in his life he was struck by that affliction. He had to give the guy credit for his scary bit.

"And Dr. Siskin," the caller continued. "I do know what it is to feel a woman's love. I surely do. It is not as strange as you pronounce. After all, we all have feelings, don't we, doctor?"

Siskin had shuffled the caller off as just another loony, but something about this 'Poe's' steely assurance made him apprehensive.

"What are you saying?" Siskin asked. "Is there a woman in your life?"

"Oh, yes. Something of a mad relationship, I would say."

"Mr. Poe, if you are who you say you are, is she in danger?"

"Doc, it's just Poe. And aren't we all in danger when we are in love?"

This time it was Tory who broke from his silence. "So, Poe, my friend, do we have a name? Who is the lucky girl?"

"Perhaps, Tory, some other time, but it's good to know that you care."

"Of course," Tory said, oblivious to the caller's derision. The computer board was flashing wildly. The entire world was calling in, Tory thought happily.

"We'd like to hear how things are moving ahead between you two lovebirds," he added.

"Oh, you'll hear from me again, Mr. Tombs," the caller said. This time the scorn was evident in his voice. "Why not plan on it?"

Before Tory could respond the connection went dead.

BONES

"**D**o you think this asshole knows who he was talking to?" Detective Thomas Sullivan asked PJ Bones.

"Well, Tory Tombs may find a new meaning to his name if he continues to play around with Poe," Bones replied.

The two men hunched over a steel-gray metal table in a meeting room set aside for the 'Poe Murders,' listening to a recording from Tombs' show. His interview with Poe had spiraled throughout social media.

"Our killer is not a shy man," Sullivan remarked.

"Yeah, I'm sure that's not one of his personality traits," Bones said.

Poe was out from the shadows only to electrify the nonstop chatter that swept across tweets, posts, and the Instagram crowds. Inhabitants of the dark web were especially fervent fans—"The Butcher 'live,'" how cool was that! Poe was no longer a figment of news reports, but a real voice and psychotically dangerous. A rock star.

"Would you believe the crazies are coming out of the woodwork cheering this guy on?" Sullivan said, shaking his head. "Look at what's popping up."

Bones scrolled through a website tagged "Liberate Serial Killers," with a gallery of mug shots. A 'Who's Who' of killers serving life sentences or are residing on death row.

Bones pointed to one photo he recognized. "This guy, Gary Ridgway. Remember him? He's the national record holder. Ninety-three victims."

"Yeah, 'The Green River Killer,'" Sullivan said. "Real scum bag. Targeted women 'in the trade' and runaways out in

Seattle and Tacoma. Told police he was 'pretty good' at strangling his victims. Then he raped their corpses."

"Jesus!" Bones said.

"He got a plea bargain deal. Serving life somewhere out in Washington."

Bones waded through Ridgway's criminal report along with his police confessions. "Hey, it wasn't all bad," Bones said derisively. "He painted trucks for thirty years and won an award for perfect attendance on the job."

"Maybe one of these Internet nuts would like him as a neighbor should they set him free."

It was then that Captain Trevor Cooligan came by with a sheaf of papers, looking even more peeved than his usual self. He got right to the point. "A manhunt is already underway," he stated. "We have no option. We get this son of a bitch."

Cooligan's marching orders were not any different from his earlier ones, though with one stark addition: find the cop killer and shoot him dead if he dares to blink. The second half of the order wasn't stated but clearly understood.

Cooligan threw Bones a furious side glance. He wasn't about to hide his contempt for the man. McBain would still be alive if it wasn't for Bones' reckless stupidity—not that Cooligan would get an argument from Bones. He should have listened to McBain and waited for backup before charging onto Poe's property. Bones would carry that guilt to his grave.

"Sully, any leads tracking his phone?" Cooligan asked.

"No luck so far, Captain," Sullivan said. "He's probably using a burner."

"So, what's next?"

"Ultrecht said that he plans to call in again. This Tombs, he's a jerkoff, but we are monitoring his show."

"There's no 'we' here, Sully," Cooligan said. "Bones should not be here."

Cooligan gave Bones another hard glare, then the lines around his eyes softened.

"I'm going to pretend that you are invisible out of respect for Phil McBain. You guys were tight, but if I get wind that you've fucked up this investigation, I promise I will slowly cut off your balls."

Sullivan and Bones stuck around the room afterward, eying a large portable bulletin board that was set up with photographs of Poe's victims.

"Our boy has had quite a run," Sullivan said. "Ultrecht has been at it for almost three years. Started with the Knox woman. She's the only one to survive…I guess you know that."

Bones sat silently, staring at Clara's photos taken after her attack. He winced at the close-ups, the photographer zeroing in on Clara's wounded neck, a bloodied mass of serrated flesh. It was astonishing that Clara had survived the assault.

"But we are getting a bigger picture now," Sullivan went on. "Ultrecht used the backyard at his cabin as a cemetery. We found Tre Simon and the Graham woman. We also unearthed about twenty dead animals. Judging from the look of them, they were tortured. Old graves, when Ultrecht was a kid."

Sullivan shook his head, trying to wrap his mind around such evil.

The picture gallery was pinned in dated order. Victims in their death masks, along with their mutilated corpses. Anne Sweeny, the teacher, her body found at Ultrecht's Harlem apartment. Bones would never forget the sight of her half-skeletal face, her dead eye peering out. Other images were not any less horrific.

"The coroner concluded that Tre Simon and Jenny Graham were buried alive," Sullivan said. "Hard to believe, but the Graham woman might have been better off than her husband."

Bones could hardly bring himself to look at the three photographs of Travis taken at Ultrecht's cabin. His face, twisted and grotesque. How he must have suffered trapped in that bricked-in crypt.

Separate from the other photos was a picture of a dead Phil McBain after the vultures had finished with him. For the hundredth time, Bones silently begged his friend for forgiveness.

"Get your ass in gear." Cooligan barged into the office, red-faced and terse.

"We traced a car, an old Buick, to our man. Port Authority got the plate heading over the GW bridge. Looks like he made his way past the Delaware Water Gap. We think he's somewhere in and around Wilkes-Barre. The feds are on their way. So are we."

SULLIVAN

Sullivan and Bones were in the lead car racing across I-80 toward Wilkes-Barre. A car suspected to belong to Poe had been spotted at a local motel on the outskirts of the city. Local police had been notified and had already formed a perimeter around the motel with orders to wait for the NYPD and the feds.

Sullivan's car careened through downtown Wilkes-Barre, past Kings College and the rail station. The city had a tumultuous history, with locals still recalling the devastating flood back in the '70s that killed over a hundred residents and leaving hundreds of thousands homeless. Then industries started to fold and with it came the collapse of the city's economy. Perhaps that's why residents were nonplussed seeing the line of police cars with lights flashing making their way through the city. They weren't about to let this trouble get in the way of their day.

Sullivan sped past an outdoor mall before coming up to the Old Wagon Wheel Motel. The place had seen better days with its flickering "Vacancy" sign welcoming guests. Only a few cars were parked alongside the two tiers of rooms. Even more rooms were located on the back property. A rusted chain-link fence circled a small cracked empty pool with a sign, "Swim at Your Own Risk."

"Reminds me of the Bates Motel," Bones said wryly as Sullivan pulled up to the front office.

"Yeah," Sullivan said. "A first-class resort for our psycho."

"Do we need to wait for the FBI boys?" Bones asked.

"Not a chance," Sullivan said. "Poe is ours."

Lulu, with a cigarette dangling from her lips, nodded to the two men as they exited the black Suburban. She needed no introductions, pointing to the back wing of the motel. "Number thirty-two," she said, handing Sullivan a key. "Try not to break anything."

"Thanks..." Sullivan said.

"Name is Lulu."

"Yeah, Lulu," he said. "Did you see our guy this morning?"

"Can't say I have. Police showed me a picture. Might be the guy who came in last night looking a bit tuckered out. Can't be sure."

"Did he say anything to you?"

"Well, he did look a bit preoccupied, but none of my business... Gotta say, a good-looking guy, nice goatee, and spoke polite-like."

Sullivan warily eyed the woman, then turned to Bones. "Let's go."

The detective, followed by a half-dozen men from his squad, took the stairs to the second floor and circled to the back end of the motel. Room thirty-two. They didn't bother with the key. Sullivan wasn't about to announce himself.

The team burst into the room with guns drawn.

The room was empty with dust balls hovering in the air. The place smelled of mildew. The place hadn't been lived in for days, likely weeks.

"Fucking woman!" Sullivan, fuming, stormed out of the room. Then he stomped over to the front of the motel. Lulu was standing outside her office with another cigarette to her lips.

"Any luck, officer?" she asked off-handedly.

"Where the hell is he?" Sullivan simmered, barely holding back from throttling the woman.

"Detective, I only know what I know," Lulu said calmly.

"Do you know what he does to women like you?"

"Well, I can only imagine," she said.

Sullivan thought he caught a flash of a smile.

"Sully, he was here," Detective Joel Einleger said, rushing over and pointing to a room three doors from the front office. In his hand was a leather file. "Looks like our man left something for us."

Sullivan, his face beet-red, glared at Lulu.

She looked back with as much innocence as she could muster.

"Take her in," Sullivan ordered Einleger before turning back to Lulu. "We have a few questions to ask you. Maybe your memory needs to be jogged a little. We can work that out for you."

Lulu shrugged. "I'll just go get my purse."

"You might also want to take along your toothbrush," Sullivan said.

POE

Chapter 16
'A Dream Within a Dream'

I admit, a close call at the motel, but I blame myself for letting
these police get so riled up, storming into the place. So, my
tease at that idiot's show had gotten under their skin. That and
the killings, naturally. I suppose I let my guard down
underestimating their determination. No doubt those boys
also wanted to seriously avenge the death of one of their own.
And to think, I was saved by that woman—some horrid
creature that ran the dump. I assume she felt she owed me
some loyalty after that disgusting afternoon together. It was
enough though to get her over to my side. I saw from my
window that she had come through. Police revved up on
testosterone, charging to the back of the motel.

Then she called my room.

"They're here, sweetie," she said, as if I needed the
warning. "There is a cellar next to the office. It's where we
keep our supplies and equipment. It leads underground to a
side street exit. You might want to take it."

Before leaving, I felt obliged to leave my police friends
a short note.

"All that we see or seem. Is but a dream within a
dream."

Edgar's poetry.

Perhaps they might appreciate Edgar as well.

It also occurred to me that PJ Bones might be part of
the posse and maybe appreciate other stories of mine, writer
to writer. I had several chapters that I was saving specifically

for him. I was sure he'd be interested. A good story is hard to put down, after all. Especially one about Clara though it remained unfinished. Endings are elusive, particularly when it involves two protagonists such as PJ Bones and myself, both wanting the same woman with neither willing to share. So it was inevitable how the story must end. One of us must die. There was no other way. And so I made the decision just who that one should be.

BONES

PJ Bones trudged back to his West End Avenue apartment, drained from a tense day at police headquarters. It had been two days since the failed raid at the Old Wagon Wheel Motel. The trail for Poe was at a standstill. Bones was tired, allowing himself to imagine a late candlelit dinner with Clara that evening accompanied by some soft Sinatra. He was not laying bets, but he held out the hope for a romantic night with her.

Clara was only more of a mystery these past weeks moving wildly between mood swings. Sex was more a furious clash of bodies leaving their bedsheet drenched in sweat. A carnal scent permeated their bedroom, a sexual intoxication that only aroused Clara more. And then she would be at him with her mouth and fingers, stroking, probing, bringing him back inside of her.

Then there was the "other" Clara, dark and dangerous, with her spitting expletives, in one instance, ripping apart their bed pillows, detonating a burst of feathers that coated the room. Her rage was palpable, reminding Bones of people he'd confronted as a cop on the streets, trapped in the throes of their madness. Still, he could not escape the burning desire he felt for the woman, caught in her web.

Bones entered the apartment, instantly aware and uneasy that the place was still. No dinner or Sinatra. And no Clara. She hadn't answered his text earlier from the office. He tried again, waiting a minute for Clara's response before going into the kitchen to pour a drink. Three shots still failed to ease his nerves. Then he went into the bedroom, setting his sights on a hot shower.

The bedroom was as he'd left it that morning, except for a note, folded in half, taped to the mirror. And then a déjà vu moment, the flash of memory. This note had no place there, just an unwanted message. He snatched the paper from the mirror. Two words. "I'm sorry." There was no emoji this time, nor did Clara bother to sign the note.

Bones felt the breath punched out of him and dropped down to the bed. This was not like the first time she left him. This felt coldblooded. A dagger to the heart. There was no escape from the message—this cruelty—that she had stuck to the mirror.

Bones saw that Clara had cleared out quickly, leaving only a few personal belongings behind, including a necklace that he'd given her months earlier for her twenty-fifth birthday. That night she was the woman he wanted to love, the flames from a birthday cake flickering about her innocent face. An angel image. Bones had never been happier. The emerald-jeweled necklace reflected the color of her eyes. She was so utterly entrancing. They walked hand-in-hand to the bedroom and made love tenderly, as if their joining made them both whole. And then, remarkably, Clara told Bones that she loved him. And he believed her.

"'You have witchcraft in your lips,'" Bones whispered dramatically, conjuring Shakespeare's *Henry V*.

She threw back her head and cackled, then hunkered into a witches' crouch with her hands reaching out like claws. They both cracked up and fell into each other's arms.

Bones picked up the necklace from her jewelry stand. His sorrow suffused with dread. Clara was suffering, and Bones thought he could save her from her demons, but he had failed; their love, a fiction, much like his made-up stories. Clara was gone again. He knew that this time was different, the reality hitting him squarely in the face. Clara Knox had left to be with *him*. Poe. The man who tried to kill her.

Bones was certain.

He recalled that other time. Poe, taunting him over the phone, contemptuous, whispering in his ear that he and Clara had met in Riverside Park. Bones had buried the thought— this impossibility—but now the picture of Poe and Clara together hurtled into his consciousness, piercing his mind.

Just then, his cell phone buzzed in his pocket, startling him. He reached for the phone, instantly feeling idiotic for coming to such a preposterous notion.

"Clara!" Bones exclaimed.

He heard a second of sound. Not a word, but a rasping titter meant to taunt him.

Bones felt a cold stillness in the room.

"Poe—where is she?" he snarled.

Not that Bones expected an answer and nor did the caller offer one.

POE

Chapter 17
'Clara, My Love'

I am a believer in fate. Not the kind dictated by some invisible force but by my own will. I am the one in control of my destiny. So was there ever a question whether Clara and I were meant for each other? Need I respond? I admit, I was first swept away by her beauty and my passionate desire that she be my first. But I see clearly now that my knife was never intended to cut deep enough into her throat to bleed out her life—that she needed to survive. How else could she have chosen to return to me? To be my lover.

Yes, our relationship got off to a rocky start and then the insult taking up with PJ Bones. I abhorred him, his arrogance, taking my Clara for himself. I might have done away with him at the cabin, burying him under the sand with his friend. But I let him live—perhaps a weak moment on my part—but he never could have Clara. She had only used him to find me. And now she has.

As I said, Clara and I were bound together by destiny.

The heat from Clara's body washed over me after we were done. Even if I had wished, I could not have restrained Clara's ferocity, her brutality, pummeling my body until I could no longer bear the assault, releasing myself inside of her, both of us screaming out our pain and pleasure. Afterward, she rested her head on my chest, though I still felt her blood wildly pulsing against my body.

"I wanted to kill you for what you did to me that day," Clara murmured.

"I know, Clara, but not now, my love," I said, stroking her hair.

"I can still feel your touch on my neck," she whispered.

"Yes, I passionately loved you, even then."

I reached my hand along her smooth alabaster skin. Her naked form was nothing less than that of a goddess. The only deformity, the jagged scar across her neck, and, for a moment, I regretted having marred such beauty, but the feeling did not last long. I understood the strange path to our reunion. It was the knife that brought us together.

This time was wholly different from our first intimacies at her apartment with Clara trembling from my touch. And then at the hospital when she was dazed and pliable from the drugs. Her deep green eyes now revealed something more mysterious, more foreboding—a killer's eyes. Perhaps that explained why our fucking was so furious.

"Now, aren't you glad I lived?" Clara asked as she nuzzled closer, her dark hair flowering on my chest.

"Of course, Clara," I said. "We were meant for each other, forever."

Clara slightly lifted her head, her eyes locked onto mine, and nodded.

BONES AND SULLIVAN

Bones and Sullivan spent the morning in the squad room reading through Poe's manuscript that he'd purposely left in his motel room. Bones had added the Tre Martin "chapter" to the pile. He had not touched the pages since Poe's unwelcomed package arrived at his apartment. The two men divvied pages with Poe narrating his killings in the first person. Chilling, mad acts of depravity. And always his "mentor," Edgar Allan Poe in his ear, inspiring him on his murderous forays. The stories had a common characteristic—there was no mercy in Poe's bloodletting. None. All that was left of his victims were their tortured bodies. Now these dead peered out from their photographs pinned to a large police corkboard. Ghosts that haunted the two men scrutinizing their sorrowful deaths.

The latest manuscript had been retrieved after the raid at the Wilkes Barre motel. A "gift" from Poe, taunting his pursuers. Bones sifted through the pages coming to Clara's stories. Poe beckoned him to read on—the brutal knifing at Clara's apartment and then a later chapter when he hunted her down at Washington Square Park.

> ...I found Clara sitting there on the park bench, writing in a notebook. She looked so peaceful and even more beautiful than I remembered. I stripped off my shirt revealing my tattooed body. She would notice me then, and I waited patiently, catching her attention with my eyes, I saw her shock from across the

park. Her eyes were as wide as saucers—those exquisite eyes! She sat there, absolutely still for the moment, but then she began screaming, bolting up from the bench. I think she was yelling out something about her "killer," which, of course, was exaggerated. I laughed aloud at the sight of my beloved Clara racing towards me. We would need private time later for such a rendezvous. And, so, I hustled back to my car, and left her there, still screaming into the air...

Bones felt weighted in his chair, immobile. Clara had come home that night in a frenzy with her bizarre story. Clara saw the doubt in his eyes, and she was right to have felt betrayed. He had not believed her.

Sullivan nudged him on his arm. "Hey, Bones, you okay?"

The detective needn't have asked. He'd seen that tormented look a thousand times before on the streets.

"Yeah. Just thinking about Clara. I wasn't much good for her, was I?"

"Hey!" Sullivan said sharply. "What would Mac say? Get your head on straight! Then make this right."

"Yeah, but, Sully...will we ever make this right? Just too much ."

"Well, we're deep into it," Sullivan said. "But we have no other choice, Bones, do we?"

PART FIVE

PART FIVE

TOMBS AND POE

Tory Tombs was about to go live for his weekly internet radio program, fiddling with the computer at his desk. He was feeling pretty good having landed Larry Inglewood advertising his used car lot. Tory decided on his go-to topic for "Tombs' Talk." Conspiracy theories. His listeners liked to make stuff up and then swear their crap was true. They were nuts, but Tombs relied on them for a lively hour.

The show started with the usual boring chatter about the UFO sighting in Flora, Mississippi. Then the nugget that the FBI killed the wrong bad guy in a back alley in 1934 instead of the real John Dillinger. "The guy lived into the '60s," proclaimed the caller. Stanley from New Rochelle, spoke in a hushed voice of "a secret chamber" carved into Mount Rushmore behind the head of Abraham Lincoln that contained hidden treasures. That one happened to be true! And Tory was ready to add his prodigious research to the conversation, informing Stanley and his audience that behind Lincoln's brow was, in fact, a large doorway that led to a huge, empty chamber. "But forget the hidden treasure—you should just stay away from those Indiana Jones movies," he told Stanley.

Tory hit a computer button for the next caller. All he heard was a hiss of air.

"Hello, friend?" Tory said, momentarily frustrated. He was about to move on to the next caller when the silence was broken.

"You must remember me, Tory," said a cold voice.

"Ah, yes, you must be one of the extraterrestrials from Roswell, Mexico."

Tory gave a belly laugh, appreciating his own timely humor.

"Well, I have indeed landed again on your show," the mystery caller said.

"Pal, so what do you have for me?" Tory said, already impatient with the caller. "Lots of folks trying to get to me tonight." Larry Inglewood wasn't the only one selling, he thought.

"It's not 'pal,' but Poe," the caller said ominously.

Listeners could hear Tory suck in air. His killer was back.

"Mr. Poe. Uh, you are the one they are looking for."

"Tory, I told you last time I was here. It's just Poe. You must get that right. And I assume you are not asking me a question, only asserting a fact."

Tory could not miss the menace behind the voice.

"Ah, Mist...Poe. You are wanted for, ah..."

"Yes, yes, let's not be shy, Tory. Murder. You must remember. Why you even invited me back to your show. I assume I'm still welcome, yes?"

"Um, but I thought you'd be kind of distracted, given, you know, the attention you're getting."

"Never too busy to talk to you, Tory. And, yes, I've become something of a celebrity. They are calling me 'The Butcher.' Doesn't really work for me, however."

Tory blew out a breath, his nerves kicking in. "Yeah, thanks for calling in, Poe. Um, I'm not sure that I should be wishing you good luck."

"You're not going to let me go already?" Poe said. "Think of your callers. And, what, no thank you for last time? Tory! You made a bit of a name for yourself after that one."

"Yeah, ah, thanks..."

"That program with the doctor. Quite the expert about women who fall in love with serial killers. I had to weigh in then. And look who I've brought onto your show with me this time. Wouldn't you like to talk to *my* lover?"

"Mr. Poe..."

"It's Poe. Last time, Tory."

Tory felt the shakes coming on harder. He stroked his chin, then looked down at his computer board. Every caller light was lit.

Then his cell phone buzzed.

"What the hell is going on, Tombs?" Larry Inglewood of 'Larry's Used Cars' shouted into the phone. "You've got a maniac on?"

"Larry, I need to get back. Later." Tory cut off the call, realizing that he had lost his lone advertiser. His head was swirling.

"Well, Tory, you sound a bit anxious," Poe continued. "So, would you like to meet Clara?"

"Clara...who?"

"Clara Knox. She has an interesting story. We didn't quite hit it off to begin with—it happens that way with new relationships—but we are now inseparable."

"Ah, the lucky lady," Tory said, at once regretting his joke.

"Hello, Tory." The voice was tinged with the Irish. "This is Clara."

Tory was speechless. For a second, he considered that he was being pranked. Maybe this person was even his ex-wife, Miriam, disguising her voice and out to get him. She liked to get under his skin with threats about his absent alimony payments.

Tory frowned, not buying his own conspiracy theory. The two people on the other side of the phone were deadly serious and weirdly threatening. He pushed aside the shakes and tried out his Anderson Cooper imitation.

"So, how did you two lovebirds meet?" was the best he could come up with.

Clara snickered at his ineptitude. "Well, Tory, a long story. Not your typical romance. You see, Poe was out to kill me. That was our first relationship."

Tory faked a laugh. "A good one, Clara," he said, his anxiety rising. "But, uh, seriously, our listeners would like to know your story. How, um, did you...hook up with Poe?"

Clara's voice hardened. "Well, Tory, I was just a college student at the time. Poe broke into my apartment. He took out a long knife, then cut my throat. I should have died, but I didn't. That sums it up."

Poe broke in. "But you are with me now, aren't you, my love?" he said.

"Yes, all's well that ends well, as you like to say," she said.

Tory swallowed hard, feeling flush at the lovers' chatter, while also imagining his listenership skyrocketing. The flashing lights on his board gave him a bit more confidence. Larry Inglewood could go fuck himself. Sponsors would be lining up outside his door after this interview.

"Well, so you're like the Prince of Darkness, Poe," Tory said lightly. "And the two of you, a modern-day Dracula love story. Poe, you don't have fangs to suck her blood, do you?"

Tory nervously chuckled into the mic. Normally he would be pleased with his innate improvisational skills—just the thing that defined his on-air talent— but his comment was met with dead air on the other side of the call.

"So, I am a vampire then, Tory?" Poe whispered menacingly. "A Prince of Darkness, is that how you describe me? Speak about my Clara in such a manner? Could you be any more dimwitted! More insulting!"

Tory took a quick breath, dread setting in. Apparently, Poe, or whatever he called himself, was less than appreciative of his on-air aptitude. "Well, I'm just saying that both of you seem to be made for each other. No offense."

"Offense taken," Poe hissed. "Stupid man. Can your feeble cretin brain possibly fathom eternal love?"

"Well, Mr. Poe...I mean..."

Tory heard a rush of air.

"Um, Poe? Clara Knox?" he called out anxiously.

Tory was aware of his heart racing.

"What's with these psychos?" he spurted out, instantly wanting to grab back the words, but it was too late. He shivered in the foreboding stillness of his apartment.

"Well, folks, now a word from Larry Inglewood's Used Cars," he told his listeners. He could not stop his voice from shaking. "For the lowest prices on cars in town, it's Larry's."

Tory cued a commercial featuring Larry Inglewood announcing his "spectacular" annual used car sale that was "set to expire in 24 hours."

Tory then lurched over to his bathroom, fell to his knees, retched, and threw up his guts onto the floor.

CLARA AND POE

It had been a week since Poe and Clara made their way through the pitch-dark night into the foothills of the Catskill Mountains in upstate New York. The area had some history being a short distance from the town of Woodstock. Poe was interested in staying out of sight in their stolen car. Snaking through a narrow forest road, he passed by a few isolated homes. The only sign of life was smoke rising from chimneys. Winter was fast approaching with families huddled inside. He and Clara would be free from prying eyes.

Poe lucked out coming up to a deserted cottage. The place must have been a summer retreat now abandoned for the winter. It didn't take much to break in. The cottage was a huge step up from his old cabin out in Long Island. The family had left a neat home with a large fireplace and a stack of logs, along with a stock of canned foods. Prints depicting the English countryside decorated the walls.

"Ah, so our lovely honeymoon hideaway, yes, Clara?" Poe laughed.

Clara ignored the remark, noticing a deer head that peered down from above the front door. Another creature that had its throat cut.

Poe and Clara settled in, their days and nights mostly spent underneath a quilted cover on a feather bed in the cottage's small bedroom.

It had been Clara who suggested that they contact Tombs' show.

"Don't you want the world to know of me, Poe?" she teased.

"And why should I want to share you with anyone else?" Poe asked.

"Perhaps to prove that even a killer can be loved."

"Ah, Clara, but I am loved by all my victims. I see it in their eyes."

"But they are dead, and I am alive," Clara said. "I want to be with you when we tell the world."

Their interview immediately went viral that night with social media turning into a hornets' nest of online buzz. There was the Twitter jabber about Clara using her wiles "to captivate the beast." She laughed at the idiocy but thought the trolls were onto something.

"I see we are being compared to royalty," Clara said, skirting through more Instagram noise.

Poe looked over her shoulder. "Yes, Henry VIII and Anne Boleyn. The man was besotted by his lovely lady, but he still couldn't stop himself from using his sharp blade to do away with her."

Clara mulled over Poe's comment. "Yes, that does sound like you," she finally replied.

"The man was insulting, though," Poe said testily.

"Tombs?"

"Just a cretinous fool. The insolent name-calling. Dracula. Prince of Darkness. Trivializing us. He was having his fun, I suppose. I am inclined to pay him a visit."

Clara turned to Poe.

"I have other plans for us," she said matter-of-factly.

CLARA AND POE

The crescent moon was low in the midnight sky, and its silver glow shined through the cottage window illuminating the naked lovers lying on the four-poster bed.

"You were never meant to die by my hand," Poe said softly to Clara, nestled in the crook of his arm.

Clara did not respond, strangely silent, and staring outside the cottage window. She was absently tracing her finger over the large black raven that covered the top of Poe's left arm and shoulder. The bird's eye had been destroyed by McBain's bullet giving the creature an even more terrifying look.

There was a lightness to Clara's touch that aroused Poe, but he felt uneasy. Clara was lost in some distant thought. It was not the first time she retreated from him after they were done.

Poe again stirred as Clara trailed her finger to the tattooed faces and inscriptions stamped on his body. Dead and imaginary figures, their names scripted in calligraphic black ink. Images of Edgar Allan Poe with Eliza Poe and Virginia Clemm Poe—Edgar, his mother, and wife. together. Others were phantoms from Edgar's imagination—Eleonora, Annabel Lee, Berenice.

Clara rested her finger on more recent images. A tattoo of a beautiful, dark-haired, green-eyed woman. Underneath the image was inscribed, 'Mary Jane.' Her likeness was followed by expressionless pictures of men and women that were roughly punctured into Poe's skin. Each had a name: Anne, Tre, Travis, Jenny.

"You are running out of skin, Poe," she said flatly.

Clara resumed her search of Poe's body, pausing under each of the tattoos. Poe wondered what she must be thinking. His eyes were half-closed as her fingers moved lower, stopping at an image of a mournful-looking woman. This tattoo had no name.

"Mother," Poe murmured. "She never did want me."

Then he laughed harshly.

Clara continued down to Poe's shaft, gently stroking it, feeling it harden. Poe responded instantly, turning to Clara, mounting her, crushing her under his weight. His eyes glinted wildly, reflecting the silver moonlight bathing his face, gazing at Clara's passive beauty. She had returned from the dead after his knifing, much like Edgar's beautiful Ligeia, to be with him. They were meant for each other, as he always knew. He felt her body pulsating under his, waiting for him to begin—and then he did, furiously driving himself into her. She remained still until she no longer could. Animal sounds exploded from her lungs in their frenzied fucking. To Poe, it was music to his ears hearing the screams arising from his lover's throat.

The bedroom was now deep in the shadows. The midnight moon had drifted past the window, its last rays of light mixing into the darkness. Poe was on the edge of sleep, satiated, as Clara left the bed to go the bathroom. When she returned fifteen minutes later, Poe was already deep in sleep. Clara then leaned over the bed and viciously slapped him across both sides of his face.

The hard blows snapped Poe into motion. He shot up from the bed, set to lash out, and he would have struck Clara had it not been for the look on her face. She seemed transformed with her hair now tightly tied back. Her scrubbed face bore red blotches. Clara reminded Poe of the woman he had met at Bellevue hospital, grim and severe.

When she spoke to him, the timbre of her voice was low and whispery as if telling Poe her deepest desire. And when she did, Poe was astounded—not that he objected to her demand, only that he never dreamt that Clara would utter such a command.

"We need to kill him," she told him. "PJ Bones must die."

CLARA AND POE

"**Y**ou want to kill PJ Bones!" Poe repeated.

"No, I want *us* to kill PJ Bones," Clara replied.

"It seems that I must be an influence on you."

"Poe, I'm not here to amuse you," Clara said. "This needs to be done."

"To ask the obvious—why?"

"He failed me. He's just pathetic."

"So, in what way did he fail you?"

"Bones was supposed to have found you. Then I was going to kill you."

Poe, bemused, shook his head. "It looks like neither of those plans worked out."

"I'm still thinking about it," Clara said faintly smiling.

"Well, you almost succeeded tonight," Poe said. "I must say that fucking you is a most pleasant way to die."

"Yeah, I appreciate your...survival instincts," Clara said. "Maybe I should let you live a bit longer."

Poe shrugged, losing patience with the banter. He had gone along but felt that Clara was somehow mocking him. Did she not take him seriously? He was about to make that point when Clara seemed to read his mind.

"I'm serious, Poe. I want us to kill Bones."

This time, Poe asked sternly, "Why kill your old lover?"

Clara's face hardened.

"Men have always failed me. They want one thing from me. My cunt. They are helpless, needy, worthless. Not understanding at all. I give them what *I* want. Bones was the worst of them, a horrible romantic. Telling me that he loved me; living in some fantasyland. And I wanted to puke each time I looked at his pitiful face.

"But you wanted to kill *me*," Poe said.

"Yes, I did. You also needed to penetrate me, and you did with your knife, cutting me like some patch of meat for your liking. Opening my throat to create your own cunt; taking me for your pleasure to satisfy yourself. Oh, how you got off on me that day in my apartment. Only that I didn't die in your bloodletting—my living left you frustrated and enraged, didn't it?"

"Yes, I did want you to die then," Poe said pensively. "But not now, Clara, not now...and you, what do you need?"

"I still need to finish what was started. Kill Bones. I must rid him from my past. And Poe, you know that you need him dead, too. You can never have me unless you do."

"Why not do this without me? Take him to bed. Then cut off his head. That should give you what you want."

"Poe. What satisfaction would that be? Such an act is over and done with, meaningless. I need more."

Poe leaned back on the bed. "I understand," he said quietly. "Bones should see his death coming slowly. A revelation, moving from light to dark. Yes?"

Clara nodded. "Exactly. A slow and agonizing awakening. He must realize the inevitability of that moment."

Poe stared at Clara, his black eyes shining in the darkened bedroom. He was still unsettled and confused by her demand.

"Bones' death. And that will satisfy you, Clara?" he asked. "You will want nothing more?"

"Only to have this misery end," she said.

BONES

The irony was inescapable. Bones might well have credited Edgar Allan Poe for inspiring his alter ego, Sam Rock. It was the famed writer who had invented the "hard-boiled detective novel." His detective had the extraordinary ability to solve crimes through his observations and analytical mind, a process he called "ratiocination." Bones had looked up the word, coming from the Latin "ratio," for "reason."

Bones had been turned on to Edgar Allan Poe's work in his college days. He was of course the master of the Gothic short story though Bones was more intrigued by his fictional sleuth, Chevalier Auguste Dupin. Dupin's deductive prowess was so effective that London police used his techniques to investigate actual murders. At least, that was the legend. Even Arthur Conan Doyle credited Poe for his Sherlock Holmes.

And, so, Bones had the writer to thank for helping him give life to Sam Rock with his own finely tuned investigative sense. Both he and this murderous maniac inspired by the same man. Yes, a perverse irony, he thought.

Bones could have done with more inspiration at the moment. Sam Rock was still at a standstill tracking down his serial killer. Bones had tossed the previous twenty pages, his climatic ending simply contrived to give his readers what they wanted. Clarity. A world in order. A righteous universe in which good overcomes evil. A satisfying ending that validated his readers' hardwired beliefs, and illusions, that justice ultimately wins out. That bad people are destined to be defeated, helpless against the moral weight of humanity. That unadulterated bullshit.

Bones gazed into the empty space of his apartment. It wasn't the first time he'd felt troubled for posing such fictions, but he understood that's what his readers demanded of him. That somehow he, Sam Rock, could vanquish the real homicidal monsters that crawled into their lives—the Bundys, Gacys, Berkowitzes, and Geins. Gein was said to have inspired *Psycho*, though even Norman Bates had nothing on the "Wisconsin ghoul" who skinned his victims' corpses, using their flesh for masks, lampshades, and other assorted keepsakes.

It is why Clara had come to him, only to see him for who he is—just a storyteller, powerless and weak.

Bones reread his manuscript pages, trying to make some narrative sense. Nothing about his killer appeared to fit. His attacks were seemingly random. He was deeply psychotic, and Rock faced too many unanswered questions. How could he capture a maniac whose mind was so diabolically absent of any human impulse? Why such cruelty when he lashes out? Humans don't forage streets stalking their prey, waiting to ruthlessly strike, and then leave bodily remnants of their savagery for all to see as emblems of their depravity. So how could Rock logically find a way to defeat *this* killer when all reason and morality failed to exist?

Sam Rock was at a dead end.

Bones bent over his keyboard. Then he reached for his bottle again. Bones found truth there that he couldn't find when he was sober. That ordinary human beings are tethered to fragile codes that dictate their everyday thoughts and behavior. But who is to say that it isn't the killer that more honestly reflects our truer selves? A primordial creature that scratches and claws and kills in order to dominate. Someone who is not born out of love—a quaint myth—but out of power, taking his rightful place among the weak. Those who refuse to accept him, contrive a vocabulary to define him—he is the psychopath—and think themselves safe, protected by men with badges, walls with iron bars, and wooden chairs that send two-thousand volts of electricity into the human body. As if any of these flailing attempts could possibly defeat him. Someone unshackled from a moral world, free and powerful and unleashed.

A drunken philosophy that made perfect sense to Bones. And he was convinced that Edgar Allan Poe, a fellow alcoholic, understood this truth as well, his consciousness of evil resonating beyond the grave and rooted in the likes of Poe.

BONES

It was after midnight when PJ Bones received two calls, both within fifteen minutes. He had finally managed to get some sleep when the first call jolted him awake. It was from the Portland Police Department, his old friend, Sergeant Jack Nolte. The news was distressing. Becky McBain was back in rehab after an overdose.

"She was out on the streets and shot up some decidedly bad heroin," Nolte told him. The sergeant had been his partner and McBain's back in the day before heading out west.

"Christ, Jack, Becky is all of twenty-years-old," Bones said grimly.

"Yeah, she's grown up way too fast," Nolte said. "She was fortunate this time. It was a bad OD; she barely made it. The judge gave her a choice—the Columbia River Correctional Facility or clean up in rehab for ninety days. This was her third go-round. He made it clear that there would be no fourth chance."

"She's had it real rough," Bones muttered, more to himself.

"The girl's lucky not to be dead in some gutter," Nolte said gravely. "Maybe rehab will save her life."

Bones cringed, knowing that another rehab stint was not the answer for Becky McBain. She was struggling, imprisoned with her own demons, seeing no way out. He understood that place all too well.

"I saw her in New York for Mac's funeral," Bones said. "A terrible blow for the kid."

"Mac was a good man," Nolte said somberly. "You know, she hadn't seen her dad since Sarah's accident."

Nolte and Bones knew that part of the family history with the horror of Sarah's death. And the pain it continued to inflict.

Their conversation lapsed into a long moment of silence.

"Let me know if I can do anything," Bones said at last.

"Sure, PJ."

Bones appreciated his former partner. He had been by his side in New York when the scandal went down with the department.

"You know, Jack, you were right to get out of Dodge back then. Best move you could've made."

"I was glad to see you moving on as well, my friend," Nolte said.

Bones was unable to hold back a wave of melancholy. He needn't tell Nolte that he had never moved on. That he still lived in a world that offered him no relief, no joy. That life was just a day-to-day battle to stay afloat aided by his whiskey. His own addiction.

"Yeah, Jack. Thanks for letting me know about Becky," Bones said, pausing, then pushed the phone's red button ending the call.

It was only a few seconds later when the phone chime sounded again. Nolte getting back—some last thought he had wanted to tell him. Bones tapped into the call.

A female voice greeted him.

"Hello, PJ," she said.

BONES AND CLARA

Bones simmered at the sound of Clara's voice on the other end of the call. The same damn nonchalance she carried at McSorley's the night he'd bumped into her. He had been drunk and furious, her toying with him. Then losing it, punching out a photographer. Afterward, Clara pretending she was back in his life. Ending it all a few months later with a note she tacked on to a mirror, "I'm sorry." Shorthand to tell him to go fuck himself. Burning him, again.

For Clara, time was seamless. She could loop back into his life at any time with all the past shit forgotten. Now the midnight caller, thinking of another way to play with his head. She was so very good at that.

"So, how are you, PJ?"

Just a laugh-riot opening.

And Bones told her so.

"What the hell, Clara?" he snapped. "What do you want now?"

"I need to talk, PJ," she said.

"Not interested."

"PJ, I'm sorry, but you need to listen to me."

Bones shook his head. He promised himself to rid Clara Knox from his mind, his being—not that he was succeeding.

"So, why the call, Clara? It's late, and you must be tired from your publicity tour with your boyfriend. By the way, how is fucking Daemon Ultrecht doing these days? I mean, how do you *like* fucking Daemon Ultrecht these days?"

"You need to talk to me, Bones," Clara said sharply.

"Whatever happened to just good old 'PJ'?" he said. "I guess we are on more formal terms these days.

"PJ—please, listen."

"Actually, I'm tied up now," Bones said acidly. "Working with the NYPD to find this insane piece of garbage. Remember? The fellow who cut your throat? You once had a hard time with him. I guess bygones be..."

"PJ..."

"Clara, we have nothing to say." Bones was having none of Clara's bullshit. "Talk to your fans on social media. You're hot now, and I imagine millions of guys jerking off to your online pictures. Careful though with Poe. He's the jealous type."

Bones felt the silence across the connection and thought Clara had hung up. Then he heard her sobbing.

"Clara, no way!" Bones yelled. "You are not capable."

It was enough to stop Clara's tearful entreaties. Her voice was more familiar now. Distanced and cool. Back in control.

"Bones, I need your help," she said matter-of-factly.

Bones stared into the phone and heaved a breath. He knew he could never turn her away, bewildered how easily he could fall back into her grasp.

"What is it that you want, Clara?" he murmured.

Clara then told Bones what she needed him to do, and when she finished tapped out the phone.

Bones listened to her silently, dumbfounded by her call.

On the other side of the line, Clara grimly smiled. It was all going as planned, she thought.

CLARA

Clara and Poe woke at dawn. She let Poe take her again, then showered, dressed, and got ready to leave. If all went well, they would both be back to the cottage in a few days.

Clara donned a pair of sunglasses and a pulldown knitted cap before wrapping the lower half of her face with a woolen scarf. She was properly hidden. Both she and Poe had mapped out their plan earlier. "Ah, such poetic brilliance," Poe told Clara.

But it would be risky, exposing them.

"There's an all-points out," Poe reminded Clara. "Stay invisible."

"You do the same," Clara said. "And Poe, no trouble."

They both understood the code. There were plenty of law enforcement eyes looking out for them. Poe's sketch— this from Clara's old description—hung on police bulletin boards across the state. Clara's picture likely stood next to his.

Poe was the first to leave that morning. The Greyhound bus stop was a mile walk away. The bus was headed to New York.

Clara left the cottage soon afterward. She would need a hitch into Woodstock's main bus station some six miles away. She gazed at herself in a mirror and knew that the ride was not going to be a problem.

The country road outside the cottage was dead quiet before a driver coming by in his 4x4 pickup saw her wave. He stopped short to give her a lift. Clara slowly unraveled her scarf, flashing a coy smile at the young guy as she entered the cab of the truck. He blushed bright red, and Clara could see him swallowing hard. He barely said a word on the twelve-minute ride into Woodstock. The town had been made famous for the long-ago rock music festival—not that the event was ever held there, but some forty miles away on some dairy farm. More of life's fictions, Clara thought.

She made her way to the Woodstock bus depot and waited an hour for the scheduled bus trip to Topeka, Kansas. From there, she would take a local bus to the small town of Willow Brook, some thirty miles away. Clara welcomed the long cross-country trip, safely nestled, and strangely at peace looking out at the changing landscape that took her across rural America with its farmlands and wheat fields that stretched on endlessly.

Clara had made two phone calls a day earlier. The first was to tell Rose that she was coming home to visit. The call had been punctuated by long, silent pauses. Nothing that Clara could say to Rose would explain why she had vanished—it was well more than a year now—without a word. Whatever small talk Clara initiated was met with her mother's clipped, pained responses.

Clara had disappeared from Rose's life but was still the main topic of Willow Brook's rampant gossip. Rose had shuttered herself behind closed doors, living with both the shame of her husband, who had long before deserted her for his teenaged lover, and now her daughter, someone, somehow, mixed up with a notorious serial killer. Here on the phone, Clara, the daughter she so loved, was finally reaching out to her. And coming home.

Billy Bruster was also shocked, looking at his cell phone, seeing a number that he had memorized years back and may very well have been tattooed on his brain. Even now, the number had the same effect of speeding up his heartbeat. He found his hand shaking before punching in the call. On the other side was Clara.

"Hello, Billy," Clara said.

Billy took a deep breath. "Why, Clara Knox," he said, trying to muster up his cool. "Long time, no hear."

"Yes, I should have called sooner. I've thought about you over the years. It's been too long. You know you were my first love, Billy Bruster...and I've missed you."

Billy was back to his seventeenth year of life. He, the football star; she, this unreachable, perfect beauty. Clara Knox, impossibly, had been his girlfriend. She possessed him, and he felt helpless caught under her spell. He recalled that one night in the back seat of his Mustang at the drive-in. The car windows had been fogged by their body heat, tongue kissing and his frantic groping. He had reached under her blouse and felt the firm sponginess of her breasts. He wanted her badly, slipping his hand beneath her dress, but she quickly put the brakes on, slapping his hand away from her body, drawing the line. It was only afterward in his wet dreams did he ever fulfill his fervent yearning for Clara Knox.

Clara's call had instantly ramped up his old craving for her.

"I have a favor to ask of you," Clara said, nudging Billy from his memory.

"A favor?" he said, confused. "I mean, sure, what can I do for you?"

"I heard you have moved on. That you're a welder."

"Yeah. I work for my pops."

"That's great. Father and son. Well, I need you to build this...thing for me."

"Well, what sort of thing?"

"Kind of hard to explain. I'll text the drawing to you," she said. "Maybe you could help me out. I would be very appreciative."

Billy closed his eyes, the sweet familiarity of Clara's voice enveloping him.

"I'll be in Willow Brook in two days," Clara continued, "and was hoping we could get together. But this would have to be our secret. I can't let anyone in town know I'm coming. Only you and my mom. I think you can understand why. Just the two of us. Old times."

Billy knew, like everyone else in town, of her notoriety. Like some apparition, Clara was coming back to Willow Brook and into his life. He was suddenly hyperaware of his heart thumping. She could have anything she wanted from him. And, maybe, there was still something between them. At least that's what Billy told himself after Clara had hung up.

The bus pulled into the Willow Brook terminal in the dead of night, bringing Clara back to her home. She remembered the last time she set foot in the town. More than a year had passed since that evening when she overheard Rose and her doctor on the phone. The talk had been about putting her away. Then her quickly packing and getting out of Willow Brook.

Clara thought of her mother. Rose had tried to be so steadfast after Clara's attack, but her mother's façade cracked each time she looked at her mutilated daughter, turning away before Clara could see her break down. Rose had been desperate to find her help, but she was out of control. The tantrums; the cuttings; the small acts of violence. She was unrecognizable from the girl she'd once been. Then leaving her mother without a word, ignoring Rose's phone messages over these months. And even so, Rose kept calling. Clara tapped into the messages before erasing them. Each the same one. Rose telling Clara she loved her.

Clara knew she could never return to that time and place. She was no longer *that* Clara, someone she could only vaguely recollect. That person was gone forever. Clara was relieved now that she understood what she needed to do. She planned to carefully make her way home, stay hidden from nosy neighbors. The next day, she'd meet up with Billy and collect the package he'd promised her.

Clara felt oddly serene. The travel over the many miles had made her feel surprisingly tranquil. She was grateful to her mother, loved Rose deeply, but her world had become far too complicated and treacherous. There was no question that Rose would be badly hurt if she brought her mother into her life. It was better this way.

Still, she had to come home.

Rose deserved better from her daughter, but Clara knew that when she came to the door of their small two-bedroom home off of Main Street. Rose would hug her, vowing this time to never let her go back. "You will stay, Clara. Everything will be all right." That's what Rose would surely say.

And then Clara knew she would break Rose's heart again when she left the following day, saying goodbye for the last time.

It was early the next morning that Clara boarded the Greyhound bus to make her way back to Woodstock. She struggled with the heft of the four-foot box that she carried to her seat. Billy Bruster had come through. Clara had given her old boyfriend a lustful kiss to thank him, leaving Billy shaking at his knees.

Chapter 18
'Killer Eyes'

I knew I was taking a chance, but I had no choice coming back to New York City. Clara was intent on her murderous scheme—my influence had apparently rubbed off on her. I must admit, a brilliant plan. Killing PJ Bones—while honoring Edgar.

I was sure that Clara would do her part in Kansas, but there also was more for me to do. Specifically, I needed the "tools" that I'd secreted under a floorboard in my old Harlem apartment. A fool's errand, perhaps, but what is a surgeon without his knife? It wasn't as if I could go to a local medical supply store and request specialized blades that allowed for fine-tuning cuts into the skin. It made no sense using a knife that carelessly severed and killed a patient. Not when it was necessary to sustain life, keep the heart beating, at least for the short term. Death is more than a physical end but a state of mind that a person must come to grips with slowly.

At least this was the philosophy that gave meaning to my work.

I was well disguised, shedding the wig and mustache while opting for a beret, scarf, and a dark top coat that I picked up in a Woodstock thrift store. No doubt I conveyed a foreign elegance. I was concerned though that I came across as a bit snooty among the blue-jean crowd of passengers also on the bus to New York's Port Authority terminal. I started to second-guess my decision to take the bus, but driving a stolen car into the city was asking for trouble. I recalled my poor

Buick, no doubt impounded, a sacrifice that was disheartening. I had fond memories of that car and the experiences we shared. I imagined the police had also discovered the nitrous gas mechanism that had come in so handy with Jenny and Travis.

The three-hour trip gave me time to contemplate this next venture with Clara. She seemed excited at the prospect of us working together, and I expected that killing Bones would bring us closer. Life is full of surprises. Clara had used Bones to somehow find me and, well, she succeeded. Of course, I did not entirely trust Clara Knox. She has given me her body but not her eyes. Those green eyes of hers that shine. Killer eyes. Something I am familiar with. Still, Clara consumed my thoughts on the bus ride to New York. I still ached from the previous night. It had been difficult keeping up with her brutal aggression in bed. She overwhelmed me. I wasn't sure who this Clara was—she was more than a mystery, but dangerous.

And I have never loved her more.

Chapter 19
'Back in Harlem'

I was on guard coming into the Port Authority. The cavernous terminal was bustling and I had my feelers up striding by teams of cops patrolling the place. I left the building quickly and found a waiting cab. The day was overcast with a storm approaching, a condition that matched my own.

There was something about the city that provoked me, daring me to act out. I passed throngs of people scurrying through the streets while my cab headed north along Eighth Avenue. I might very well have chosen any one of them at a different time. And yet these good citizens sauntered along without the slightest notion that they were being watched. They lived their lives in such blissful ignorance with no idea that I also lived among them. Such foolishness.

I needed to be more focused approaching Harlem. I had the cabdriver leave me a few blocks from my old apartment building but realized this might have been a mistake. I was hardly invisible on the streets in my beret and topcoat and better suited for a mugging. Even so, the switchblade in my pocket assured me that no one was going to mess around and still insist on breathing.

I also carried my house keys, letting myself into the front door of the five-story walkup. I immediately bumped into a neighbor from a downstairs apartment. He looked puzzled, trying to match this well-dressed stranger to his memory. He couldn't quite figure me out as I hurried past him to the stairwell. I came to my old apartment, the front door still covered in yellow plastic police tape warning residents to stay away from this crime scene. I checked the hallway and all was quiet. Then I cut the tape with my knife and entered the apartment.

I was somewhat taken aback. The place looked sunken in as if it had been beaten down by the police. Walls were covered in black granular powder used to detect fingerprints, and my prints were highlighted everywhere. No doubt the police had already matched them with my juvenile records. On top of one wall were Edgar's words that I had once carefully inscribed.

"The boundaries which divide Life from Death are at best shadowy and vague. Who shall say where the one ends, and where the other begins?"

Words that still inspired me.

Even the police desecration did not ruin my intimate memories of the place. The coffin I had built for Anne Sweeny still stood in the corner with the lid upright against the wall. I went over to look inside the empty box and could see the deep scratches in the wood that Anne had clawed. I found myself suddenly reminiscing of our time together. She had been a lovely woman, though being entombed in the coffin might well have inhibited her best self.

I needed to push away the nostalgia and move along. I went over to a console table, swiveled it aside, and ran my hand against the floor plank. Edgar had inspired the hideaway with his story about the killer who buried pieces of an old man under the floorboards—not that I could hide a body under the floor; city apartments were just inadequate for such a plan. Still, I managed to carve out a narrow space beneath a slat and now wedged the board up with my switchblade. The surgical knives were laid out in size order as I had left them. The blades were gleaming, and I was pleased to have them back. Then I piled them carefully into a small hardback case that I had brought along.

It was at that moment that I sensed someone stirring outside the front door. I pocketed the case in my overcoat and slid over and looked through the peephole. My downstairs neighbor again. Portly with a hang-dog face, he was one of the building's lowlifes that I hadn't paid any attention to in the past. I was giving him my attention now. I opened the door and he quickly stepped back, his eyes wide as saucers. He looked at me as if he had been suddenly electrocuted.

"You, *you're that guy*!" he shouted.

I saw that he was holding in his hands a strip of police tape that had been ripped down from the door.

I might have taken the opportunity to drag him into the apartment and slice him into small pieces, but this wasn't the right time.

So, I smiled.

"Friend, nice seeing you again," I said politely. "You put on a little weight, yes?"

Then I edged by him to take to the staircase, only he had something else on his mind. I was stunned as he ran toward me and idiotically dove at my legs, trying to tackle me to the floor. He was yelling something about "the butcher," with his small fists hitting my legs. I bent down and lifted him by his round head and saw the fear in his eyes. This little hero. I slipped my hand into my coat pocket for the switchblade. Then I slit open his stomach. I didn't think the cut was fatal but would unleash a gusher of blood that might get him thinking differently. He stared at his stomach, screamed, and went into shock.

The noise brought neighbors out of their third floor apartments and into the hallway. The scene was getting loud and messy, not what I was looking for at all. I started shouting. "A doctor! We need a doctor!" I took out my phone and pretended to call.

"That's Freddy," an elderly lady said, sidling up to me. "He's in 2F."

"Yeah, well, Freddy tried to end it all," I said. "Just called 911. Paramedics are on the way."

The woman gingerly kneeled and stroked Freddy's head. Freddy was moaning loudly, his blood spreading like wings from his body. I revised my earlier prognosis. Freddy was as good as dead.

Residents from neighboring floors were making their way to the scene, huddling around the man bleeding out on the floor.

I found myself surrounded and needing to make a quick exit.

A young Puerto Rican guy hovered on my shoulder.

"Hey, didn't you once live here?" I turned and saw he was narrowly eyeing me. "Hey, aren't you that guy on television that the cops..."

I scowled, pushing past him, and bounded down the steps and out the building. I hit the streets and was lucky enough to flag a passing cab. I told the driver to hustle to the Port Authority, that I would make it worth his while. He grunted and took off. I realized that I had lost my beret in the scuffle and that my topcoat was wet with Freddy's blood. It was good that the coat was black, hiding the stains, but blood was already puddling around me on the back seat.

By the time the cab approached midtown, I could see a phalanx of police cars barreling up Park Avenue, lights flashing, sirens on fire, warning drivers to get out their way. If I didn't know better, I would've thought the city was under attack. And I suppose it was. I laughed out loud, impressed by my own resiliency, perking up the attention of the cabbie. He peered at me with shifty eyes in his overhead mirror. I gave him the peace sign and he grunted again, no doubt thinking I was another nut-job passenger.

He veered in front of the terminal to let me out, and I paid with the promised generous tip. I was inclined to stiff the guy given his attitude, but cabbies always remember the passengers that leave them flat, and it was best to stay invisible with all the commotion around—not that it mattered. The guy would discover his bloodied back seat soon enough. I can't imagine him being too happy with me then.

I had an hour wait for the bus to Woodstock. It was clear that the police presence had been ramped up around the terminal. The cops were already on high alert for a serial killer and might well have already been notified about a tall, bald man in a black overcoat wanted in connection with a homicide up in Harlem. I made my way through the huge station and quickly discarded my coat. Then I slipped into a shop and bought a Yankee cap and blue windbreaker. It was the best I could do on the run.

I slowly strolled over to the departure gate on the other side of the terminal, casually passing a two-man police team that gave me a squinty look. I responded with a "Good afternoon, officers" greeting that seemed to ease their suspicions.

An hour later, I was on board a bus back to Woodstock.

BONES AND SULLIVAN

PJ Bones and Thomas Sullivan had gotten word that afternoon of a killing in Harlem. Some sixty-eight-year-old janitor had been stabbed to death in a fight at some apartment building. Another murder north of 110th Street that normally wouldn't have interrupted their morning plans coordinating the hunt for Poe, but Sullivan's attention perked up, glancing at the report. The building's address at Frederick Douglass Boulevard was familiar. Poe's old building.

"What do you make of that?" Sullivan asked Bones, pointing to the report.

Bones checked out the address in the homicide report. "I might just want to stay out of that neighborhood," he said caustically.

"Yeah, still a bizarre coincidence. The homicide took place on the third floor. Wasn't that the same floor that Poe lived on?"

"Right, but he moved out in a real hurry. Not likely he was homesick and looking to pay a visit."

Sullivan grunted. The coincidence at Poe's apartment house was bothering him.

Bones was also wrestling with his doubts. How likely was it that two murderous assholes were living in the same building? Poe ditched the city with every cop after him. Why would he return to his old apartment?

It was then that Matt Roberts called. The taxi commission official bypassed any niceties. "Sullivan, are you sitting down? I thought you might be interested in some bad news."

"Yeah, I'm already sitting," Sullivan said. "And I'll add your bad news to a big stack I already have on my desk."

Sullivan could hear Roberts take in a breath before he began.

"One of my men came back looking like he was about to have a heart attack. Just apoplectic. The back of his cab was soaked in blood. He didn't realize the problem until he picked up a couple of tourists. They freaked out finding themselves sitting in the slop."

"Christ, Matt. What did the cabbie say?"

"Well, he was sure it was this weird guy he had previously picked up in Harlem. Dropped him off at the Port Authority Terminal. He might be the guy you're looking for."

"The suspect in the Harlem homicide?"

"I'm talking about the serial killer that you asked me about last time."

"Your man thinks he saw *Daemon Ultrecht?*" Sullivan exclaimed.

"Sure sounds like him. Tall, bald, black eyes. Menacing type. At least that's how my driver described him."

Sullivan and Bones stared at each other from across the police desk. Poe was back in New York?

"Matt, did Ultrecht seem hurt? You said blood was all over the back seat."

"That was it. He was laughing to himself in the back of the cab. Something he heard in his brain, I guess. Sicko. That blood must have belonged to someone else. Your forensic guys will need to make that match."

"So, where is the cab now?" Sullivan asked.

Robert gave directions to the taxi lot. "Yeah, I know the routine," he said. "Don't touch anything until your men show up."

"That's right. We'll be getting back. And thanks, Matt."

"Just get this sucker."

Sullivan hung up his desk phone, turning to Bones.

"How does this make sense?" Sullivan said. "Coming back to his apartment, then knifing some guy in broad daylight with an audience around."

"Unbelievable," Bones said, shaking his head. "If it's him, he was thinking of getting out of the city, and fast. We need to reach out to the PA cops. We might get lucky."

Sullivan still was perplexed. "But why would Poe come back? He knows that every cop would like to get their hands on him."

"Yeah, I don't think it's nostalgia," Bones said. "He was looking for something in the apartment."

"Then why this Freddy Jones?" Sullivan asked. "Slicing him open in front of the world? C'mon!"

Bones told Sullivan the simple truth that befell so many victims. "The guy was just at the wrong place at the wrong time with the wrong guy. He somehow got in Poe's way."

Sullivan skimmed through the report on his desk.

"Our guys at the 28th Precinct found entry into Ultrecht's apartment. They checked the place. Nothing there except for a floorboard that had been pulled up. Likely something that Poe had once buried there."

"Nothing that was once alive, I hope," Bones said dryly.

Twenty-four hours later, the Port Authority investigation report came to their desks. PA police had found a topcoat, scarf, and beret that someone had dumped into a garbage bin. The clothing was drenched in blood. Surveillance tapes had also recorded a man exiting a retail shop wearing a Yankee cap and a windbreaker before making his way through the terminal. At one point, the man is seen stopping momentarily to say something to two cops on patrol, giving them a short wave. The tape then shows him entering Gate 17 at 3:27 PM.

The Port Authority schedule listed the 3:33 PM bus leaving the gate to Woodstock, New York.

BONES AND SULLIVAN

Sullivan and Bones sped up to the town of Woodstock, one-hundred-ten miles north of Manhattan. They pulled into the town center in the late afternoon and parked next to a candle and craft shop. Across at a small green, a dozen residents had formed a drum circle and were happily thumping away. Nothing else was moving too fast in the town trying to hold on to its hippie roots. The only distraction was the staccato sound of a siren piercing the air. It was coming from the Woodstock firehouse.

Police Chief Brad Cooke hurriedly greeted Sullivan and Bones outside of police headquarters, a church-like, two-story building that butted up against the town hall. Cooke was on the move and told the men they could talk in his car. He was needed six miles outside of town—a forest fire was burning out of control and there might be victims. The police chief knew the two men were from "the city" after a call informing him that a suspect wanted in a multiple-murder investigation might be hiding out in the Woodstock area. Their investigation would have to wait. The fire spelled big trouble.

Bones and McBain piled into the back of the chief's squad car as Cooke hit the gas, careening out of Woodstock with the car siren blaring. Eight minutes later, they may as well have arrived in hell.

The inferno had razed nearly five miles of woodlands and showed no sign of abating. Engine companies from neighboring towns had responded along with a small army of volunteers. They soon were beaten back, helpless against the vortex of flames that made any approach to the firestorm impossible.

Cooke bounded out of his police car and rushed up to the fire chief. "Tuck, what's the plan?"

"Not a damn thing we can do on the ground," Fire Chief Frank Tucker said. "State authorities have been contacted. We'll need to first tame this thing from the air."

Tucker pointed to a slew of air tankers that just had arrived and were circling the smoke-filled skies. They could see the lead plane bank to the left, dropping a flood of pink retardant over the conflagration. It was followed by three other tankers raining their chemical mix onto the burning woods.

"Not sure if that made much of a difference," Tucker said tensely.

The flames only seemed more emboldened shooting from the trees into the high sky. Any hope of containing the fire's spread was dashed as wind gusts spawned plumes of fire and swirls of thick smoke forcing firefighters to further retreat.

"We're going to have to let this beast burn itself out," Tucker told a knot of his men.

"There are people in there!" shouted one of the civilian volunteers.

The fire chief exhaled. Tucker was also envisioning the hell that existed behind the wall of fire.

"Yes, I know," he said quietly.

BONES AND SULLIVAN

Sullivan and Bones slept restlessly that night at a local B&B, meeting up with the chief in the morning. Bones' old instincts were kicking in. Somehow, Poe was part of this disaster and, if true, then so, too, was Clara.

Brad Cooke confirmed his fears, reporting on the investigation.

It had taken the previous day and a night for the fire to die down enough to allow firefighters into the smoldering ruins. A half-dozen homes had been swallowed up by the conflagration. In one, the remains of two bodies were discovered. They were nothing more than blackened, skeletal figures.

"It was arson," Cooke said bluntly. "Started in the house where we found the bodies. Looks like a double suicide."

Cooke held up photographs of the victims. Bones could not avert his eyes from the pictures: two bodies fused together, twisted in a macabre embrace, their bones melded by the heat of the blaze. Lovers locked in each other's arms—a final, horrific perversion of their union—as if they had been punished for their sins.

"These two are likely the ones you are looking for," Cooke said. "I'm not sure what forensics can tell you. Their bodies were nearly pulverized by the inferno. I guess this is the way they wanted to go out."

"What makes you think suicide?" Bones said testily.

Cooke squinted at Bones, puzzled by the man's peevish attitude.

"Well, the place was locked and loaded, ready to explode," Cooke said. "Lots of combustibles around, then they deliberately ran the gas. The place was nothing more than a bomb. Judging from how we found these lovebirds, heavy breathing would have set the place off. That and a match."

"So, you think this was some lovers' suicide pact? Bones said angrily. "Doesn't add up,"

"I thought you guys would be thrilled with the result," Cooke said. "Finally got the bastard."

"Yeah, Poe is dead." Sullivan paused, then turned to his partner. "And Bones, it's tough about your woman."

It took a second for Sullivan's comment to register with Cooke.

"*Your* woman?" Cooke said, astonished, staring at Bones. "Did I hear that right?"

Bones' face darkened, wanting nothing more than to take off from this town and get back to New York. "Hey, she wasn't *my* woman," he snapped. "Yeah, I knew her. So that's that. Just another victim as far as I'm concerned."

Sullivan immediately regretted bringing up Clara. He held up both hands, a peace gesture.

Cooke was not about to let it go. "Well, she wasn't a victim as far as I'm concerned. These two nearly took out families with them. Families with kids. Those folks barely got out of their homes alive. Lost everything. I'm not in the mood to feel sorry for this bitch, whoever the hell she was."

Bones clenched his fists. He was in no mood for the chief's opinion about Clara or anything else.

Sullivan put a hand on his partner's shoulder.

"Hey, Captain, thanks," Sullivan said. "Too bad we couldn't get to you sooner."

"Yeah, a real shit-show," Cooke said tightly.

Sullivan turned to Bones. "Let's get back to the city, PJ," he said quietly.

Bones didn't bother to reply and stormed out of the office.

Sullivan waited a moment then also headed over to the door. "Let me know if you come up with anything else, chief," he said.

"Hey, detective," Cooke called out. "Did you ever figure out what made this maniac tick?"

Sullivan shrugged, leaving the question hanging in the air.

Cooke was back to his usual business that afternoon, filing away the ugliness of the previous day. He shuffled through papers on his desk, becoming irate at a town council budget report for the coming year. Bottom line—no raises for his men. He needed a word with the mayor. He then opened an envelope, an invitation to speak at the Vets Lodge the following month. He put the invitation to the side. Next was a single-page, missing persons' report. Another one of those MP notifications. A young couple hiking out near Bearsville, about six miles away, was reported missing. Cooke shook his head at the two pictures of the young man and woman. These hikers ought to read their trail maps before heading out. The police chief got up from his chair to tack the notice onto a crowded corkboard. Then he went back to his desk to sort through the rest of the pile of papers.

BONES AND SULLIVAN

Sullivan was behind the wheel on the long trip back to the city. He and Bones had hardly spoken a word since leaving Woodstock, both men lost in thought, reliving the events of the past twenty-four hours.

"I don't believe, it, Sully, this suicide pact," Bones said glumly, breaking the silence. "That can't be Clara. It is not what she had in mind."

"What she had in mind?" Sullivan said. "What the hell does that mean?"

"She reached out to me on the phone, wanted my help to get Poe," Bones said.

Sullivan, turned from the wheel, glaring at Bones. "And you didn't think that this was something you should have told me about?"

"She didn't want the cops involved. This was something else. Between us."

"Incredible," Sullivan said, shaking his head. "What part of your body were you thinking with, Bones?"

Bones exhaled. "Mac said the same thing to me."

"Well, we are both right."

Bones stared out the car window, absently taking in the passing countryside. "I still don't believe it. This is not what she wanted."

"Hey, PJ, listen. Clara was damaged goods. Face it, the hard truth. You know that as well as I do."

"Sully, we are all damaged," Bones said bitterly. "How is it possible to get through this scummy life of ours without getting fucked up? All the bull we bought into at the academy to 'preserve and protect,' to 'live honorably.' Hysterical stuff."

"Well, I happen to believe in that 'bull,'" Sullivan snapped. "And I think you do, too, PJ. Listen, I'm sorry about Clara. Truly. No secret about you two. It's all over every precinct in the city."

"I guess there goes my reputation," Bones said grimly.

Sullivan grunted, finding no need to revisit Bones' past life with the NYPD.

Bones opened the car window and closed his eyes, letting the cool air wash over him. Not that there was any escape from the grotesque photographs that played in his mind. Images, real and unreal, that haunted him.

Clara. Her blackened skeleton, embracing Poe.

Rising from the burnt ruins, and laughing at him.

PART SIX

BONES

Bones' sleepless, sweaty nights gave way to his drunken days. If there was any clarity in Bones' inebriated state, it came from conjuring his father's last moments of life. Again, he was back with Liam Bones at the window ledge on the seventy-fifth floor of the great tower. This recurring nightmare that flooded his mind as he downed another whiskey shot. He could plainly see his father's face, so strangely composed, knowing that his life was not worth hanging on to—why stick around only to be brutally clobbered by a shattered world? The enveloping inferno seemed a fair ending to his miserable life. Yeah, Dad, better to make the leap—to be the one to decide and fuck the reality of that decision. To take the next step and fly with the air screaming in your ears, accompanying your own screams purging from your body, with gravity accelerating your descent as you plummet to the ground for those twelve seconds of sheer nothingness. Still, you must have felt unencumbered from your life's unhappiness until it all ended with a thud. Your body broken into a hundred pieces with your flesh and bones hitting the pavement at one-hundred-and-twenty-miles-per-hour, you little more than a blot of body tissue and bone matter on the sidewalk. Even all the king's horses and all the king's men couldn't put Humpty Dumpty back together again.

Bones remembered loving that nursery rhyme when he was a child. Back when he had a father he wished had loved him.

Bones took another drink.

In his stupor, Bones pictured Clara, another person in his life that chose to jump to her death. She in the arms of a psychopath. Free choice, so who was he to tell her otherwise? Bones thought about *her* insane leap into nothingness. What the hell was the difference? She was dead. The final insult. She also couldn't be identified. Just another human being blotted into nonexistence, reduced to a skeletal horror, as if she were some nameless remnant from an archeological dig around Mount Vesuvius. He recalled that the volcanic blast was 100,000 times more powerful than the combined blasts of Hiroshima and Nagasaki. That was enough to kill her. Clara Knox. That was her name. The woman he loved.

Even in death, she possessed him.

Bones staggered to his bedroom and fell onto his bed. He was spent, bled out, but knew that he would not be allowed to sleep. Too many phantoms hovering about him. Even when he finally drifted into some semi-conscious state, they were all there, beckoning him into their world. To take the leap. Just one more step. One last primal scream before it ended. It would be better than living in this continuous loop of memory. Liam and Clara and Mac, and all the rest of the fallen he had known. After which, these ghosts would take him again to the seventy-fifth floor of the South Tower telling him that he had a way out of this life of his. Just one more step.

BONES

His cell phone rang at seven that morning, sending needles into his brain. Bones had blacked out the previous night, his mind finally having had enough of consciousness. Drinking into oblivion was his substitute for sleep. Still in a stupor, he clumsily reached for the phone.

"Hello, Mr. Bones," the female caller said.

The stranger's voice was enough to shake Bones back to some degree of sobriety.

"Yeah, what the hell do you want?" he said.

His brain was still on fire as he tried to place the caller.

"This is Rose Knox, Clara's mother," she said.

Clara's mother? A cold slap awakened him from his vaporous gloom.

"I got your number from a Detective Sullivan...after he told me about Clara."

Bones rolled up from the bed, but his legs gave way and he fell back onto the mattress. He could feel a pounding headache starting to make itself known.

"Yes, Mrs. Knox, I'm very sorry about Clara," Bones said solemnly.

"It's just Miss Knox. Mr. Knox is nowhere in the picture. Just kept the last name to make it less confusing for Clara. I suppose that doesn't make a difference now."

Bones could hear the Midwest steel in her voice. Rose Knox was not about to show any emotional wavering. He might very well have been speaking to Clara.

It had been five days since Woodstock. That sickening day. The bottle had been his only escape, only now Clara's mother was on the phone.

"Your daughter was a wonderful woman," Bones finally replied, regretting how trite he sounded.

"Mr. Bones. I know who my daughter is...was. And, yes, there was a wonder about her, but she was severely ill. She never recovered from the assault. Became someone I didn't recognize. I loved her deeply, but a mother's love wasn't enough for her."

Bones nodded into the phone. He understood all too well. He held back from telling Rose Knox that *his* love for her daughter was also not enough. Not nearly enough.

"As I said, I spoke with Detective Sullivan, who told me that Clara died in a fire," Rose said. "He didn't say much of anything else, but all those people, you know, on the internet, have made my Clara into some sort of monster..."

"Miss Knox, you shouldn't pay any attention to those parasites. They never knew Clara. Their drivel is just a way for them to feel better about themselves."

"I appreciate your kindness," she said. "But you had a relationship with Clara. You knew her."

"I did love Clara," Bones said quietly. "To be honest though, I don't think I ever knew her."

"Then I am sorry for you, Mr. Bones," Rose said. "It could not have been easy being in love with my daughter."

Rose Knox was a most unusual woman, but Bones was still confused about what it was she wanted from him.

Rose got to her point. "I am calling, Mr. Bones, to ask you a question."

"A question...and what is that, Miss Knox?"

"Clara spoke about you when she came back to Willow Brook that last time. She told me that you were a good man. That she believed in you. She never did have men in her life that she could say that about."

Bones shut his eyes, powerless to stop Clara's ghost from entering his mind. The booze had helped, but here was Rose Knox opening that door.

"Clara also told me that you would help her," Rose continued. "What was that about, Mr. Bones?"

Bones wasn't sure what to say.

"She believed that somehow I could save her," he said finally. "But I was too late. I'm very sorry."

Bones heard what he thought was a sob coming through the phone. A quick beat of emotion that was instantly suppressed.

"I was also wondering if you might join me for a memorial service for Clara," Rose said, the steel back in her voice. "Clara deserved a proper service. A proper goodbye."

Bones sighed. He could not refuse this woman. "Yes, she does deserve that."

"Thank you, Mr. Bones," Rose said. "You were someone who cared about my Clara, loved her..."

Bones paused, gazing at Clara's ghost beside him.

"I still do, Miss Knox," he said softly. "I still do."

BONES

Willow Brook might have been a town born from a Norman Rockwell painting, though Clara once told Bones the place better belonged in some *Twilight Zone* episode. This small-town USA was inhabited by aliens intent on creating chaos by way of their unceasing gossip—creatures that were, in reality, once her friends. Almost all of them were there at the memorial service and still living in Willow Brook.

Bones presence had an immediate effect as he walked into the chapel. He sensed lines of eyeballs checking him out from across the pews, that and the tittering talk coming from some young women huddled in the corner of the sanctuary.

The service was all about "Willow Brook Clara." The vivacious high schooler that everyone loved and admired and was envious of—a person destined for something special. So said her former friends and classmates that took to the podium. Bones listened, bearing with their mostly saccharine and disingenuous eulogies. He suspected that Clara's old friends were more interested in spreading vicious gossip about the Clara who left Willow Brook for the perilous, foreign enclaves of New York, prattling on how they weren't surprised at all how she ended up.

Bones then noticed an older man sitting in a corner pew. He recognized him from a photo Clara once showed him. Wendell Knox. Her father was considerably older than his photograph, with a shock of white hair, bent and tired and sad. Sitting next to him was a young girl, maybe fourteen or fifteen with red hair and freckles. Clara and the girl had inherited their father's emerald green eyes. Clara had told him the story: her father's affair, then bolting out of town with his pregnant seventeen-year-old intern named Sahara. Rumor had it that Sahara soon met a musician and left her dad with the one-year-old. She had grown up to be this pretty teenager.

Bones chose not to feel sorry for Wendell Knox, not with all the pain he'd caused for Clara and Rose. He also decided not to reflect too deeply on the man's transgressions given his own sins.

After the hour-long service capped by the church chorus's rendition of "Amazing Grace," Bones went up to Rose, who thanked him for coming. As usual, she was short on sentiment, but he could see her eyes brimming. And then he leaned over and kissed her on the cheek. The move surprised them both with Bones unsure whether to apologize for his overstep. Rose then took his hand in hers.

"Thank you for being here," she said again, and wistfully smiled.

Bones nodded. They both knew that he had no choice but to come to Willow Brook. Perhaps Clara's ghost would let him rest now.

Bones picked up his coat and hat, moving past the aisles crowded with Clara's old friends still watching his every move. Then a man came up from behind to introduce himself. He said his name was Billy Bruster. Bones recalled his name—Clara's boyfriend in high school. He found it hard to connect her to this crew-cut bruiser.

"Mr. Bones, I know you and Clara were together."

Billy was already visibly anxious, unsure what he was doing approaching PJ Bones.

"But Clara was in town a couple of days before...she died. She called me earlier from wherever she was, letting me know she was coming back home. To see me."

Bones was mystified. "To see you? Why?"

"Well, that's it. Mr. Bones. I admit that I still carried a torch for Clara. She's always known how easy it was to get me fired up about her."

Bones nodded knowingly, not at all surprised at Billy's comment.

"But then she asked me to build something for her. Just weird. She had an idea—a drawing—for this sort of—'thing.' That's what she called it."

Billy pulled from his pocket a rough pencil sketch of a long iron rod that was joined to a bulbous-shaped piece of metal. The other end of the rod was connected to a steel plate. The drawing also included a picture of what looked like a crank and motor.

"I had no idea what this was for," he said nervously.

Bones sensed something foreboding in the sanctuary. He looked at Billy, pale and troubled. Billy felt the sinister change in the air as well.

"Mr. Bones. I know all about Clara and the maniac and the stories they are telling about her," Billy said. "Honestly, I don't believe any of that crap, but I was knocked for a loop to see her here in Willow Brook. Then she was with me, all friendly-like as if we were back in high school. She asked whether I could help her, me being a welder. I agreed to make this thing for her...whatever it is."

"What is it that you think you made, Billy?" Bones asked, intently eyeing the drawing.

"I mean, it looks like one of those long rods that swing under an old fancy clock. You know."

"Yes. I know."

"Mr. Bones..."

"A pendulum, Billy. You built a pendulum."

Both men stood there, trying to make sense of this thing that Clara wanted from Billy. Enough so to return to Willow Brook.

"And there was something else she told me she needed," Billy said. "A chemical compound we use to break down metals."

Bones waited for the rest.

"Sulfuric acid," he said tightly. "Clara said she needed sulfuric acid."

Bones' face tightened.

"I probably should have walked away from Clara given all the talk about her, but she has that way about her, you know. Well...had a way about her."

"Yes, I know," Bones said. "Anyway, it makes no difference now that she's gone."

"I guess," Billy said, hesitating. "I still miss her though."

Bones understood, patted the man on his shoulder—the only sympathy he could muster—and turned to leave the chapel.

Gusts of cold air struck him as he stepped outside. Bones was glad to have come here. Rose Knox was a remarkable woman. But his talk about Clara with Billy Bruster gnawed at him as he left the chapel. His gut feeling was telling him something was wrong. He shook his head. Even in death, Clara haunted him.

He just needed to let her go.

BONES

It had been three weeks since his trip to Kansas. Bones was feeling better, finally, leaving Clara's ghost behind and finding refuge in his work. He had pushed aside the drinking and already the mental fog was fading. There were still the struggles with his fifteen-hundred words a day, but he was determined to finish what he started. Find closure to his book along with this chapter of his life. And move on.

Bones saw an email had come through from Milo Beckett. They had hardly spoken in weeks. Beckett was more interested in writers willing to write. Bones was past his contract deadline and his agent's patience. So, the obligatory email, roughly the same message each time, asking where the hell was the manuscript? This time the message was not italicized, a sign that Beckett was losing steam with him. Bones shrugged. He told his agent that he was getting closer. Again.

Then his phone went off, the chimes jolting him from his daydreaming.

"Hey, just checking in," Thomas Sullivan said. "Hadn't heard from you in a while."

Bones wasn't surprised by the call. Sullivan had made it a point to stay in touch since Woodstock. It was the last time the two men had seen each other. Bones had gotten to appreciate the detective hiding beneath his gruff demeanor. Sullivan reminded him of Phil McBain. Another tough guy. Good heart.

The men talked for a while, keeping Poe and Clara out of the discussion. Sullivan mostly did the talking. Rising crime in the city. More budget cutbacks to the department. Same old, same old.

"Just thinking one day getting out to Woodlawn," Sullivan mentioned in passing, leaving unsaid an open invitation to Bones. It wasn't the first time he'd brought up the Bronx cemetery where Phil McBain was buried.

"Yeah, we should do that," Bones said, feeling a wave of guilt.

"Well, will give you a call sometime."

And that's how they left it as they hung up.

Bones thought about his old friend. He could hear Mac, his sardonic voice imparting his Celtic wisdom over a pint of dark ale, telling him to get his shit together. Then he would threaten to kick him in the ass if he didn't start moving on with his life. Bones had promised himself to go to the cemetery, but he had enough of death. He needed more time to find some sense of peace, and then he'd visit Mac.

Bones leaned back to his computer, trying to get his mind in sync with Sam Rock's—but his concentration was interrupted by a rustling sound outside his apartment door. He got up from the desk and ambled over, poking his eye into the peephole. He saw Mel, the building staffer, walking away toward the floor elevator.

Bones opened the door and saw the letter Mel had just delivered. The envelope rested on the door saddle, pink and welcoming, the kind that contained the usual Christmas card, but it wasn't yet that time of year.

Bones brought the letter inside the apartment. It was addressed to him but with no return address. He carefully unsealed the envelope. It contained a single unsigned Post-it with an image.

An emoji.

The face had two dots for eyes and an umbrella-shaped mouth.

A frowning face.

POE

Chapter 20
'Leaving Woodstock'

I didn't have a good feeling at all after New York and only had myself to blame. I had been too sloppy. The public knifing, dodging the police, then dumping my bloody clothes for the windbreaker and Yankee cap. How lame was that? I see that I'd fired up the tabloid front pages again along with the social media rabble, but it wasn't publicity I was looking for. I had other matters on my mind.

So, a change of plan. I needed to hightail it back to Woodstock. It wouldn't be long before police tracked me there. Clara was not sympathetic when I called and told her about my outing in the city. My beautiful Clara certainly had a sailor's mouth when she's angry, but this was no time for a lovers' quarrel. We both needed to adjust on the fly.

The hikers had been no match for my easy smile and invitation for some fresh water. Lacing the drink with roofies did the trick. The old reliable. It was disappointing not to have spent more time with them. They seemed a nice enough couple and we might well have bonded, but life was not on their side. I tied them face to face in a lovers' embrace. I thought a nice touch. There was the usual "I-don't-want-to-die" pleading from the girl when I doused them both with the gasoline. She needed to get over it and face reality. I admit that the plan was ragged with no subtlety. It just would have to do for the short run, but I gave myself props for thinking on my feet. The two would suffice as stand-ins for Clara and me.

I'd found what I needed. Two large bags of ammonium nitrate fertilizer used for gardening that the owners had stored away. I also managed to siphon gas from a neighbor's truck the previous night, filling a five-gallon can. I was not a big fan of Timothy McVeigh's, but the mix would do the trick.

The gas oven had nicely filled the cottage as I left my new friends looking all terrified and such. I didn't expect quite the blast when I hoisted the torch into the place. The explosion sent me flying. It shook me up for sure. I imagine the hikers also had a rough time.

I flagged down a driver speeding by, and he stopped short seeing the woods ablaze with the cottage burning in the distance. And then there was me, looking like the panicky survivor. Then I called the Woodstock firehouse to give them the bad news. Just a terrible firestorm raging in the woods outside of town. They should come quickly.

POE AND CLARA

Poe was glad to see his childhood home still standing after all the running around on the property by the police—not that he was the nostalgic type, only that the crumbling cabin made for a perfect hideout. The surroundings were all too familiar with the dirt yard, the dense woods, and swamplands. Poe could see the sandbar from the cabin. A stranger might mistakenly take the stretch of sand for an oasis in the middle of the dark swamp waters. Of course, looks were deceiving as Poe liked to joke.

His childhood home had lost some of its character after police had dug up the yard and found Tre and Jenny's bodies. No doubt they'd had their work cut out for themselves removing Travis' corpse from the fireplace and then raising McBain from the swamp. Poe laid bets the NYPD was not coming back even if they suspected he was still alive. What deranged person on the run would take up residence again in such an uninhabitable place? He laughed at the thought.

Poe was suddenly alert. He saw a figure coming up to his place from down the road. Then he smiled. Clara had returned after her trip to Kansas.

"My love, welcome," he called out as she came up to the cabin. He had contacted Clara in Willow Brook to tell her of the change in plans. Forget returning to Woodstock. They would meet here. Criminals returning to the scene of the crime, he joked.

Clara gave him a jaundiced look as she sagged onto the porch steps. She had been traveling straight for the past twenty-four hours, moving between the cross-country bus trip back to New York and then the cab ride out to Long Island.

She had told the driver to drop her off at the old cemetery, getting his condolences while keeping him away from Poe's house. The two-mile hike to the cabin wasn't made easier with the large package that weighed her down.

"This shithole never looked better," Clara said derisively, scrutinizing the dilapidated cabin and pockmarked grounds.

"Well, as they say, home sweet home." Poe grinned, pressing up to her on the cabin steps.

"Your 'home' looks more like a bad accident," Clara said, pointing to the yellow police tape that wound around the cabin and much of the property.

"I thought it gave the place some charm," Poe said dryly.

Clara smirked. "Well, no doubt this is the last place police will look to find us."

"Why would they be looking for us at all?" Poe asked. "We are both dead. Died in the fire."

"It was stupid, Poe," Clara said sharply. "First the guy in New York and then those other two. You were supposed to be invisible. Woodstock was so very fucked up. That was not our plan."

"I had no choice, Clara," Poe said. "New York was unavoidable—some good citizen playing hero. An idiot. Then the police were onto me. The Woodstock fire covered our tracks. The bodies did."

Poe touched Clara's cheek. "We are better off being dead," he said.

Clara turned her head, peering out at the swamp waters and the distant sandbar. "Dead," she repeated absently.

Poe glanced down at the sealed box next to her.

"I see you were successful, yes?" he said.

Clara let go of a previous thought.

"What do you think?" she said testily. "Billy Bruster was easy."

"Yes, I imagine he's still walking around with a hard-on. Probably believed he had a second shot with you."

Clara thinly smiled. "Yeah, some big man on campus. Billy told me after our graduation that his fondest high school memory was fondling my breasts. So sad."

"Well, you do have memorable tits, Clara." "Yeah, well, you should know," Clara said caustically.

"Of course." Poe let out a short laugh. "I'm deeply appreciative."

Clara rolled her eyes. "Poe, get your mind focused now. We have serious work to do."

"Yes," he said, patting the box sitting between them. "Do we have everything?"

"Billy was good for one thing. This looks perfect for our plan."

Poe leaned over and opened the box. Then he pulled out a four-foot-long iron rod attached to a rounded metal piece. The shaft was fixed to a two-foot-square steel plate. The box also stored a small motor with an on/off switch. And a wooden crank.

Poe got to his feet and held the contraption over his head, watching the rod swing freely from the metal plate.

"I'll need to first brace the plate into the barn ceiling and then reconnect the shaft," Poe said.

"So, this will work?" Clara asked.

"Yes. But then we'll need to find another *incentive* to motivate Mr. Bones."

Clara stared icily at Poe.

"That was not part of the plan," Clara snapped. "It is not necessary."

"We need to make sure he shows up," Poe said.

"Bones will come," Clara said. "He has no choice, really."

"And what if he brings the entire NYPD with him? What then?"

"Poe, leave this to me!" she said sharply. "I *know* PJ Bones."

Poe narrowly eyed Clara. "I hope you are not misjudging human nature," he said.

Clara's jaw tightened. "Bones will come—he will come for me. We don't need to complicate this."

Poe paused. "Of course he will," he finally said.

"And Poe. No other *incentive*. Do you understand?"

"Of course, Clara. I understand perfectly."

Chapter 21
'The Stalking'

Clara was a sensible woman, but she did not understand human nature. That was my specialty. People like PJ Bones seek to save "the innocent" from the likes of me. Not someone like Clara Knox. She was too... complicated. I could not count on his make-believe hero complex or his pathetic feelings for Clara. I planned to give him some other reason to come find Clara and save her.

At the crack of dawn, I quietly slipped out of bed, glancing over at my lover. Clara was an angel when she slept. Then I made my way out of the cabin and climbed into my father's old truck.

The risks were in front of me, but, hey, what is life about if not taking the jump? I headed west on the expressway to a massive mall in Nassau County named after a president. I was counting on the Santas, the Christmas shoppers, and all the tinsel and piped-in happy ho-ho-ho crap. Enough to make you puke, but a good cover. Always best to strike when the fools were distracted.

Still, it was risky business driving the run-down Chevy with its twenty-year-old expired plates. I'd managed to get the thing running, but it was easy enough to see it catching the eye of some industrious cop. I had already killed a cop, so one more would hardly make a difference, but why stir up another hornets' nest—not yet anyway.

I expected the truck would work well enough for the one-way trip to the mall. The other risk was making my snatch in broad daylight. Really for amateurs, but I saw no point beating myself up. Every plan needs a bit of tweaking. I admit being a bit annoyed with Clara's attitude. She needed to go with the flow.

I did my best with the disguise sporting a hunter's cap over my wig. I even fashioned a phony beard, hardly a convincing cover, but I figured that a shopping mall wasn't the first place cops would be looking for a serial killer, and mall security wasn't exactly the FBI.

Next was finding "the right one." I relied on my old formula. Someone vulnerable and accessible.

I arrived at the shopping center and managed to find a parking spot. Holiday shoppers were already in full throttle that morning, so the place was jammed. I made my way into the mall, the consumer catacombs beckoning customers with the promise of material bliss, a façade meant to shield them from their monotonous, insignificant existence.

It was tough going with the bustling crowds, and I was growing impatient and thinking I had made a mistake coming to the place. That is when the brunette with a long ponytail sauntered by. About twenty-five, busty, a swing to her hips. Likely had an attitude that she was hot shit. Well, no matter. I followed her for the next half-hour. She was already loaded down with a few stuffed shopping bags but wasn't through, making her way into a cosmetic shop. I peered through the window and could see her examining a line of lipsticks. She picked up one and coated her lips in blood red. A prophetic sign. She was the perfect choice.

I followed her down an escalator and out to the parking area to the far end of the lot. The woman seemed happily content as she opened the door to her Corolla, putting her bags in the back seat. She never knew what hit her when I tackled her onto the seat.

I could see she was about to scream but the knife to her face shut her up pronto. Then my standard punchline. "Quiet, and you won't be hurt." I could see hope shooting from her eyes. Maybe thinking she just needed to give up her pocketbook, maybe the thousand dollars' worth of Christmas crap.

She played it cool until I applied the chloroform. Then she struggled with the wet cloth on her blood-red lips, that familiar terror in her eyes. About fifteen seconds later, I suppose the pleasant smell of the liquid made her relax before the chemicals finally knocked her out.

I took the car key locked in her fist and left her sprawled in the back seat. Then I settled in behind the wheel and made my way onto the Long Island Expressway for the two-hour drive back to the cabin.

Clara was waiting as I pulled the car into the yard.

"Poe, we don't need her!" Clara shouted, furious at the sight of the unconscious woman in the back seat. "Why fuck up our plan?"

Clara glared at me with those steely killer eyes. She always had a mind of her own—that's what I loved about her. But she just did not understand human nature.

I wondered what PJ Bones would think to find his lovely Clara alive. Kind of a mix of relief and hatred, I imagine. But would he risk playing the hero once more after what had happened to his detective friend? And this after Clara left him high and dry, only to be with me? Salt on the wound for sure.

"She will help us with our virtuous Mr. Bones," I said. "Besides, I can use her assistance over at the barn."

"I have my way to bring Bones here," Clara snapped. "Take her back, now!"

We spent the next few minutes going back and forth, but there was no sense in arguing. I threw my arms out as if to concede the battle, and told Clara I would return the woman to the mall after dark.

It was enough to satisfy her. "Good. Better this way," she said.

By then, the woman had come around, overhearing our conversation through the car's open window.

"Thank you, *thank you*," she cried out.

Clara grimaced and nodded to the brunette. I thought she was about to apologize for inconveniencing her. I held back a laugh and went over to the poor woman and stroked her face. She needed some comforting.

The woman jerked back as if I'd tased her.

Clara narrowly eyed me, still angry, and silently turned back into the cabin, leaving me alone with our guest.

The woman stared at me with her deer-in-the-headlight look.

"Everything will be all right," I whispered in her ear.

Then I gave her a reassuring smile.

POE

Chapter 22
'Edgar's Pendulum'

I felt a twinge of regret having lied to Clara. It was wrong deceiving the woman you love—and I was passionate about Clara. I had hungered for her when she was away in Kansas, growing more bitter each day by her absence. I might have cut up that Billy Bruster for having once touched Clara, but we'd needed him for our plan. And, PJ Bones, well, he had no idea what fate awaited him. But soon.

This woman would give Bones another reason to play the hero. I could not count on Clara alone to lure the man. "He will come to find me because he has no choice," she'd told me. I understood her absolute confidence, caught in her spell as well, but our Mr. Bones wasn't a fool. He had been burnt too often. And I had no use having his police friends storming in, all interested in seeing me dead.

Bones would surely come now, alone. Even with the tough guy attitude, he believed in the hero crap he wrote. Saving the innocent. That wasn't Clara.

So, I waited that evening. Clara was still recovering from her long trip and had gone to bed. I bid her a good night, assuring her that I would soon take care of the woman. I wasn't exactly lying. Clara was suspicious but too tired to continue our argument.

I slipped out of the cabin and made my way through the dirt field, careful not to trip into the deep holes left after police had exhumed Jenny and Tre's bodies. Then I went into the old barn on the property. There was the young woman, wide awake, strapped to a steel platform where I had left her. She started to squirm when she saw me approach but calmed down once I put a finger to my lips. Maybe she felt assured that she was going back to her boring normal life that night. I understood, given my promise to Clara. Of course, the woman swore that she'd keep our "misunderstanding" secret. I expressed the proper gratitude for her discretion, though I might have been less than candid about my intentions. I still needed her assistance. I mean, all successful ventures require some sacrifice.

But we had some time to kill before then.

I found out her name, Lorelei Swallow, from her driver's license, and smiled at a few pictures of her cats that she also kept in her wallet. No boyfriend apparently, but I did come across a SAG card, so Lorelei was an actress. Likely the femme fatale. She with her sleepy seductress eyes and come-hither attitude.

I came up next to her and she became twitchy, maybe thinking I was about to take advantage. But I didn't want to rush things and was more interested in chatting. You know, break the ice.

"Have you ever read Edgar Allan Poe?" I asked.

"What, Edgar...who?"

I thought she might be pulling my leg. But she wasn't, so a bit disappointing.

I pulled out my well-worn book of short stories.

"Lorelei, listen to this one," I told her. "Edgar was a great storyteller. And what a perfect night for his story. I mean, you being here—it's as if Edgar's tale has come to life. It's about a prisoner, tied onto a platform just like the one you are on now, and then the strangest circumstance as he faces a huge pendulum suspended above him. Oh, but I am giving away the story."

Lorelei, her brow crinkled, gave me a confused, worried look.

"I don't know what you mean," she said quaking. "What are you talking about?"

"Listen!" and I began to read.

> ...Looking upward, I surveyed the ceiling of my prison. It was some thirty or forty feet overhead...There was something, however, in the appearance of this machine which caused me to regard it more attentively. While I gazed upward at it (for its position was immediately over my own) I fancied that I saw it in motion. Its sweep was brief, and of course slow. I watched it for some minutes, somewhat in fear, but more in wonder....What I then saw confounded and amazed me. The sweep of the pendulum had increased in extent by nearly a yard. As a natural consequence, its velocity was also much greater. But what mainly disturbed me was the idea that it had perceptibly descended. I now observed—with what horror it is needless to say—that its nether extremity was formed of a crescent of glittering steel...and the under edge evidently as keen as that of a razor...

> Down—steadily down it crept...It vibrated within three inches of my

> bosom! I struggled violently, furiously...Down—still unceasingly — still inevitably down! I gasped and struggled at each vibration. I shrunk convulsively at its every sweep. My eyes followed its outward or upward whirls...they closed themselves spasmodically at the descent, although death would have been a relief, oh! how unspeakable! Still I quivered in every nerve to think how slight a sinking of the machinery would precipitate that keen, glistening axe upon my bosom.

"Excuse me, mister." Lorelei had intruded on my recitation. "But when can I go home?"

I guess I was taxing Lorelei's patience. Obviously, she did not fully understand the story. Or her place in it.

"Of course, I always imagined what it would be like—to witness Edgar's masterpiece!" I said.

I turned back to Lorelei. I didn't think she was listening.

But it was time.

I left her side and went over to a tall ladder. I climbed to the top of the barn. Then I removed a bedsheet that draped the large mechanical piece.

"Look. Edgar's pendulum." I called out to her. "And not an ordinary one, I can assure you. Incredible, yes?"

I stepped down from the ladder, and we both spent the next minute gazing at this strange object hanging ominously from the barn ceiling. I had to admire my handiwork even if

Lorelei seemed much less appreciative. I suppose that was to be expected.

"*Please*, I just want to go home," she cried out.

"Yes, you will be home soon enough," I assured her.

Lorelei continued to gape at the looming iron fist twenty-five feet above her. I saw a flash of recognition on her face. Lorelei finally understood. And then she started screaming, wildly shaking, trying to free herself from the straps tying her down. I could see the fear lighting up her eyes. She was seeing Edgar's story differently now, and no doubt bad thoughts were flickering in her mind.

"Oh, my god!" she gasped.

I nodded, gratified that she was giving me the proper respect.

"Now let me show you how it works," I said. "See, that pendulum is held by a metal plate that I've attached to the ceiling. This switch turns on the electric motor that starts it in motion. This crank allows me to lower the pendulum, so you can get a really good look as it comes closer. Let me show you."

I pushed the switch to the motor and the pendulum started to whir and then slowly begin its swing. Within less than a minute it was forcefully cutting across the air. Lorelei seemed hypnotized, her eyes following the sweep of the metal shaft. I then rotated the crank handle and the pendulum dropped several feet. The move startled Lorelei, and I could see her face had lost all color. Edgar's nightmare was coming to life and descending upon her.

"Please...don't..." she cried out.

"Oh, you might be wondering about the sharp bottom of the shaft," I explained. "These are the razors from my private collection." I didn't want to boast, but it hadn't been easy cutting the metal edges from my tool-set and then soldering them onto the bottom of the pendulum.

I turned the crank again and the pendulum fell another foot.

Lorelei lurched as the monstrous mechanism plunged closer toward her.

"Dear lord in heaven. NO, NO, NO!"

Lorelei's distress was understandable, but she must have found clarity to her life knowing that her death was imminent.

"I think it's better if you take a closer look," I told her.

Then I taped Lorelei's mouth. There was no need to create a racket and disturb Clara's sleep.

I went back to the crank handlebar. The pendulum's powerful swing drew sharply closer to the woman. In that moment, Lorelei reminded me of one of those forest creatures I'd captured as a kid, caught in my trap, crazed, frantically trying to break free. There she was, her body snapping back and forth on the platform—did she really believe she could escape from the descending blade? I suppose she needed to try.

I waited a moment and turned the crank again. The pendulum continued on its unrelenting downward path. Lorelei lifted her head transfixed at the sight of my splendid mechanism about to slice her open. Suddenly, she was back in motion, violently pounding her head against the steel platform, her screams muffled by the tape.

The razor-sharp blade glinted as it flashed by Lorelei's face. And, then, she was still-bound, all fight was gone. I could see that Lorelei had finally come to grips with her fate, the time when she was about to die.

Then I turned the crank handle and the pendulum dropped one last time.

POE

Chapter 23
'Poor Lorelei'

I expected that Clara would be enraged when she awoke that morning. I brought her coffee in bed and then told her that Lorelei had stayed the previous night. It was odd though when we walked into the barn afterward. Clara stared at what remained of Lorelei Swallow, her mutilated body hanging off the platform where I'd left her.

Clara's silence was unnerving.

"Poe, this was not our plan." she finally said. "This was not meant for her."

"Well, it is satisfying to see that it works," I said, taking a closer look at the pendulum still embedded in Lorelei's face. "But I will need to make adjustments."

It hadn't gone perfectly. The pendulum had swung erratically once it hit Lorelei, creating a slew of haphazard cuts to her body and head. The razors were intended to saw straight through her chest bone to sever her heart. A simple clean surgical cut. Seven, eight swings would have done it, but the pendulum was not stable enough at its metal base to prevent it from moving wildly.

It looked like Lorelei had been attacked by a half-dozen chainsaws.

"This is a mess," Clara hissed. "Her face is unrecognizable."

The blade had cut Lorelei's face into separate pieces, looking much like a puzzle that needed to be joined together. A pity, I thought, given her once-good looks.

"Every bit of flesh and tissue has been cut off her chest," Clara said bitterly.

Clara glared at me and maybe even considered strapping me down to the platform. She might have if she hadn't loved me.

"The woman has just been butchered, Poe," she said. "What kind of person would do this?"

I assumed Clara knew me better by now.

"Well, she can have Tre's old grave," I said, a conciliatory gesture on my part.

Clara's body coiled, and I thought she was about to strike me.

Best to move on, no use arguing over spilled blood, I was about to tell her—but I didn't think she'd appreciate the joke.

"There will be no more surprises, Poe."

Clara's face had turned vacant except for her translucent eyes. They glistened sharply. Like daggers, as the expression goes. And I felt a chill standing next to her.

BONES AND SULLIVAN

The suspected kidnapping out in Long Island at first did not get Thomas Sullivan's attention. That would be the business of the Nassau County police now looking for a fire-engine-red Mazda CX5 belonging to a Miss Lorelei Swallow of Long Beach. She had been last seen as a shopping mall and was reported missing. The search of the mall parking lot found an abandoned, beaten-down Chevy truck with expired plates that was tracked to the late Edward Ultrecht, the father of Daemon Ultrecht, both reported to be deceased. It was that last piece of information that got Sullivan's attention. Then the detective called PJ Bones.

Bones was finally clearheaded, safely ensconced in his fiction and off the booze. He even thought he had figured out his serial killer. He wasn't especially happy with his heroic conclusion, but at least the pieces fit. Sam Rock triumphed, the killer was caught, justice prevailed. Bones expected he would be done after polishing up the pages. Milo Beckett wasn't exactly jumping for joy at the news—his contracted writer was now four months late on the promised manuscript—yet relieved nonetheless.

But here was Sullivan on the phone.

"Bones, you might be interested," Sullivan said tersely. "Our friend might be back."

"What do you mean?" Bones said.

"It means we were wrong, PJ," Sullivan said. "Dead wrong."

Sullivan told Bones about the missing woman and Ultrecht's truck. Could Poe be alive? And if that was true, was Clara?

Not that Bones was entirely shocked to hear the news. He had decided not to tell Sullivan about the anonymous Post-it message—a frown-face emoji—willfully erasing the note from his memory. That and everything else about Clara Knox. He needed Clara dead to survive. In his mind, he insisted on it.

Sullivan interrupted his thoughts. "We already got a court order for the exhumation up at Woodstock. My hunch—the bodies are not our two. We were too quick to believe they had been killed in the fire but the forensics were inconclusive."

"Sully, you don't have anything," Bones said sharply. "They looked quite dead to me up at Woodstock. And if they were alive, why would they make themselves known now? With the heat off, they could just be gone."

"Bones, these are sick individuals. Poe *and* Clara. They can't stop. And if they are still breathing, we will find them and then there will be no holding back."

Bones understood the message. The NYPD was most interested in retribution.

"You're way ahead on your skis on this one," Bones said. "The only thing you have is some old truck and a missing person. You've added that up to conclude that Poe and Clara are alive and on the prowl. And then randomly kidnap a woman, a Lorelei Swallow, in broad daylight at a shopping mall. I wouldn't even use this detective work in my book."

"Well, PJ, I got a bad feeling about this one," Sullivan said plainly. "And I think you do, too."

"Damnit, Sully, I've had enough of Daemon Ultrecht and Clara Knox," Bones snapped. "They are dead and buried as far as I'm concerned. I've moved on. I didn't realize just how deep into the shit I was before. I barely made it out of that hell. I need to stay out."

"So, you think all this is over for you then?"

Bones heard Sullivan's unspoken message.

He was also deserting Mac.

"Poe and Clara are dead, Sully. Case closed."

"I suppose it is for you," Sullivan said wearily. "But I don't think so."

BONES

PJ Bones agonized over whether the ghost of Clara Knox would finally leave him in peace. She haunted him. With all the other ghosts. Some existential joke that was his life. He thought he could find an escape into his fictional world, and so he wrote his books. This was where he found resolution. The world could be made right. And all it took was three hundred pages of lies.

But Clara Knox. She may very well have been a fictional character that somehow had materialized—poof, a dream girl that loved him. He had let his guard down believing she actually existed. Needing her to fill the void. This Clara.

He should have known better.

With Clara gone though he stood a chance. The fire that killed her had freed him from her grasp. It was over, finally. This woman—his obsession—that had taken over his life. But then her siren's call. The anonymous Post-it. Then Sully's call—and the possibility that she was still alive! He swiped away those possibilities. Better a ghost than someone he could touch and feel. Someone too real. He was better off believing in things that he could just make up, feeling safe in his lies.

So, when his phone chimed later than evening, he refused to answer the call…ringing, ringing…but he knew that she would never leave him in peace…ringing, ringing…until this was finally over…ringing, ringing…

There were no safe lies he could hide behind…ringing, ringing…

Only the reality that existed on the other side of the call…ringing, ringing…

He never stood a chance…
And, so, Bones picked up the phone.

BONES AND CLARA

Bones was astonished at first, seeing her sitting at the corner table as he entered the dimly lit restaurant tucked away in Garden City, a well-heeled Long Island community. Clara Knox was very much alive. A ghost in the flesh. He walked over to her table and sat down across from her. A glass of red wine was already waiting for him.

Clara looked older than Bones remembered. Gone was her buoyant innocence that enchanted him that evening long ago at Barnes & Noble. And then everything else that happened that night. Her porcelain face was paler than he remembered, but still this Irish lovely. When she spoke, the lightness of her voice was gone. Bones supposed that was the price for hanging around with a serial killer. He found nothing funny about his observation, just confused why she had called. What Clara wanted from him. And why he had decided to come, after all of this.

Clara reached across to take his hand, gently squeezing it, welcoming him back to her life. Bones remembered the spark from her touch and felt that energy spike through his body again. But he needed to survive and pulled his hand away.

"What am I doing here?" Bones asked angrily. He had no intention to make this a lovers' reunion.

Clara looked across the table, measuring her words. "I need your help, PJ."

Bones fixed his gaze on the woman. "I seem to remember that you called, asking for my help," he said. "That was before you died in the fire."

Clara's face tightened. "PJ. You were going to help me."

"But, Clara, why would you think I would ever help you now? I saw the corpses you left behind in Woodstock."

"That was Poe," Clara said quietly.

"And the missing Long Beach woman? Where is she now? Lorelei Swallow, I believe that's her name. Have any idea?"

Clara hesitated, then dabbed at her eyes with a napkin.

"Clara, spare me!" Bones seethed. "What makes you better than your lover?"

It was then a waiter came by, prepared to recite the restaurant's "special" entrees. Bones waved him away. He wasn't planning on staying.

"Why are you here then?" Clara asked.

"That's the question I had for you," Bones said.

"I told you on the phone what I needed from you."

Bones could hear the coolness back in her voice.

"Then you will never see me again," she said.

Bones looked across the table, the candlelight flickering off Clara's face. He fought to suppress old feelings starting to take hold of him again. He was little more than a cliché. Some middle-aged, worn-out writer out of control in his own life's fiction—not that the revelation did him much good looking across the table at her. This Irish lovely.

He could not find a way out.

Bones shut his eyes, shaking his head absently. Before saying another word, he reached across to the wine and drained the glass.

Bones' first thought was that the port wine had a salty edge. He licked his lips, trying to make sense of the taste, but then he understood. His instincts told him to fight the feeling as the room started to spin, but by then it was too late.

Clara threw some cash onto the table, quickly moving over to Bones' side. The roofie had hit him hard, maybe too hard, and Clara was worried that she wouldn't be able to navigate Bones outside the restaurant. He had at least seventy-five pounds on her, all dead weight, as she stood him up and placed his arm around her shoulder.

"An easy drunk," she told the waiter, pointing to the wine glass. Clara added a wry smile, hoping her jest landed.

Patrons nodded sympathetically at the slight woman contending with her inebriated husband. The blue-blooded Garden City crowd likely agreed that the old boozer didn't deserve such a stunning young wife.

The maître-d' smiled tightly, opening the door for the two patrons. Certainly, good riddance, making a mental note of the pair for future reference.

Clara managed to bring Bones into the parking area and then bundled him into the Mazda CX5, Lorelei's car. Bones was on the edge of consciousness, mumbling. "Wher'r we go...?" But his world went dark before he could finish his question.

Clara strapped him into the front seat—she couldn't have him bouncing around the car. She let out a deep breath, taking a moment's satisfaction before starting the car. Everything so far was going according to plan.

POE, CLARA, AND BONES

"You did well, my love."

Poe glanced over at the unconscious man slumped over on the front seat of the car.

"Bones is just so helpless," Clara said disdainfully. "I told you. He couldn't resist meeting up with me at the restaurant. It didn't take a minute for your roofie to hit. Tough getting him out of the restaurant but we have him."

"Yes, the Special K is, well, special," Poe said, grinning. "I remember that Tre Simon also enjoyed it."

"This is different for you, isn't it?" Clara said.

Poe frowned. He hated PJ Bones. His arrogance, his fame, and then there was Clara. The thought of this man with her so easily enraged him. But there would be time enough for Bones, and he would savor the moment.

"This is different for *us*," Poe said. "And then there will be no turning back after tonight. We will be one and the same."

Clara silently gazed at Poe.

Poe was exultant that Clara would finally live in his world. "Normal" existence was an impossibility. She belonged with him, sharing his contempt for those nice people with their nice homes and nice children, their nice illusions—so desperate to hold onto the fantasy that the world was safe and sane.

That is, until he came to visit.

Poe glanced at his childhood home pressed into the hard-dirt piece of land. This is where he grew up among the swamp creatures. He, too, was a predator. The kids at the children's home sensed his threat, which was true, and that he existed in the shadows, which was also true. So, they called him names, scurrying by him, wishing that he would go back to where he came from. They didn't count on the fact that he would one day come out of the darkness and be ever-present in their lives. And here he was—the raven, powerful, deciding who lives and dies.

Clara would certainly understand. They belonged here, together. They were bound forever.

Poe inhaled, letting the cold winter air fill his lungs. He felt alive, the anticipation of what was to come that night animating him. Bones' death would be perfect. Edgar might very well depart his grave at Westminster Hall in Baltimore to spend this evening with them. Here was Edgar's brilliance—his pendulum—made real. And it was he, Poe—the living incarnation of Edgar's imaginings—that would bring his mentor's dreams to fruition.

Poe barely held back from shouting out to Edgar. The moment was rapturous. He would celebrate later, but first there was work to be done.

Then Poe went over to the car, releasing Bones from his seat belt, a move that caused him to sag and fall from the car to the ground. Poe signaled Clara, and they both took hold of Bones' legs, dragging him across the rough ground and jagged small stones and into the barn.

Bones groggily broke from his stupor, choking on the yard dirt he had swallowed. Lifting his head, he squinted at his two captors standing above him. It was Poe bending over to tie his hands and feet. His predicament was coming into focus as he fixed his eyes on the barn ceiling. A large, odd-shaped, metallic object hung from the barn ceiling some twenty-five feet above him. Bones tried to make sense of it when Poe pressed a wet cloth to his mouth, momentarily suffocating him. Then his head began to reel again before he slipped back into the dark.

Bones was roused from his chemically-induced blackout. Poe, standing atop a tall ladder, was hammering a metal plate into the ceiling, the noise filling the barn.

Poe glanced down to see Bones stirring on the barn's dirt floor.

"Just making this steady for you," he called out. "It made a horrific mess the last time we used it. I promise, you will be killed much more efficiently."

Bones struggled on the rough floor trying to free himself. He rolled over, striking a large canvas bag. The bag lay prone on the floor, opened at the top. The mangled head of a young woman was sticking out.

Bones hollered. The drugs and chloroform had nearly paralyzed his vocal cords, turning his protest into incomprehensible noise.

The dead woman's face had been cut in large slices, each piece misaligned with the next. Her forehead and eyes tilted to the left side of her head while the woman's nose and mouth seemed on the edge of falling off her face. Only her chin was in place. A ghastly, grotesque death mask.

It was then that Clara came into the barn. She looked over at Bones squirming next to the corpse, and snickered. "Well, PJ, I see you found your new lover," she said. "To think I ever let you fuck me."

Poe climbed down from the ladder, suddenly inflamed. Clara's comment had set him off. A picture now carved into his brain. Bones, his cock inside Clara, believing that she was ever his.

Clara held up her hand as he bolted over. "Not yet, Poe," she said evenly. "We will have our revenge soon enough. Let him first suffer and contemplate what is to come."

It was just enough to calm Poe down.

Bones, still drugged and frantic at the sight of the dead woman, garbled something unintelligible to Clara.

"So, at a loss for words, PJ?" Clara mocked. "Very unbecoming for a writer of your stature."

Clara then turned to Poe. "Our plan is for midnight, yes? Will you be ready?"

He nodded sharply. "Yes, the apparatus is secure now. I expect the blade to cut right through his breastbone and into the heart, severing it in half. So, how perfect a symbol is that for us, my love?"

"Yes, Bones has serious issues with his heart," Clara said stonily. "Always falling in the love with the wrong women."

Bones had stopped flailing about the dirt floor. He was resigned to rest next to the mutilated body that once contained the life of Lorelei Swallow.

POE, CLARA, AND BONES

Poe eyed the iron mechanism anchored to the barn ceiling, satisfied with his work. Clara had left. She needed to prepare herself for their midnight hour. They agreed it was the most appropriate time to bring about Bones' death.

Through a wide hole in the barn roof, a harvest moon cast an eerie glow into the barn. That sinister moon reminded Poe of that night in Woodstock, with the celestial orb spotlighting their carnal battle. Tonight, he and Clara together would destroy the man who had dared to intrude into their lives. How glorious that PJ Bones be the sacrifice to bind their eternal love!

Bones was sprawled out on the barn floor more alert now. Poe grudgingly appreciated the man's courage. He seemed reconciled to his fate. Poe had tired of the screams and pleadings from those others, content to have someone so accepting, surprisingly composed.

Poe curiously observed Bones, who was silently studying *him*. He was again struck by the man's cool bearing.

"Did your parents know that they had brought a freak into the world?" Bones said at last.

The barn instantly stilled.

Poe glared at Bones. Then he pulled a switchblade from his pant pocket and bent over his prone captive. He laid the blade across his prisoner's cheek.

"The steel feels cold, Bones, doesn't it?" Poe said darkly. "Now imagine how cold your body will become buried under the earth, food for maggots that will be overjoyed by your presence. Of course, you won't feel a thing, but it's worth thinking about the end of your meaningless life. Perhaps even appreciate these final moments before your heart is carved from your body."

"Daemon, I've always appreciated your Edgar Allan Poe impersonation. You've got it down. But face it. You are pathetic. How does it feel being such an unloved, repulsive monstrosity who comes in his pants when he kills?"

Poe squinted, stepping back from Bones. Something was wrong. The arrogance of this man. The smell of fear absent.

"Soon, Bones." Poe hissed. "It will be midnight, the witching hour for your death."

Bones smirked, looking past Poe toward the open barn door. Clara stood there, stock-still, staring at the two men.

"It's almost midnight, Poe," Clara finally said. "It's time."

Poe nodded, but he wasn't completely at ease. He had patiently bided his time these past days. Clara's plan was brilliant, luring Bones to this place. And here was the final act—but this scene is not what he'd pictured. Bones' insults and contempt bleeding out to him. His mocking contempt. Baiting him. Poe had held back from cutting his throat. Bones would feel his blade soon enough and finally understand his power. Still, he felt enraged by the man's arrogance.

Poe impulsively kicked Bones in the ribs, raising him to his feet. Then he pulled him over to the platform. It was still streaked with Lorelei's dry blood. Poe prodded Bones onto the steel slab, cinching his bound hands to a wood post before strapping down his body.

"Ah, just one more thing," Poe said. He leaned over, ripping apart Bones' shirt, exposing his torso. "Now keep still when the cutting starts. Otherwise, you will be chewed up. Better a clean slice into your body."

Poe tapped Bones on the center of his chest. "We are counting on this particular spot," Poe whispered darkly.

Bones narrowly eyed the iron fist pointing down at him from the ceiling.

Clara watched silently. Poe found her sphinxlike composure strange, but he understood—first kills are soul shaping.

It was time.

Poe turned from Bones to a switch affixed to a wood beam and snapped it on. A motor near the platform started running, the sound humming through the barn. Poe could feel the heavy pendulum begin to rock, a movement hardly perceptible at first. Slowly, the shaft gathered momentum with its mechanical swings growing wider. Poe gazed at his creation, momentarily transfixed by its hypnotic sway.

Poe waited a minute before he reached for the crank. He turned the handle and the pendulum began its slow descent from the ceiling. He waited a few minutes before another turn sent the shaft several feet closer to the platform below. It was easier now to see the pendulum's bulbous head. Visible were the glinting razors that protruded like shark teeth from the outer edge of the head.

"These blades will do a nice job for you," Poe told Bones. "I expect eight swings will be enough to fully open you up, but let's not rush ahead. We need to savor your precious final minutes."

Poe paused and then turned the crank again.

Bones started to twitch, keeping his eyes on the scimitar that now swept ten feet above him.

Poe grinned. Bones must finally be coming to grips with his horrific end, no doubt remembering Lorelei's dismembered face. Bones might have thanked him for stabilizing the pendulum with the blades aimed straight to his heart.

Poe chuckled at his joke. He grabbed the crank handle again, dropping the pendulum a few more feet, the swoosh of the mechanism cleaving through the silence in the barn. The sweep of the shaft was relentless, its descent unstoppable. Within a minute the pendulum swing was flashing within a foot of Bones' body. Bones let out a sharp yelp. His first sound since he was strapped down. Not so much a word, but a cry for mercy. That, at least, was Poe's interpretation.

Poe was radiant, his face gleaming from the moonlight snaking through the broken barn roof. He was ready for the night to end. And, finally, be forever free of PJ Bones.

"Bones, this is good. Now is not the time to hold back. You will feel better if you let it go. I promise not to hold your feeble grasp of life against you. You were always weak. Never good enough for my Clara. You must have known that. And that is why you are here. To die in her presence. To put an end to you."

"Poe."

Clara finally broke her silence and stepped from the barn's shadow.

"I will be the one."

Clara came up to Poe's side, pulling aside his hand from the crank handle.

The move was enough to startle Poe.

"Of course, Clara," Poe said, hesitating before stepping back.

Poe understood. Clara and he were meant to share this moment. Bones' death. They both needed him gone. Clara despised the man, his tortuous life, his weakness. Poe also saw through Bones' façade, his righteous anger toward the evils of the world. Dishing out the hope in his stories that "good people" were safe from the likes of him, a freak meant to be hunted and destroyed. That PJ Bones was their savior.

Bones' followers should see him now. Poe bitterly laughed.

Poe savored the cool night air seeping into the barn, waiting for Clara, and this final act to play out—to still Bones' beating heart. How perfectly fitting for her. For both of them. They would be joined forever now.

The moonlight cutting through the ravaged roof-top now hovered over Bones lying motionless on the platform. Clara gripped the crank handle and their eyes locked, a silent message passing between them.

Then Clara turned the crank, lowering the pendulum. The sweep of the large blade came within a few inches of Bones' chest.

Bones jerked sharply against the straps that held him down on the platform.

"Now, now, Bones, I can see you breathing more deeply," Poe said.

He put his hand on Clara's back. She turned to him, and Poe nodded his approval. The midnight hour had struck.

"Best to relax, try not to expand your chest," Poe said. "Hold on to these last few seconds of your life. The cutting is about to begin. The first slice will be painful of course, but not fatal. Your outer skin will be raised open. The second slice will shred what skin was left on your chest. I expect it to take five or six passes to break through your sternum. And then the prize. Your heart. Exposed. Then torn apart. Much like the rest of your miserable life."

Bones tilted his head, watching Clara. He furiously fixed his gaze on her.

"Yes, Poe," Clara said. "It is time."

Poe thought of Edgar, how proud he would be. This final chapter of his book. The death of his nemesis. His revenge fulfilled. And Clara. She is where his story began that afternoon at her apartment on Cornelia Street—he had bathed in her blood then, a sacramental bonding that foretold their future. He could see that now. Clara was meant to survive and be with him. Together, the world would come to understand the passionate, ferocious intensity of their power—and pay obeisance.

Poe instinctively touched his shoulder, caressing the raven etched into his skin. He and Clara would seal their vows with Bones' death, the knife, this time, in her hand. She, too, would feel the rush that comes with the killing.

They were so much alike.

Poe broke from his ruminations to turn to Clara. He was mystified. Clara's head was bent, her eyes closed as if in prayer. This was not a moment of sacrifice but of triumph.

The pendulum continued its sweep, a hair's breadth from missing Bones with each pass. A shadow flickered across Bones' face as the swinging blade blotted out the moonlight seeping into the barn. A second of time between the light and the darkness.

Clara then reached under her coat to pull out a small glass vial of liquid. She scrutinized the bottle as if it were a foreign object. Her brow creased, deliberating her next move.

Poe looked at her, perplexed. The time had come...

Clara unsealed the vial.

...to end the existence of PJ Bones.

Then Clara stepped in front of Poe and hurled the liquid into his eyes.

A full second of utter confusion stormed Poe's mind. It took that long for the sulfuric acid to make itself known.

Then his screams shattered the silence.

Poe's bellows rose high out of the barn and into the black sky. He collapsed to the floor, frantically crying out. One long screeching syllable of excruciating pain. He tore at his eyes already dissolving into a mushy substance. Then he ripped off his shirt, scrubbing the cloth against his eye sockets, a move that only electrified his agony.

"CLARA," Poe screamed, trying to get to his feet. *"NO, NOT YOU?"*

His body jerked spasmodically as he fell back onto the dirt floor.

A moonbeam shot through the open barn roof illuminating his twisted, convulsing body.

POE, CLARA AND BONES

Clara skirted around Poe shuddering convulsively on the barn floor. He had crumbled into a fetal position, rocking and mumbling incoherently. Clara reached for the crank handle on the wood post and lifted the pendulum back to the ceiling. Then she went over to Bones tied to the platform.

"You might have stepped in sooner," Bones said angrily. "He could have killed me."

"Poe was so enthralled," she said." I needed him first to embrace your death. To think he had won. Only to face this…"

Clara nodded over to Poe, who was suddenly thrashing about the barn floor like a broken puppet on a string. More bolts of pain had assaulted him, and he tore at his face, trying to claw away the agony of the burning acid. Then he collapsed again, insensible, muttering Clara's name over and over. As if it was the only word his brain possessed.

"That still wasn't part of our plan," Bones snapped.

"Yes, I know. This was part of *my* plan," Clara said. "And you are alive, PJ."

"This is…insane, Clara."

Clara sighed. "It had to end this way, PJ," she said. "Poe wanted me, but he knew I would never be his alone until you were gone. Not that he needed much convincing to kill you—he hated you for loving me."

"Yes, it was pretty clear how thrilled he was seeing me squirm with his damn contraption about to slash me open." Bones huffed out a long breath. "I felt a lot differently about the situation."

"I didn't want to just kill Poe—he needed to suffer," Clara said. "I wanted to make him first feel—human."

"What do you mean?" Bones asked, bewildered.

"For once in his life, he felt someone loved him. He believed *I* loved him. That we were somehow fated."

Bones grimaced.

"This was my answer. Not the blinding. That pain would never be enough, but to be so…humiliated, so powerless. So despised. By me. And before you."

"Yes," Bones murmured. He paused. "How betrayed he must feel."

Clara understood.

"I'm very sorry, PJ," she said gently.

"You thought I could help," Bones said pensively, "but I failed you from the very beginning."

"No, you did not fail me," Clara said, shaking her head. "I just needed to do this my way—and you did come through for me, PJ."

Bones stared at Clara, unable to hold back the familiar ache he felt for this woman.

Clara glanced at her two lovers. She saw them both clearly now. Bones and Poe living in their fictional worlds, locked in some eternal grand duel between good and evil, two sides of the same coin. They could neither save nor kill her, only desire her, crave her love. That was never possible. She was already too far gone in the darkness.

"I thought you could save me," Clara said softly. "But, my dear PJ, Poe's knife cut too deeply. I could never have been saved. I see that now."

Bones nodded slowly. He, too, understood. He probably always did. And why he struggled to find an ending to his story. Their story. It wasn't the killer, after all, that had eluded Sam Rock's grasp, but his lover.

Clara had always been beyond his reach.

He gazed at her. "I hope you can find some peace now, Clara. It's over. Finally."

Clara tilted her head, lost in thought for the moment.

"Not yet, PJ," she said sadly. "There is one more thing for me to do."

She then reached into her bag and took out a long blade, studying it as it lay in her hand.

"This is the one he used on me."

She gently stroked the knife.

Bones tensed, at once alarmed at the sight of the blade. What was Clara thinking? With him?

Clara touched his cheek with her bare hand.

"No, PJ." She looked at Bones tenderly.

Clara then laid the knife by his side. It would take Bones some time to sever through the straps and rope that tied him to the platform.

Bones locked his eyes on her. He knew.

"Clara, you need to cut me loose now," he said.

"Peter James Bones." Clara called out his name.

Bones again heard the Irish in her voice. Her green eyes glistening.

At that moment, she was the Clara he remembered, the woman he so loved. Even now, after all of this, Bones could not let go of her.

Then Clara reached to the back of her neck to unclasp a thin necklace adorned with a small charm, a bird soaring free in flight. She held the charm in her palm, glancing at the golden creature for a moment before resting the necklace on Bones' chest.

"Don't give up," she whispered.

"Clara…" Bones' eyes pleaded with her.

She leaned over to give him a gentle kiss. She sadly smiled.

Clara then turned to Poe, his head now buried in his arms. He was lying silently on the barn floor.

She lifted him to his feet, then led him out of the barn under the dome of the stars.

CLARA, POE AND BONES

They walked arm in arm beneath the starlit night sky as lovers might in some romance story.

"Can you see the Big Dipper?" Poe asked Clara. "I used to search for those stars when I was a kid growing up here."

Clara told him she could. It was right there, above them. She saw no reason to be truthful. Agonizing spikes of pain shot into his brain, but Poe didn't complain, content to be led out into the open night air.

They made their way through the hard dirt yard, Clara guiding him past the deep empty holes that had been dug into the ground a while back. This is when Poe could see the world and wreak havoc upon it. Now he was sightless. Knots of burnt tissue and vitreous gel leaked from two hollowed cavities on his face where his eyes had been.

"You have been unfaithful to me," he said quietly.

"It had to be this way," Clara said. "We needed this to end...this madness."

"Yes, of course," Poe murmured.

Both walked on through the woods that surrounded the property. They could hear the bustling of creatures scurrying about. Another memory for Poe. Clara was careful, helping Poe avoid the branches and divots. The air was crisp and Clara breathed deeply.

The two made their way out of the woods and to the edge of the swamp. There Clara saw the sandbar that stretched into the middle of the quagmire.

"We're here," Clara said.

Poe nodded.

Then they stepped onto the sand. The powder was firm and easy to traverse. A walk on the beach. They continued on, with the underground swamp water mixing in, the sand turning wet and thick. By the time they were in the middle of the sandbar, they no longer could take another step. And within seconds, they started to sink into the mire.

Clara and Poe stood there silently. Clara looked up at the moon, finally tracking a constellation. Now she saw it. The Big Dipper.

The moonlight reflected off the two. Poe was bare-chested, his shirt destroyed in the frenzy at the barn. His body seemed to glow with his tattooed images luminous under the harvest moon.

Clara could feel the heavy sand crawling up her leg, rising past her knees. She didn't bother to struggle. She glanced over at Poe. He also was not resisting. Clara eyed him more closely. Poe seemed serene, at peace. Clara leaned toward him, her finger tracing the outline of the raven that covered his upper arm. Poe sighed at Clara's touch, as he always did. Then he raised his head and in a powerful voice spoke to the night's black sky.

"'Deep into that darkness peering, long I stood there, wondering, fearing, doubting, dreaming dreams no mortal ever dared to dream before.'"

Clara listened, taking in the words, also thinking about the darkness.

"Even now, Edgar is here with me now, Clara," Poe said. "Speaking to us."

Clara was silent, the quicksand now up to her waist.

"Clara. Clara!"

Bones came running up to the edge of the sandbar. He had finally cut his way out from the platform. Over his shoulder he was carrying a loop of rope. He went onto the edge of the bar, feeling it firm under his feet.

"PJ, this is the plan. *My plan*," Clara called out.

"Clara...don't."

Bones got on his stomach and crawled along the sand, feeling it starting to give way. He flung the rope toward Clara, less than an arm's length within her reach.

"PJ, it's all right," Clara said softly. "It's all right."

"Please...Clara."

"Forgive me, PJ," Clara whispered. "There was no other way."

Bones lay there on his stomach, his forehead touching the sand. And he understood his father's last moments. As he leaped from the seventy-fifth floor.

Clara also needed to be set free.

Bones lay prone on the sandbar, fifteen feet away, a world apart from Clara and Poe. They were hand in hand.

Bones finally crawled back to land, collapsing next to a tall tree, its thick branches wildly twisting above him. He sat there a long while, looking up into the black sky, silently praying to the harvest moon casting light and dark shadows against the smooth surface of the sandbar.

CLOSING

PJ Bones and Becky McBain walked among the stones at Woodlawn Cemetery. They were joined by Thomas Sullivan. The vast Bronx cemetery was a final resting place for some three-hundred-thousand souls, among them Phil McBain. Bones needed to make amends to his friend for waiting so long to visit.

"You know, he's up there wanting to give you a kick in the ass," Sullivan said to Bones earlier that morning over the phone.

"Well, maybe he will give me a break," Bones replied. "I'm bringing Becky."

The threesome skirted around the sea of unknown and well-known names inscribed on headstones. Bones gave a respectful nod, walking by a rough-hewn stone with a parchment scroll attached to its façade. The grave of Herman Melville.

This would be Bones first and last time at the cemetery. His life in New York was winding down. The apartment and car had been sold. He would be gone by the end of the week for Mexico with its turquoise waters, though he vowed to forsake the tequila. He had dried out, this time for good he told himself. He thought Mac might approve.

Bones had also finished his book, rewriting the ending. The story was better now—not that he had come to any profound conclusions. Maybe his readers would understand. Life is a struggle, that we all live in the shadowy mist, seeking to survive. There are no clear endings, just the chaos we grapple with and fight to overcome. Sometimes we even prevail to find some nub of the truth. At least Bones hoped that was possible.

His hero, Sam Rock, turned out to be a flawed man after all, also wrestling with the demons in his life, struggling to find justice. To right the world. Just doing the best he could. Bones wasn't sure whether Rock finally succeeded in either his mission or his life. He'd leave that to his readers to decide. Whatever, he had retired Sam Rock. It was better for both of them to finally move on.

Bones had also finished reading Poe's manuscript that Sully had handed over to him. A dark story of death. Poe ended his book with a few poetic lines from his mentor.

> For the moon never beams,
> without bringing me dreams
> Of the beautiful Annabel Lee;
> And the stars never rise,
> but I feel the bright eyes
> Of the beautiful Annabel Lee

Bones understood very well the burning desire that consumed Poe. He, too, could never escape the lure of Clara Knox. She with the bright green eyes.

They were together now.

Bones, Sullivan, and Becky explored the northern edge of the cemetery, at last coming to Mac's gravesite. A new stone had recently been placed atop his burial ground. It read:

> Philip Kerry McBain
> A Good Man

"That seems to sum him up," Sullivan said firmly.

Becky then bent down to place the single flower she brought that day, resting it alongside the stone. It lay next to a framed photograph of Phil McBain, sterling in his uniform.

"That's an Irish Rose," Sullivan said.

"Yes. He named me after the flower," Becky said softly. "Rebecca Rose McBain."

Sullivan nodded. "You know, they say that the flower's color is so brilliant that it sparkles like dancing leprechauns."

"I like that." Becky smiled brightly. "So would Dad."

Sullivan then cleared his throat, stood ramrod straight, the old soldier he was before his years on the force, and recited the ancient Irish blessing.

"May the road rise up to meet you.
May the wind always be at your back.
May the sun shine warm upon your face.
The rains fall soft upon your fields…"

Bones turned to Becky and also could not help but notice how she had changed. There was something about her glowing eyes that reminded him of another young woman. Both with the same lilt of the Irish in their voice.

Becky sighed, placing her hand on the stone. "I wish Dad could be here. To tell him that I was okay. I had been in such a bad place. I was so scared. I thought that I might be better off just letting go."

"But you didn't, Becky," Bones said. "You didn't take that step."

"No. I'm still afraid at times, PJ, but I'll be okay. I wanted Dad to know."

Bones nodded reassuringly. He thought about her struggles and was grateful that Becky had found a way to beat back the demons that hurt her so cruelly. That finally she had found her way out. Free from the maddening.

Bones put his arm around the young woman's shoulder.

They lingered over Mac's grave, feeling the whisper of a gentle breeze, finding peace amid the sea of stones rolling across the distant cemetery.

A Final Note to Readers

No American writer haunts us like Edgar Allan Poe. His tales of horror resonate even 175 years after his death, very much a good run for any author. He is a storyteller of his times and of ours probing the fever dreams of our lives, vividly bringing them to light (or, rather, into the darkness of our imagination). To read Edgar Allan Poe's literary works is also to see the author's life in its bleakest shades. His short stories and poetry carry the deep wounds of personal tragedy that are etched into the portrait photographs of the man. His eyes are the most unsettling, dark and melancholy, images that dare viewers to contemplate what he must be thinking at the moment the shutter is snapped. I suspect these are thoughts we'd rather not bring to mind before going to sleep.

And this is where *The Maddening* is born. It is a story that inhabits the metaphysical space between our dreams and nightmares, so very well familiar in Edgar Allan Poe's own storytelling. My "Poe" might very well have found a home in the writer's Gothic imaginings, his tattooed body a surreal reflection of his "mentor's" life (along with his own malevolent existence). PJ Bones is yet another refraction of the renowned author, a character that Edgar Allan Poe might well have recognized, besieged by alcohol and his personal demons. And surely, he would have understood Clara Knox from his own obsessive yearnings for the women in his life, also beautiful, desirous, and ultimately doomed.

I have brought some of Edgar Allan Poe's life into my story but these are small slices taken from a much larger picture of the man. Of course, volumes have been written about his contributions to American literature. Few writers, in fact, have garnered as much attention. While his short stories and poetry are celebrated, Poe was also among the first writers to explore the literary realms of science fiction and the modern detective novel (with thanks from Arthur Conan Doyle, among others). His fascination with physics and cosmology produced a cosmological theory that forecast the Big Bang theory eighty years later. Then there are his grand tales of balloon adventures and amazing technological inventions, and so on. I admit to feeling a particular kinship with the writer. Poe's cottage is a stone's throw from my own home in the Bronx, and where he spent his last years. Perhaps his spirit still lingers here, prompting me to dive into the literary underworld that he created.

So, *The Maddening* is this author's humble bow to the master, whose tales of the macabre continue to tap into our deep-rooted fears while stimulating a few faster heartbeats. Certainly, my intention as well—to have you step onto the sandbar and feel the sand give way under your feet. I hope it has been enough to shake you from the complacency of a safe reading. The ultimate pleasure for any storyteller of such tales. I appreciate that you have taken the chance.

Acknowledgments

All books have a professional family, and mine at Dark Ink has been wonderfully supportive. A special thanks to Michael Aloisi, the owner and publisher of AM Ink Publishing and its imprint, Dark Ink, for creating such a welcoming and collaborative space, and his commitment in bringing this story to life. Also, thank you to my editors, Joe Tonzelli and Louis Stephenson, for sharpening these pages and to Alicia Mattem for her evocative cover design.

Friends and family have also rallied around this book. Dr. Mitchell Saskin generously helped me delve into the psychological mindset of my characters. My family has borne the weight of my recitations despite the occasional grimace that arose from the more vivid parts of the story. So, thank you to Fred and Linda Thaler, Enid Wolfson, and the Black family— Eric, Marjorie, Helen and Sophie. My amazing 'guys', Robby and Rebecca, have also lovingly put up with their dad's mad imaginings. And my deep appreciation to Matthew Thaler, a talented screenwriter and author in his own right, whose keen editorial eye greatly helped this story take flight. The book is dedicated to Amy Wolfson, my partner in crime (at least the fictional kind). Finally, Amy can find rest from these dark bedtime tales I shared late into the night that she endured with her wry humor and, as always, loving support.

About the Author

Photo Credit: Rebecca Thaler

Paul Thaler is a former journalist and a media commentator for national and network news programs. He is the author of the critically acclaimed *The Spectacle: Media and the Making of the OJ Simpson Story*, and *The Watchful Eye: American Justice in the Age of the Television Trial*. His debut novel, *Bronxland*, was cited on Goodreads as the top-rated "Best Historical Coming-of-Age-Book." He lives in the Riverdale section of the Bronx with his wife, Amy, where they have raised their three children, Matthew, Robby and Rebecca.

CPSIA information can be obtained
at www.ICGtesting.com
Printed in the USA
BVHW082157250123
657140BV00002B/4